SHADOWING HANNAH
Sara Berkeley

Sara Berkeley has published three collections of poetry, *Penn* (1986), *Homemovie Nights* (1989), and *Facts About Water* (1994), and a collection of short stories, *The Swimmer in the Deep Blue Dream* (1992). She was born in 1967, grew up in Dublin and now lives in San Francisco. *Shadowing Hannah* is her first novel.

Acknowledgements

Big thanks to my great editor, Ciara Considine, to all at New Island Books, and to Dermot Bolger, who started every ball rolling for me. Thanks to my friends who read and commented on the manuscript: Connie, Marcy, Chris, and Kate. And thank you Talc, for making the world I write in.

SHADOWING HANNAH

SARA BERKELEY

Sara Berkeley.

SHADOWING HANNAH
First published September 1999 by
New Island Books
2 Brookside
Dundrum Road
Dublin 14
Ireland

Copyright © 1999 Sara Berkeley

ISBN 1 902602 04 8

All rights reserved. No part of this book may be reproduced or utilised in any form or by any means mechanical, including photography, photocopying, filming, recording, video recording, or by any information storage and retrieval system, or shall not, by way of trade or otherwise, be lent, resold or otherwise circulated in any form of binding or cover other than that in which it is published without prior permission in writing from the publisher. The moral rights of the author have been asserted.

British Library Cataloguing in Publication Data
A catalogue record for this book is available from the British Library

The Arts Council
An Chomhairle Ealaíon

New Island Books receives financial assistance from The Arts Council (An Chomhairle Ealaíon), Dublin, Ireland.

Cover design: Jon Berkeley
Typesetting: New Island Books
Printed by Cox & Wyman, Reading.

To my wonderful Mum and Dad

One

They ate dinner in the back room as they had for a month now. They watched the news, eating silently, fork to mouth, fork to mouth. It made Hannah smile when she thought of the two of them there and the picture they cut. Hugh grunted at the politicians and switched off when it came to the weather.

'I don't want to hear it's going to be wet and windy with an overnight freeze, do you?' he asked Hannah.

'Not now, I don't,' she said. 'There might be a freak tropical heatwave on the way, though. A meteorological signpost of global warming. Just in Harrow and Wealdstone—so we shouldn't go to work tomorrow.'

'Hm,' said Hugh. 'Better not eat any of that chocolate-chip ice-cream I bought then. Don't want to find I've grown out of my swimming trunks.'

He got up heavily and took her plate. 'Fine cuisine as always, dear girl.'

Hannah followed him out to the kitchen and watched him scoop ice-cream into two mugs.

'You eat it from mugs?' she said.

'You may not believe this,' he replied, licking the spoon, 'but I would eat ice-cream from a Wellington boot.'

'I believe it,' she said. Then, 'Hugh? I have something to ask.'

'Ask. I may relent.'

'Well, it's just that...Mo's asked me to move in with them. And I don't know what to do.'

She couldn't see his face. He was busying himself at the sink.

'Ah,' he said.

'And she wants to know by Friday, because the other girl just moved out, kind of without warning them, and they need someone quick.' She was speaking hurriedly. 'So I said I'd tell her tomorrow. But I don't know if I want to or not.'

'Why is that?' he asked, still washing dishes, still with his back to her at the sink.

'Well, y'know, being here with you, I really like it. Then—they're right near the centre, and Camden Town and all that. As well, I've never lived with girls.' She gave an awkward half-laugh and Hugh turned, wiping his hands on a dishtowel, and smiled too.

'It could be fun. All those...things girls do,' he finished vaguely, and they both laughed. 'You'd come and cook your uncle a bite to eat now and then, wouldn't you?'

'Oh yes.'

'Well then,' he raised his eyebrows.

'I suppose...' she left the sentence hanging, and then it was too late to finish it.

'I'm having my ice-cream now,' Hugh said, and he hung the tea-towel on the cooker rail and went into the back room.

She didn't follow him, but went upstairs instead, dragging her feet on the stairs like a child would. The carpet was worn through in places, she could see the underfelt. The roses that had once made up the pattern were almost white on some stairs. She pushed open the door of her bedroom and stood on the threshold looking in. It was a small room. A quarter the size of her bedroom at home. The bed was narrow, a mean single bed. It would be cool to have a double bed some day.

The thought of packing up her things again made her feel heavy and bored. She lay against the wall and eyed the photos on the dresser moodily. He was looking out at her, that photo with the towel around his neck so he looked like a tennis star, and the uncertain smile. She had fiddled with the camera, and said something that had brought about this peculiar smile, as though he was hurt but he didn't want her to see. This was the single photograph, out of the hundreds over the years, the only one that came close to capturing him. Funny thing, a photo: there he was, that moment, with that expression she had looked for again and again and never quite found. But it wasn't him. He was three hundred miles away, moving, thinking, writing. He was filling the hole she'd made. And she, on her side, lying in the upstairs room of a London suburban terraced house—she felt the opening of loss, it gaped in the stillness of the room, it emptied the chambers of her heart. She whimpered quietly and closed her eyes. *Are you careful in your denial, Hannah? Do you cover up the tracks? Do you tell the right lies?*

Two

2 February 1991.

Dear Sparrow,

I hardly know what to do with myself. My world is awfully empty without you in it. Are you careful? Burn this,

    Finch.

Hannah read it several times, as though unable to believe her eyes. Hardly a letter at all, really. Just a note. Its brevity was painful, like an open sore. The other letters had all been long, full of information, discussions of books and films, memories. Did she remember the time she had gone away on the school trip to Paris? How she had come running in, her arms full of packages, shouting 'Paris in the Spring! Paris in the Spring!'? And the time he had told her she would be a nun?

    She smiled to herself. She'd been twelve or thirteen. Came home from school and said the nuns wanted her to be one. He'd seemed faintly amused. He'd said maybe they were right. After all, she liked going to Mass, the incense, the candles. She was disgusted. She said something shocking, gross—deliberately.

    'Fucked if *I'll* ever be a nun.'

And he had laughed, and on her sixteenth birthday when he gave her those roses, so dark and tightly packed, so perfumed, he wrote on the gift card, 'For my little Sister.' The smell of the roses touched her memory, touched the open sore, and she crumpled the note and left it on the bedside table, stretching out slowly on her bed.

She'd phoned from the airport that time, after the trip to Paris. There was no one there to meet her, so one of the teachers stayed with her to make sure she was collected, and she phoned. René! His voice! And she was twenty minutes' drive away. She wanted to see him, she wanted to see him...then Daddy and Christian came hurrying in the doors and hugged her and took her to the car. Shiny and warm in the car. They edged into the traffic. Hot sun, René in twenty minutes, everything looked so green when you came back. *Home, can I be coming home, and why did I ever go away? Into the house, over the threshold, feeling like a bride, where is he?* She'd called his name, run down the passage, dizzy—*Daddy and Christian behind, René before*—he'd opened his arms, his eyes dark, he'd been waiting too! Thin bones under his white shirt; he always looked so smart in a white shirt because of his colouring. Embrace. She didn't fully understand, but balance was back, restored, *everything right, my God, I'm back.* 'Hello!' René hugging her again, *it's you, it's you, how did I ever go away, white shirt, thin bones, hug me again—*

Hannah sat up. She reached for the note and the cigarette lighter. She held the paper, tipping it sideways as the flame consumed. When it ate close to her fingers she dropped it hurriedly in the ashtray and watched it curl and blacken till the words were all gone.

Harrow. 7 February 1991.

Finch,

London's a hell-hole and I love it. When it snows, there's enough to freeze your bones, but not to ski, or even look nice; but that's the price you pay for the view of Westminster through the bare trees and the trains and the handsome black cabs on Blackfriars Bridge in the morning. We are marooned! The snow is drifting. There's ice building up inside my bedroom window. The sink pipe is frozen. Soup for dinner. Ancient two-bar electric heaters. Why doesn't Hugh get central heating, you ask? I don't think it's ever occurred to him. He is contented with his heaters and an electric blanket. He tried to make me let him buy me one, but I can't stand the things. It feels like deep winter alright. It's all orange and white and billowy out there. Downing Street was attacked with mortars today by the IRA. Nice, eh?

Feels like we might huddle up in this room till next week and never move. We don't have much food! There's a kind of excitement about snow, mixed in with the dirt of people dying in the streets. The man who often sits outside Sainsburys, hunched up, with a sign 'Sick and no bed.' Where's he tonight? In some shelter I hope. My heart goes out to him.

It says on the radio that a few years ago in February someone was out mowing the lawn. BUT SO WOT?

Nelson Mandela says sanctions should not be lifted from South Africa, in spite of an impulse (commendable, but a serious error of judgement) to reward President de Klerk's lifting of apartheid. Yes. Apartheid is reputedly lifted.

We're snow-sealed. People walk in that rehearsed manner. I just had the nicest bath in the whole world. Hugh doesn't have a shower either. He cooks over stones. He sleeps in a hole in the ground. Nelson says Winnie has strong support among 'the ordinary members of the ANC'. Who are they? She's charged with abduction: 14-year-old Stompie McKetrie. More beds have been made available for the London homeless. I've just remembered an American I met in college. He was on an exchange from the U. of Minnesota. He was on an army scholarship. He could be at the war now! I hope not. Hugh just said, 'I must write a card to a friend of mine, seeing as he's been haunting my dreams again.' So this happens to everyone. You've been in mine, as much as ever, and always the same scenario. Guiltexcitement-shamepleasure. Mixed in till there's no one separable. Is there anyone home?

Hugh's asleep now with one hand on his chest, as though protesting his innocence. So much for writing to the friend who haunts his dreams. I'm the only one in the room doing that. And this in spite of a rotten chest so I'm spitting mucus in the bathroom in between pages, and mugs of strong coffee. Yes, I hear you, all that smoking at college. But I lay awake from 4:30 till 7, a bit feverish so my brain was being rattled like dice, and on the throw, some new nightmare image would flit across the room. The lampshade became a KKK helmet, the eyes narrowed and widened and I didn't know what horrors they had seen. I said your name. Then I slept and dreamed. Want to know my dreams? Well you can't.

I saw a guy on the tube today reading *London Fields*. I wanted to lean over and say 'the end is fucking brilliant. Want to know what happens?' Finch there are so many things I want to talk to you about. What's going to happen? I'm not allowed to ask that question, am I? I don't allow it myself. I'll shut up now.

'It's just that the tears have a different colour on them now, but I miss him.' A man on the radio just now talking about the cot death of his fourteen-week-old son. The end of the news. Recession, trials, and war. One strange thing has happened. In Albania, hundreds of people worked for hours to push down a huge statue that was a symbol of communism.

'Who has the fun? It's always the man with the gun.'

Sparrow.

Three

Hugh drove her down to Camden Town on Saturday morning. Another letter in her bag, a fat one, she humped her suitcase into the Volvo's boot and settled a box of books beside it.

'I don't know how I've somehow got all these books since I came,' she said as Hugh locked the boot down. 'What—it's only been a couple of months.'

'That all?' said Hugh.

'Seems like ages. I got here eight weeks ago.' She pulled the gates open and stood looking up at the house. The usual pang of leaving. Why not stay in a place? Why always moving? But she was curious too. Living with Mo and Julia. Shaking her head slightly, she sat in beside Hugh and he started up. She wondered if he'd say something. 'It was good having you to stay,' or 'The place'll be empty.' But he just pulled out onto Byron Road and down towards the station.

Driving across London she saw the buildings and the streets and they looked foreign and strange. *Right now*, she thought, *I'm not living anywhere. This is the city where I live now, but just for this single hour, I don't really live anywhere.* She spotted the BT tower, hazy in the city air. The parks they passed looked grey, dead as winter. It was still February. For such a short month, it went on for a hell of a long time. Still, then there was March, and signs of hope. Dad's birthday on

March 10th was always the turning point, however grim the weather. And then her own, less than three months later. He always said the same thing to her on his birthday, as he opened her card. 'Just another few months now to yours.' She'd be twenty. No more teens. Starting her twenties. She felt a heaviness, an ache for something to happen or be over. *Is this all there is?* She brushed the thought aside almost before it had occurred. *Here I am, on my way to my first house-share ever. Sharing with Mo and Julia! Girls! Clothes and cooking and going out at night—silks and lace thrown over wardrobe doors...*She stole a glance at Hugh, his hands, relaxed down the bottom of the steering wheel. Wouldn't it be nicer, more comfortable, to just stay with Hugh in Harrow? She thought of the little room, the quiet—stripped bare now. And the house she was going to: the only time she'd been there it seemed full of people she didn't know. The doorbell rang; the phone shrilled and no one answered it; people came in, sat down uninvited, left without saying goodbye; everyone talked about a thousand people she didn't know.

'Where do I turn off the North Circular?' asked Hugh, and she flipped through the *A to Z.*

'East End Road,' she read out. 'That goes into the Great North Road, then Archway Road, then swing right by Archway Station, down...Junction Road, that becomes Fortress Road, and then we're there!'

'We'll have to get you driving,' he said. 'Then I can put my feet up.'

'Sure! And I can borrow the car for extended periods of time.'

'Hm. See if you can spot—ah, there we are, a sign for Camden Town.'

She felt a thrill of excitement. Camden Town! *Dear Finch, here I am, living in Camden Town.*

She watched London go by. It was so different, travelling by car. You could see life on the streets, how the city was strung together. Travelling by tube, you got no sense of how it all connected up. They passed Tufnell Park station. Then Hugh turned onto Leighton Road and she called out the house numbers.

'Up a bit, it's up the hill a bit, I came from the other end—there! Number 96.'

He cut the engine and they both sat still for a minute, waiting. Then they were both busy at once, getting the bags out, dragging boxes up the path and the front steps. She fished for the key Mo had given her.

'Will you come in for some tea?'

'Another time.' He dropped the last bag on the flagged tiles and straightened up. His breath was coming painfully from the exertion. He wiped his forehead and started down a step. 'I've got some work to do,' he said, then, awkwardly, 'You'll be alright?'

'Yeah. Fine.' She hovered at the front door, on the verge of giving him a hug. She'd thought about this moment, wondering how it would be.

'I'll be off then,' he carried on down the steps, out of her reach, fumbling for the ignition key, treading heavily on a low shrub by the path.

'Bye then!' she gave a half-wave. 'I'll phone you. Thanks!'

He didn't turn round, but waved as he opened the car door and looked up at her when he was in the front seat with the belt on. She waved again, and he nodded and slewed round to back out of the space.

There was nobody in. She stacked her belongings inside the front door and stood for a moment, listening to the silence of the house. There were water pipes ticking upstairs. A dog barked in someone's back garden. She could hear the bass line of a song through the walls. She listened hard, screwing up her eyes to hear better. She stepped from the dark hallway into the sitting room, and stood by the door, watching the flickers of light across the room as wind moved the trees outside. She could smell cigarettes. Joy Division. It was Joy Division, that hard beat coming through the wall.

Dear Finch, she thought, *this is my new place. Here I am. It's a bit lonely. Nobody's home.* She felt in her bag for the letter and held it there a moment, her fingers running over the rough edge of the stamp. Then she went back into the hall and started to move her belongings upstairs.

When he reached home, Hugh sat in his car after he'd switched the engine off and stared at the plain cement wall of his garage. There wasn't anything in the garage apart from the old white Volvo. No boxes or tools or shabby garden chairs. He climbed out of the Volvo and locked the garage doors. Inside the house, he was making tea when he found the packet of chocolate fingers, tucked behind a tin of spaghetti in the cupboard. Sellotaped to the wrapping was a note in his niece's childish hand. 'Had to hide them from robbers. Hannah.' He gave a low chuckle. In the back room he turned the television on, but he didn't even glance at the screen. He sat in his armchair, balancing the tea and biscuits on the tiled grate, and opened his paper. He sat like that until the six o'clock news came on. He watched the news, and then a sit-com, with a plate of stew on his knees. He ate a bowl of tinned fruit salad with evaporated milk as the Saturday night film began. Before it was over, he switched the set off and turned out the lights. He climbed the stairs and used the bathroom. Pausing a moment on the threshold of his bedroom, he took a long look at the half-open door to the little front room. He could see a streetlamp lighting a square of the plain white wall. He watched as the room glowed briefly with the headlights of a passing car. Then it fell black and white, as though a quick flame had flared and gone out.

Mo sat sideways a little in her chair. The table underleaf was low and she knew without looking that she couldn't fit her thighs under it without effort. She couldn't hope to cross her legs. So she sat a little sideways, it made her look more sophisticated anyway, and stirred her coffee. She lifted the spoon out and put it carefully on the scrubbed wood. Hannah watched her.

'*Fat Girls*,' said Mo, 'by Mo Royce.' She grinned, and Hannah smiled too, and waited for the story of Fat Girls. 'Fat girls have something extra,' said Mo, 'and I don't just mean subcutaneous layers. I mean something extra.' She sipped, and watched people go by on the High Street, behind Hannah. 'They're funny, or they're sweet, or they're the kind of girl you go to when you want a cry. They understand.' She laid emphasis on 'understand', but Hannah couldn't 'hear any irony in her voice. 'And the fat girl won't tell anyone that you're ashamed of the hair on your arms, or the size of your feet, or your damned heavy flow. It doesn't matter what ugliness you tell a fat girl, because she's—always—uglier.' Mo smiled again. She didn't look ugly. She was saying what she felt and it was coming out right. She wasn't making Hannah feel uncomfortable. She had something to say, and she wasn't finished. She watched two couples come into the café and pile their coats on a bench by one of the tables. She sought Hannah's eyes, found them, and held them almost all the way through what she said next. Almost to the end.

'I'm a funny girl, Hannah. I have to be. Working at the bar, at the magazine, all round, I'm a funny girl. Not very funny, but funny enough that people stop caring that I'm fat. See? Now pretty girls, pretty girls are just the same, down the other end of the scale. They have to have something extra too, because—' she leaned forward as Hannah tried to interrupt, warning her not to, 'because they have to cover up for being pretty. See really pretty girls, beautiful girls, if they have half a brain, know that they're not allowed to admit it. Not even to themselves. Cos if they do, that's pride, and the rest of us will cut them out.'

'Oh,' said Hannah. Mo waited to see if she'd say anything more. 'That seems very harsh,' she faltered.

'Yes, I'm putting it strongly, I'm simplifying. But I want to make the point: pretty girls have to have armour too, to hide behind, so they won't be accused of flaunting it.' Mo's voice had taken on a gentleness that made Hannah feel easier. She fingered the spoon her friend had laid on the table. She turned it over, rocked it a little on its bevelled edge.

'You know,' Mo went on, 'when I'm pulling pints behind the bar, fetching beers for the rugby boys and the Beautiful People and the middle-aged men who eye me up and down like a side of meat, I always think the same thing. I look them straight in the eye and think: Boy, if I told you back the sad little story of your sad little life, you'd crumple up and cry. I break them down like that, in my head, just for a second, and then I can look in their eyes when I hand them the change.' She watched Hannah, waiting for her to look up. She didn't.

'Let's go and spend,' she said at last, and reached for her coat. 'I know a great market.'

'Not Camden?' said Hannah.

'No. Camden's just for tourists now. It's full of leather and boutiques. I know a place where we can find *really* cheap stuff. Feel like shopping?' she grinned again and Hannah laughed.

'Or *wot!*' she said. Mo made her happy. She talked sense. For the first time in a long time, Hannah felt almost safe.

Dear Finch. How does it go with you? Does it go Monday, Tuesday, Wednesday? I just hope it doesn't go two a.m., three a.m., four a.m. I'm getting quite used to writing these letters in my head now.

They headed for the tube. 'It's in the East End,' Mo explained. Hannah felt brave, going out there. The East End was a wasteland after the war, she knew from her childhood. You didn't go out there unless you knew somebody who lived there.

Mo leaned close to her, over the racket of the train, and asked how she liked Leighton Road. 'Everything alright, is it?'

'Yes. It's fine. I like my room. I like being able to see a garden always.'

'Julia alright?'

'Fine. I like her.' Actually, Julia intimidated her. Tall, leggy, fond of tiny leather skirts and outrageous stockings, she seemed a dangerous presence in the house. And she had a boyfriend. Morgan was a student. He dressed flamboyantly. He drove a battered Beetle. He smoked dope with Julia. Hannah didn't think she'd ever summon the courage to speak to him. They were a fabulous pair and they seemed to lead a mysterious, exciting life. Hannah had met their kind during her own year at college. They made her feel like a worm: ugly, boring, a little slimy. She looked out the window as the tube slid above ground. London stretched on every side for miles and miles. *Oh Finch,* she thought, *don't leave me alone in this city. Come for me! Rescue me!* She drew a sharp breath, caught Mo's eye, and smiled weakly as her friend cocked her head quizzically. 'I was thinking of Morgan,' she said.

'Ah. Morgan.' Mo made a face.

'Don't you like him?' Hannah said. She was aware already how much Mo's opinions affected her, and she wasn't sure she wanted to hear Morgan's character put through the shredder. Mo was good at that. She could do it with a single word, and it made Hannah uneasy. It happened at work all the time, and she didn't like it.

'Of course I do,' Mo laughed. 'I just wonder how he and Julia keep it up. Know what I mean?'

'Yeah, right.' Hannah hadn't a notion what she meant. Sex? Dope? Something shocking she didn't know about? Her mind began to reel over the memories of the past week. She'd been living for one week at Leighton Road. It seemed like a year. And yet she still felt funny getting off the tube at Kentish Town, turning the corner onto the road, putting her key in the unfamiliar lock. She felt a pang of unease, remembering the letters. Two already. One more and it would begin to look odd. Letters were a public affair in that house. 'What does your brother do?' Mo had already asked. 'That's a bit sweet of him, writing like that,' she'd said. And Hannah had hidden her sudden hot flush of shame. She'd have to get a post office box. Somehow, it felt like the act of a criminal, a person in trouble.

'Julia's a pretty smart girl,' Mo said suddenly. 'Did you know that?'

'No. Well—I mean, I can believe it.'

'Daddy's a doctor, you know. She was supposed to follow. She got straight A's all the way up. But she's not going to do what Daddy wants.'

'But I thought she *was* studying medicine.'

Mo laughed, then bit her lip and shook her head.

'She is,' she said. 'She is. I just meant that if her Dad knew the half of it, he'd cut her allowance right away.'

'She's on an allowance?'

'How do you think she survives? Government grants don't happen to surgeons' daughters, you know.'

'I suppose she does have lovely things.' Hannah felt her knowledge of Julia shift into a new key. Suddenly she imagined a house in the Home Counties, a gravel drive, cars, stables. She thought of Julia lying in elegant underwear on the couch, lighting a Dunhill, Morgan standing at the window in his classic pose, and she felt a rush of envy. 'And she's so lovely-looking,' she added impetuously. Mo gave her an odd look, and then smiled. When she smiled like that, Hannah thought her whole face changed: she looked gentle and humorous. She looked like someone you could really like.

'So how come you have an English accent then?' Mo said. 'Did you live here before?'

'I am English,' said Hannah warily.

'How long did you live in Ireland then?'

'Since I was twelve. My Dad brought us over there a few years after Mum died. He has a sister in Dublin. She looked after my younger brother a lot.'

'And your older brother?'

'He was away at school,' she hesitated. 'When he'd finished his O-levels, we went to Ireland. Where do we get off?'

'Oh not for ages yet,' Mo said. 'So you know London?'

'Not really,' said Hannah. 'Just the part we lived in, Bayswater. I was too young to know the city really well.'

'Which feels like home then: London or Dublin?'

Hannah thought for a minute. 'I don't know,' she said. She glanced at Mo and saw the older girl seemed to be waiting for a further answer. She shrugged, wanting to end the conversation. 'I don't know,' she said again. 'I don't think about it.'

At the market, the stalls were very close together and the clothes were very cheap. Mo picked out things Hannah's size and held them up to her. 'Here, this'll look good.' Hannah was afraid to do the same for her. But she felt more and more awkward as Mo kept picking out things, holding them up against her—short skirts, the tight ribbed jerseys that were the fashion, things Mo could never wear herself; things Hannah would never usually dare to wear. They tried on hats and picked over old shoes at a junk stall. Then they began window-shopping down the street where the market was. 'In here,' Mo said. It was a shop full of silks and crazy-patterned leggings. 'Look at *those*,' Mo picked out a pair. 'Uh-huh,' said Hannah. She looked for the price tag but there wasn't any.

Mo looked at her and smiled. 'Go on,' she said.

The changing room was upstairs, in a room with carpet and two curtained stalls. Away from the clamour of the market it was quiet, muffled. Hannah felt dreamy as she tried the leggings on. She was glad of the curtain. She hated communal dressing rooms. On her own, she could pose in front of the mirror, see herself as she could really look if she had the confidence. The way she imagined when she saw herself in her mind's eye. *I'm quite pretty,* she thought doubtfully. Mo pulled the curtain across. The brass rails clinked gently. Hannah stood stiffly, looking at her friend. 'Wow,' Mo said softly. 'Wow.' She reached out and passed her hand down the curve of Hannah's waist, and over the ridge of the waistband, down, down the thigh and around. Hannah stood terribly still. *Mo is twenty-one,* she thought, *she's twenty-one.*

'They're—I think they're too much,' she said.

'I think they look amazing on you,' said Mo. 'Couldn't you splash out?' She smiled again, a slow invitation. 'You look great!'

'Mo—' she stopped. The older girl moved back a little. She put her hand out and gently tugged the curtain. Almost imperceptibly, she raised her eyebrows, but she didn't smile. Then she pulled the curtain all the way. The same tinkle of curtain rings. Hannah was shaking so much she could hardly get the leggings off, they clung to her like webbing. *I'm such a little fool,* she told herself. *Such a bloody fool.* Then she wondered, *Did that happen? Was that…? Did she…?* She felt excitement welling up, then abruptly, fear. She began to hurry, afraid Mo would have left the shop, be walking away. She straightened, pulling her jeans on, and looked at herself in the mirror. 'I look the mouse I've always looked,' she said aloud. But she ran her fingers through her hair and smiled at herself, broadly, brashly.

Four

Dear You,

I feel like writing a letter to someone I know well, so well that I scarcely need to write at all. It must be you. Or perhaps it's myself. Maybe I want to write myself a letter. What would I tell myself? Hannah, I would say—because that's my name—Hannah, you'll be alright. It'll never happen, this terrible thing that you fear, whatever it is. You won't feel pain. You won't be left out there in no-man's-land to die. What is it that hovers over me? I feel scared, Finch. Lonely. I want to reach into my future and put good things there, like pieces of furniture into a doll's house. But what are good things? I'm afraid to look at boys. I want to tell them all to fuck off, with their knowing looks and their alcohol breath, leering over me, looking down my dress. I want to say to them what Mo said: If I told you back the story of your sad little lives, you'd want to cry. But the trouble is, I feel so sad about that myself. Of course everyone's life is a sorry tale. What about mine? What about mine?

Hannah put her pen down. Her vision had blurred. She stared across at the television. It made no sense, she couldn't make out whether it was a programme or an ad. Hugh wasn't watching either. He was doing his accounts, receipts and cheque-stubs littered the floor round his chair. He balanced a heavy book on his knees and he was bent closely over it.

'You're in a bad light, Hugh.'

'I know.' He sighed deeply. 'I'm afraid to look at these figures in a light that will illuminate them fully.'

'Fancy a cup of chocolate?'

'Yes I do,' he said happily.

She slipped from the chair and flicked on the main light as she left the room. She heard him grunt in mock pain. In the kitchen, she leaned against the fridge and felt like bursting into tears. It wouldn't have been so bad if Mo had been there when she came out of the shop. Well, in fact, she didn't know how it would have been. But at least she would know now, and not be in this terrible doubt. Mo had just disappeared. And she'd been too afraid to follow her back to a house that would probably be full of strangers, where she felt she hardly belonged. She groaned aloud. What a horrible mess! She slopped milk into a saucepan. Lucky for the haven of Hugh's. Maybe she should have stayed here, safe in the shabby old house with the mugs of hot cocoa and dependable Hugh. He'd only seemed mildly surprised when she turned up for tea. 'Aren't you out painting the town all sorts of colours?' he'd said. 'Nope,' she had answered, and that was that. It was unspoken between them that she'd stay and cook him Sunday lunch. He didn't seem to notice she'd arrived with nothing but her coat. She carried in two brimming cups of chocolate. Hugh was clipping sheaves of paper with paper clips. She felt a rush of affection for him. His life seemed so simple, so clean. And there he was, in the centre of it, not asking for anything, not expecting anything. But what did he dream, she wondered? What did he think about before he went to sleep?

'Now I know what an unusually poor accountant I would have made,' he said, stacking the papers on his knee.

'Well I'd be awful too, if it's any help.' She put his chocolate down.

'It's no help at all, I'm afraid,' he said with a sigh. 'But at least you have the delightful talent of hot-chocolate-making.'

'Oh thanks!' she laughed, 'I'll put that down on my CV.'

'Isn't it time for a little backgammon?'

'Indubitably it is. I haven't pulped you at backgammon for about two weeks now.'

'They don't indulge at your new place?'

'No.' She thought guiltily of the many nefarious indulgences Hugh would not be hearing about. She wondered if he shocked easily. It was so hard to tell. 'He's a dark horse, your uncle,' Mo had said, and she hadn't even met him. She'd never thought of him as a dark horse before. Did everyone have a secret life? Suddenly, Hannah thought of Mo visiting Hugh's house. It was such an odd thought—placing someone in a new context like that. She wondered what it would be like if Mo were there now. Could she settle down to a quiet game of backgammon? Could she fit into the cosy atmosphere, no questions asked? It was hard to imagine; she couldn't make up her mind. Especially now. Such a heavy question mark hung over the afternoon. She tried not to think about it. Backgammon. Double fours, double fours. She blew on the dice like she'd seen done in Westerns, and threw.

'Yes! Well, nearly. Five and four. But that's fine. I blow you away here, and then I…blow you away…*here!*'

'Ooh,' Hugh threw dice he couldn't use; he took off his glasses and began cleaning them with his sleeve. 'It appears as though I'm losing. Must be some dirt on my lenses.'

'Must be.' She threw again.

A second time, he threw bad dice. 'Dice are a mystical thing,' he said ponderously, peering at the board.

And Mo with René. How would that be? She tried to picture her new friend with him as she had always pictured everyone she met. He was the gauge, the measuring stick. But she found she didn't want to picture them together. Her mind shut down on the image. She couldn't put anyone beside him. Even in memories, he stood alone. Her father and Christian hovered in the background like ghosts, only René had focus in her past; the rest of the world was blurred around him. Trying hard, she couldn't remember a single time he had mixed: not with her friends, no friends of his own, always just the two of them. Was that really how it always was?

'At last!' Hugh had thrown double threes. 'How nice!'

She knew instinctively that Mo and René would be a dangerous mix. Mo was dangerous enough on her own. She winced, hearing the muffled clink of the brass curtain rails. The girl was already curious about René. What does your brother do? she had asked. Christian didn't seem to interest her. *It must be something invisible that emanates from me,* Hannah thought with a growing sense of unease, *something unconscious I communicate. Maybe it's like what animals smell. A spoor. Something warm, feral.* A shiver ran through her. *Maybe, with certain people there will be no hiding it. I'll give myself away to them without even knowing I'm doing it. People like Mo.*

'That's very kind of you,' Hugh said. She had moved without noticing two places she could have caught him.

'Oh,' she made a gesture of resignation.

'But I can't promise you'll receive any gentleman-like treatment in return. In fact, I shall now proceed to clear the board.' And he did. Hannah was silent. She didn't want to play backgammon any more. She felt a mood settling on her that was familiar and ugly, a mood she hadn't experienced for some time—not since before she left home. She felt bitter. Vague impressions of the past crowded in on her, oppressing her with the irritation and sadness they had aroused in her at the time they occurred. Why had she never noticed that nobody she knew knew *him*? There was nobody she could talk about him with, nobody to give their impressions of him. She sat back in the armchair and stretched her legs and arms out carelessly. Hugh cleared the pieces into their box without a word. Hannah watched him, wondering what really went on in his head. Even he couldn't really know René terribly well. And if he did, it was hard to introduce her brother as a subject without discomfort. She turned a few thoughts over in her mind. Imagine if she were to ask Hugh something surprising, something out of the blue? There must be things that would jog him out of his habitual easy humour. She had seen him thoughtful, sombre, but she had never really seen him confronted with something that forced him to step aside from himself and *react*. She had never challenged him in any way. She had striven to maintain the status quo.

He looked up and caught her watching him. He raised his eyebrows.

'Hugh,' she said slowly, already obscurely ashamed, not wanting to continue. 'Can you remember what you did…' she paused, then continued blindly, 'the night Mum died?' She watched him anxiously, afraid of his answer. When it came, it was thoughtful, measured.

'Yes. I remember very well. I sat here, in this very chair, where I am now. I played cards.'

'Cards?' she repeated.

'I played Patience. All night long after your Dad called.'

There was silence. She tried not to imagine it—Hugh, in that very chair, playing cards into the early hours. Had he cried? Did he bury his head in his hands? Weep aloud? It was too awful to imagine him jogged out of his placid demeanour—she grappled with her own half-memories, the house full of people, the awful heaviness over everything, and the unnatural brightness of the neighbours, patting her on the head, and René's arms, his white shirt. She felt tears coming and fought them back. She mustn't cry now because it would be wrong, all wrong. Hugh would misunderstand. It was too long ago.

She stood and put her hand to the back of her neck, manoeuvring her head as though it were tired. 'Good night,' she said, and smiled briefly. Hugh said nothing until she reached the door, though he looked as though he was about to. But he must have changed his mind. As she turned the handle, he said 'Goodnight Hannah,' mildly, kindly, just as he'd always said it.

It hardly seemed as though she'd been asleep two minutes, her nose stuffed and her cheeks stiff with dried tears, when she heard the distant shrill of the telephone. René! It must be! No one else could be calling in the middle of the night. She pulled on her jersey. She must get to the phone before Hugh. Stumbling downstairs, it occurred to her how heavily her uncle slept. She had seen him nod off on Sunday afternoons in his armchair. He slept deeply, his asthmatic breathing making sleep sound laborious. She flipped the main light on in the back room and scrabbled round, blinded, for the phone.

'Hello?'

'Hannah? Hello?' It was Mo, sounding as if she'd been laughing a lot. 'You haven't come to the party. Why haven't you come?' There was a lot of noise in the background. 'Hello? Is that you Hannah?'

'Yes, it's me. Hi. Mo, I—' she sat on the edge of the armchair, hunched up, pulling at the telephone flex. 'I didn't feel like it. I came back to my uncle's.'

'I know you came back to your uncle's, Silly, I'm phoning you there.' Mo giggled. She was drunk. 'What made you do a shy and retiring thing like that, then?'

'Well,' Hannah felt she had to shout to be heard above the din, but she didn't want to wake Hugh. 'I thought after this afternoon, I thought, you just...I couldn't find you.' She screwed up her eyes. The middle of the night.

'Well of course you didn't know what you thought,' Mo's voice was authoritative, but somehow kind, as though she were gently reproving a child. 'But it's awfully late. Were you asleep? I only called because I was worried. Come home tomorrow, won't you? Hannah?'

'Yes. I'll be home. Is the party good?'

'It's appalling,' Mo giggled again. 'Legs everywhere. Someone fell out the bathroom—wups!' There was a moment of confusion, a few loud hellos, then Mo seemed to wrestle the phone back from someone. 'That was Jeremy,' she shouted, laughing and talking at the same time to someone at the other end. 'He wants to—ooh! I say! Now he's making rather a rude—Jeremy! Stop that! I've got to hang up now Hannah. Promise you'll be home tomorrow?'

'I promise. Night Mo.' She laid the receiver slowly back in its cradle. It was terribly quiet. Somewhere in London was the party: loud, uncontrollable, spilling out on someone's lawn; open doors, bottles everywhere. She hugged her knees and stared at her bare feet on the hearth-rug. 'Glad I'm not there,' she murmured, curling her toes tight and stretching them out again. She looked across at the chair where Hugh had sat playing Patience the night her mother died. She tried to picture it again, the slow laying out of the cards in diminishing rows, the flat sound as he turned them out in threes, black on red, queen on king, building on the aces. She wondered what he had thought about, losing his only sister so suddenly like that. A quick calculation—he would have been thirty-four. Just three years after losing his mother. Her grandfather had died before she was born, when Hugh was in his teens. She thought about him in each of these lights and then as the young brother of her mother. When he was still in college, her mother was already married and a mother. When she herself was born, Hugh was just in his late twenties. He'd always seemed old to her, but she thought of the books she'd found on his shelves, gifts from her mother, signed 'Happy 24th Birthday'. On Hugh's 24th birthday, René was already a year old.

She sighed deeply and rested her forehead in her hands. The only way she could ever really see her mother now was in memories built around photographs and the single, jerky home-movie her father had taken in their garden when she was about six. This was her mother, then, standing on the lawn in a cotton dress, laughing, pushing her loose hair back from her eyes. She was laughing at Christian. The camera swung down to the baby, sitting naked on an old rug, grabbing at his own bare baby toes. Then it lurched back up to her mother, six-year-old Hannah beside her, holding her dress, squinting up at the camera. Her mother looked into the camera and said something and laughed. She screwed up her eyes in the sun, laughing, and then she just smiled, looking straight at the camera, until the ratchet squares bobbed up the picture and the reel was over.

Hannah woke into an atmosphere of suburban Sunday, and lay for a while listening to it. Voices on the street outside, church bells, smart heels on the pavement—she could picture everyone in their Sunday best, out for the paper and sweets for the kids. It all seemed so proper and clean. She thought of the flat on Leighton Road. It would be littered with full ashtrays, empty milk cartons, clothes, there was probably someone sleeping on the couch. And Mo: she'd be in bed, dying of a hangover. Suddenly Hannah felt tremendously light-hearted. She threw back the covers and stood hopping from foot to foot and shivering as she dressed. She ran downstairs, jumping the last three, and burst in the kitchen door. Hugh was eating porridge, the paper propped against a full carton of milk.

'I'm just in time to cook your bacon!' she said extra cheerfully.

'Indeed,' he said, still reading. As she poured the oil in the frying pan he added, 'Very perky this morning.'

'Yes,' she said, 'I'm feeling very pleased with myself because I didn't go to a party last night and get polluted and wake up feeling like death on a plate.'

'I see.'

Dear old Hugh, she thought. *What a sweetie.* She threw in an extra slice of bacon, and began to picture how she would nurse Mo through the hangover. Absolutely no bacon. Or porridge. Big thick sandwiches, doorstep hunks of white bread and processed cheese, white lemonade, that sort of thing. She could go shopping on her way home. She felt a bit guilty, though; maybe she should stay with Hugh for Sunday lunch. But she knew if she mentioned it, he'd say mildly that he didn't mind. She set his bacon down and took away his porridge bowl, pleased to be doing this for him. Then she took her own mug of coffee and sat down between the table and the fridge. Hugh smiled at her.

'So what's your grand design?'

She laughed.

'Oh, cure Mo's hangover, save the world.'

'Olympic gold-medal bacon cook?'

'That's just a hobby though.'

'How's work going?'

'It's boring.' She drew her legs up, resting the heels of her shoes on the rung of the kitchen chair. 'I'm still filling in for this girl. It's been a month now. The temp agency doesn't think she's coming back. She went barmy or something, I don't know.'

'So the job's yours if you want it.' It was more of a flat statement than a question, but she was still a little surprised. Hugh never inquired about things.

'I suppose so.' He didn't ask, but she added anyway, doubtfully, 'If I did want it,' and then, 'Tell the truth I haven't been thinking about it.' She put her mug down, felt the cheerfulness ebb. Hugh cleared his throat and shuffled back his chair to take his plate to the sink.

'What do you think I should do?' she said, stopping him from moving away with the plate. He looked at her and for a moment, she was sure he was about to say 'I really don't know dear girl,' and she felt ready to be disappointed, let down by his taking it so lightly. But he pursed his lips a little and said simply, 'I think you should go to college. Have some fun. Study something you enjoy.' She was so surprised, she let him stand and gather the dirty dishes and bring them to the sink. Then she said tonelessly, 'I already tried that.'

'And you didn't like what you were studying?'

'No, it wasn't that.' She stopped. This demanded an explanation, something she couldn't give. 'It was boring too,' she finished flatly. It sounded unconvincing, and she felt tired of the subject, endlessly tired as she had at home, after she'd dropped out, during all the arguments, all the scenes and attempts at explanations. Now it all came back: the feeling that all she knew for sure was how to hold out against them all. But Hugh was different. He said nothing now, as though he sensed her mood changes, the undertone of defeat and defiance. She fiddled idly with the sugar in its bowl, thinking again of Mo. The scene in the dressing room seemed a long time ago. Had it even happened to her? When she thought of Mo she felt curious, a little excited, dangerous. It was all out there: what was she waiting for? She stood up. 'I'm going back into town this morning,' she announced, a little louder than necessary.

'Are you?' said Hugh.

'I'll come out next weekend, or give you a call during the week.'

'Yes.'

She hesitated at the kitchen door. With his back to her and his hands in the washing up, he seemed large and shabby, like a great bear. He must have sensed her standing there, for he turned his head and they exchanged a look she could not describe to herself. Nothing passed between them, yet it cut her to the heart. She left the room hurriedly, subdued by the expression on his face. It was as though he were thinking of something entirely different; as though he had forgotten she was there. He looked as if he were dreaming of something she could never imagine.

Although she purposely took her time, she could feel a sense of urgency to be back in Leighton Road. She lived there now! Things happened there. Interesting people came round. Soon they'd stop wondering who she was, and just accept her. She wondered: did they think 'Oh, someone Mo brought home'? She was such a central person, Mo. If she brought someone home, people respected that. *But I'm not important,* Hannah thought to herself. *Better not to be. Too out in the open.* René always said, 'You stay in the doorway Hannah, neither in nor out.' She had liked that, though she wasn't sure if he meant it as a reproach. *Maybe you'd like Mo after all,* she thought, but she doubted it and it troubled her.

Leighton Road was quiet and intensely sunny. She brushed by the overgrown tree at the gate with a sigh of pleasure. Her key fitted smartly in the door. No one seemed to be up. She checked the front room for visitors, then rested the bag of groceries on the kitchen table. Propped up against the toast rack was another letter, which she pocketed quickly without even examining the postmark. There would have to be a post office box, whatever the expense. It was just conceivable that Mo's curiosity would run to opening a letter eventually. She stood looking out the kitchen window at the massive jungle of weeds that was the back garden. Then she went upstairs to see if Mo was awake.

Mo was asleep, and so was the person beside her. Hannah shut the door carefully and stood a moment on the landing. Was it? She'd hardly seen. Just a shape under the bedclothes. She felt small and stupid. The letter burned in her pocket, she didn't want to read it. What was this feeling of betrayal for? She went into her own room and flung her jacket on the bed. She stood in the middle of the room. There was nowhere to go. The unopened letter drew her eyes to it, she stared at her jacket pocket as though she could imprint the contents in her brain just by staring. Letter after letter, they never stopped coming — it was like an endless, fragmented conversation and she no longer felt in control of it. For some time now, she realised, the picture she had of him had been shifting. It was almost imperceptible, but now she tried to fix her thoughts on the change that had taken place. René. She brought him to mind, she conjured him, and it was an effort, like drawing from memory. There was a stock of memories, she stored a whole headful; but somehow, he came to her now in a suit, dapper, serious. Recently, it had always been in this dark suit, funereal, she didn't know why, and he wasn't smiling. He looked as though he had never smiled and never would. She became uneasy, there was a note of reproach in his voice, though she couldn't make out anything he was saying. Just the sense. Reproach and disappointment. A hot sense of having displeased him, a fear of his displeasure. *Why? It was never like this...I did what you wanted, I went away...*

She sat on the bed and pulled her knees up close. She never wrote to him about the anger. She never said that waking from these dreams she would be clutching the sheets not in fear, but in anger. She woke cursing him, wishing him pain and immeasurable unhappiness. She put her hands to her face. It shocked her now, to bring these thoughts to the surface, from where they had been hiding. She felt guilty thinking them, but it was like at school when she'd done something wrong: it was guilt mingled with the pleasurable fear of being caught.

There were two people now: the René in her dreams, flint hard, unyielding, and the René she kept before her when she wrote to him, when Hugh mentioned him, on the rare occasions when they spoke on the telephone. *If I dream*, she thought, *I can't help it. Those dreams are out of my control. It's not my fault.* But she knew now that it was pleasurable to think of him like this—cold and disappointed, somehow thwarted. She wondered again what he'd do if she got a boyfriend. Instead of the shudder this thought usually provoked, her unwillingness to imagine, this time she felt a delicious thrill of fear. She pushed the image further: they were together, in the front room at home. He was in his shirt sleeves, he took her by the wrists, he was angry, furious about something. He shouted. She saw the veins stand out on his forehead, he held her wrists so tightly it really hurt.

But where was this coming from? She couldn't ever remember him being angry like that. Only quiet. Always reasonable, always repeating they must stop if she didn't like it, asking her to tell him if she wanted it to stop. She tried to remember a single occasion when he had shouted or been angry like that, and she couldn't. When he was angry he'd talk more quietly. But he listened, he always listened. In her dream, he shouted, out of control. He'd never *been* out of control like that. Always in possession of himself. It was one of the things she loved about their times—how for those few moments at the end she could always break through the control and see him, exposed, without his walls, completely himself, oblivious and lost. Then he would come back, come out of it, their secret stronger and one of the best, the most exciting things she could imagine in life; and more locked down, faster between them; no need to talk, just a look could pass between them...

There were sounds from downstairs, Mo's name called, then her own. Julia was home.

Hannah got hurriedly off the bed. She felt excited, purposeful, just in the mood for Julia. She hoped there was someone else, that Julia had lots of people with her. Stopping in the middle of her bedroom, she could make out a few voices in the hall. She went out onto the landing and hung over the bannisters. They were balancing coats on Mo's antique coat-stand that was always falling over. She called down 'Hellooo!' Julia looked up and smiled.

'There she is!' she turned to her companion. 'See? I told you she was a lovely thing!' Another face turned up and Hannah saw dark hair and a cravatte, a strong face, Julia's type. She drew back, laughing, pleased in spite of herself, delighted with Julia's compliment. What an amazing, a *peculiar* thing to say! She came downstairs slowly. There were three people in the hall. She hadn't noticed the other boy but now he stared at her curiously. She smiled.

'I bought muffins,' she announced. There were exclamations of approval and they trooped into the sitting room.

'Morgan's making tea,' Julia said. She sat in a low armchair, stretching her long legs out. Hannah saw the tops of her stockings under her little red jersey skirt. 'Missed a party, Hannah' she said, and smiled broadly. 'Wasn't it,' she turned to the dark-haired boy. He was lighting a cigarette. He screwed up his eyes, said nothing.

'Mo home?'

'Yep.'

'Home alone?'

'Nope.' Hannah was pleased she could be shown to know and not to care either way.

'Thought not.' Julia laughed to herself, as though over some secret. 'Lord, that was a party.'

They talked about the party and Hannah half-listened. Half her thoughts were probing the avenue she had explored earlier. She allowed many vague possibilities to touch her imagination. She thought of him in pain, lying in pain, and she was looking down on him. She stood above him, a leg either side of him, her feet touching his hips. His hands were behind him, handcuffed behind him, so he was powerless. He was asking her to free his hands, commanding her to, but she knew she didn't have to. And yet, as she looked down on him, she knew she didn't want him in pain. The last thing she wanted was his pain. It was a destructive dream, and she was glad to put it aside and join the conversation, have muffins and coffee and feel the day slip into one of those long afternoons where nobody moved from the room; where the conversation turned in on itself in tight little circles; where everything was cripplingly funny and she thought, *I wish I could preserve this, I love these people, this will never happen again.*

Mo came downstairs at last, with a boy she called Bit, who seemed to pay more attention to Julia than he did to Mo. Mo didn't seem to mind. They opened some wine, and soon the light was going and they were all a little drunk. Then someone rolled a joint and Hannah smoked for the first time, feeling this was the finest day, a perfect time, with good and evil in exquisite balance, and poised, ready to fall across her life like a ball-and-chain. But when it swung down, she felt, she would already be far away.

Towards midnight, people left, and Julia went away somewhere too.

'Get your letter?' Mo said. Hannah was lying staring at the ceiling. She frowned, remembering the unread letter.

'Yes. Forget where I put it now.'

'That your brother again.'

'Yes.'

'My brother wouldn't write to me if I gave him fifty quid and a stamped addressed envelope.'

There was a long silence.

'Bit's funny.'

'D'you think so?' Mo propped herself up on one elbow on the couch.

'Mm.'

Mo lay down again and after a while said reflectively, 'I think he fancies you.'

'Rubbish.' Hannah sat up. The room was a sickly yellow. Mo was watching her.

'Well don't sound so disgusted. You just said he was nice.'

'I said he was funny.'

'Did you leave someone back in Ireland, Hannah?'

'No. No one.'

'Ever?'

She stood up. The room was a mess. Cushions, books, crumbs—someone had spilled wine. She assumed her most nonchalant voice. 'I'm going to bed.' She smiled briefly at Mo and went upstairs. She climbed straight into bed, fully dressed, and pulled the covers up over her head. When the eiderdown shifted, her jacket slid onto the floor. She heard it fall and lay with her eyes shut tight, trembling, waiting for sleep.

She didn't see Mo the next morning. She left the house without breakfast and arrived at work at exactly nine o'clock. All morning she hardly moved from her desk and she didn't go out for lunch. All morning she did the idiotic jobs she'd been assigned. At least a hundred times during the three hours before lunch she thought how boring work was. At twelve-thirty she left. 'I'm not feeling well,' she told the section manager, and she felt so unusual that it was almost true. Her throat was tight. Her breath came in short painful sobs. Walking in the street, she felt tears come. First she tried to stop them, then she turned into the park. *I'm crying in the street,* she thought. *Is that terribly wrong?* After a while she calmed down and when it occurred to her to go to the pictures, she felt quite cheerful.

The cinema was huge and plush, blue-green, like underwater; thinking of the number of steps she'd come down, she realised it must actually be right down under the street. A huge underground cavern with the ordered rows of velvet seats, the pinpricks of light glowing and dimming, the slight creaking of the curtains coming across, baring the screen. The writing on the screen rippled, unblurred, moving up when the curtains were clear of it. A warning to patrons that there are nasty things in the world. Handbags are stolen. Pockets picked.

Hannah kicked off her shoes surreptitiously and flexed her toes over the soft carpet. She hoped no old throat-clearers would come and sit near. The twenty people were well spread out over the cinema. A few were reading. Feeling one with them now, Hannah took out her book and read a few pages in the yellow light. A couple of times she felt the lights were dimming before they actually did.

The film was undemanding, comfortable. There was no violence and no overt sex. She hardly took her eyes from the screen and when it was over she would rather not have had to leave the cinema. Once outside, though, she felt the novelty of being on the streets an hour earlier than usual. She wandered into a few clothes shops and found herself looking at the kind of things Julia wore. She wondered if Julia was at home. She kept strange hours; Hannah wasn't sure when she ever went to college. She certainly never saw her studying, though her books were everywhere and most of her friends were students. Still feeling odd, she took the tube from

Tottenham Court Road and walked up Leighton Road in the rain. There was a light on. She hoped Julia was home. Julia didn't ask questions all the time like Mo did. She didn't seem to care about anything.

Julia was sitting at the kitchen table. She was studying, there was a lamp on the table, and she wore glasses Hannah had never seen before. The room felt different, there was a studious, ordered air, and Hannah had the impression of walking in on a scene that occurred every day, while she was out.

'You're early,' Julia said. She looked totally different in glasses. And she wore a sweater and jeans. Her hair was drawn back.

'Am I disturbing you?' Hannah felt humbled by the sight of this Julia, so serious. She remembered the conversation with Mo. *If her Dad knew the half of it, he'd cut her allowance right away...*

'No. I'm finishing up. Want to make me a coffee?'

'Look at that,' Hannah filled the kettle, watching the rain. 'It's turning really heavy. I just got back in time.'

'Leave work early, did you?'

'I left at lunchtime,' said Hannah. 'I went to a movie.'

'Quite right,' said Julia. She was clearing up her books. She didn't seem to think it an odd thing to do, to go to a movie instead of being at work. 'Care for a G&T?'

'Why not. I'll just get out of these shitty clothes. I *hate* having to wear a skirt to work.'

'It doesn't make sense to me,' Julia said. 'It's only a magazine. It's not as if you have to meet clients or anything.'

Up in her bedroom, the rain beat viciously against the window, but Hannah felt a kind of happiness. She picked her jacket up off the floor, took the letter out, and put it beside the bed. *The heart betrays the head,* she thought. *If only the head knew, what would the head do? The heart can't help it, the heart can't help it.* The letter would be full of memories, full of half-questions, unstated feelings. It weighed on her already. She didn't want to open it. She put on her oldest jeans, looked at her straight hair in the mirror. It could look okay, tied back like Julia's.

They drank two gins before cooking dinner, and they drank two after, and Mo didn't come in.

'You see the thing about Mo,' Julia said, 'the thing about Mo is that she thinks she knows about everybody. Because people tell her things, because she's a good listener. And so she thinks she's got it all down. But she hasn't. She doesn't know about me, really.' She lit a cigarette and blew out the smoke. 'And she doesn't know a thing about you.'

Hannah lit one too. She felt like smoking and drinking and talking all night. 'I think I'm going to give up my job,' she said.

'See?' said Julia. She smiled. 'See? Nobody knows about you.'

'Well you haven't known me very long. Mo only asked me to move in because you needed someone quick and she knew me a bit from work.'

'No she didn't.'

The two girls stared at each other for a minute. Hannah was trying to figure something out. Did she like Julia, or was there something too dangerous about the girl? Certainly there was danger, but was it bad?

'She asked you because she fancies the pants off you.'

Hannah felt like laughing. *Fancy-pants.* It was something she used to call people when she was a kid. She used to think it was rude, way back then. *Fancy-pants.*

'I know,' she said. She caught Julia's eye, and smiled. There was a new expression on Julia's face. She didn't look knowing and sophisticated any more. Hannah laughed softly. 'I know,' she said again. She looked out the window, at the black square with rain runnelling down, and felt Julia's eyes on her.

'So how come she was in bed with Bit?' she asked.

'Jeremy?'

'No...that's his name? That was Jeremy?'

'That was Jeremy.'

Julia got up and went to the fridge. She made two more drinks, sloppily, keeping her cigarette between her teeth, and her eyes slitted against the smoke.

'If I were to start telling you the whole story,' she said, through the cigarette, 'I think we'd be here until at least—what day is it now? Forever, anyway.' She carried the drinks back to the table. *I must be drunk*, Hannah thought. *Funny, it just feels warm. But I'm only as drunk as I know I am.* Julia was arranging things on the table.

'This is Jeremy,' she said, moving her glass forward, 'and this is Mo,' she moved Hannah's glass. 'This is Richard, Morgan, Harris, and this is me. This is Louise. Ever meet Louise?' She moved the salt and pepper and some glasses until they were all in a ring. 'And this is a brief summary of the entire *ménage* from day one.' She began swapping glasses round in an orderly way, then she moved them randomly until they were all over the table. Then she put them slowly back. 'Get the picture?'

'It must be confusing.'

Julia sat back and sighed deeply, resting her elbow on the table and her chin on her palm.

'It's fun. Or it used to be.' She stopped and bit her lip. The room fell silent. It had even stopped raining. There was no music next door. Hannah had one finger at her jawbone and she was moving her head slowly from side to side, so that, as her head moved, her finger traced the line of her jaw, right up to below her ears on either side, to where the bone ended and her finger could slide in and feel the vein. René said if you pressed both sides hard enough, at this tender place, you'd stop the blood going to your brain. *Then where would we be?* she thought. She stopped tilting her head and concentrated on separating the two images, the René she knew and the one before her now: a stranger she knew so well she could name his desires. *Cronus took his sister Rhea to wife*, she thought, piecing the words together carefully, *and ruled Elis. He took her to wife, for whom the oak is sacred. And he swallowed his children by her, because of the prophesy.*

Where had that come from? A story he'd told her? A letter he wrote? It was as though she had memorised it. A poem at school or something. *Because of the prophesy.* What was the prophesy?

'Do you know the Greek myths?' she asked Julia.

'Is that what you were dreaming about?'

'There's something in my head and I don't know where it came from.'

'It was probably something they beat into you at school. Did they beat things into you at school?'

'I liked school,' Hannah said dreamily. 'I liked coming home from school and reciting what I'd learned.'

'Golly. My Mum used to have to stand over me all the time or I'd skip homework and go riding.'

Hannah could see the front path where they'd lived when she was very young. It had always seemed immensely long.

Years later, they passed by once, and it wasn't long at all. She preferred the memories.

'So you're interested in Jeremy,' Julia said.

For a moment she felt like denying it, but she was too weary. She said nothing. She tried to picture Jeremy's face but she couldn't. Instead, she saw herself in a huge empty hall, in a white dress, dancing in a slow circle. René led her in a wide, lazy circle, the music coming from far away; it was getting late, it was close to dawn, it was no time at all—the hushed, eerie hour at the end of the night. They would dance like this when there was nothing else left to do.

She felt sorry now. She'd been moving away, she hadn't even read the letter yet. Foolish, it was foolish to start believing she was free. Who was Jeremy? Some raw-faced student. Who was anybody else? There was no one else.

'Time for bed,' she said woodenly. Her head felt thick now. She enunciated with care because she wanted to. 'Think I'll turn in now.'

Julia lit her last cigarette. 'Stay with me while I finish this.'

Hannah stared at her. *And who are you, she thought? I suppose you expect me to pour out all my little secrets. Just because everyone else here is completely fucked up. As if I wasn't bad enough myself.* But she took the lit cigarette when Julia offered it and smoked it for a bit.

'What did your parents think of you coming to London?' Julia asked.

Hannah thought for a bit. She didn't want this conversation now. She sat on the edge of the chair and took her glass up.

'My father didn't mind,' she said. 'My mother's dead.'

'Is she really?' Julia was surprised. Then she said with interest, 'Do you think she sees you? Do you think she can see us now?'

'No,' said Hannah. 'I don't.' Julia was drunk, that was obvious. She was probably quite drunk herself. She no longer felt the other girl was superior to her. She just felt tired. There was no need to be polite any more. In fact, the ruder the better. 'I think that's a fucking stupid idea,' she said aloud. Then she smiled. It felt like the most honest thing she'd said all night. The perfect note to leave on. No more irrelevancies. She stood up.

'I'm going up to bed now so I'll get plenty of sleep and wake up in time to cross the city to my ridiculous and futile job,' she said. 'My profound thanks for the liberal gins.'

'You're quite perfectly welcome,' answered Julia. 'And may I wish you every success in quitting your job as soon as decency allows.'

'Who cares about decency? Not me, that's for sure.'

'Absolutely right. Then we'll really have something to drink to.'

It was easy! She could leave any time she wanted to. If only everything was that simple. But on reflection, everything probably was. She climbed into bed. There was the letter, still on the bedside table, but she would definitely read it in the morning. No more pretending she didn't care. *Why was the oak sacred to Rhea?* she wondered, just before she fell asleep.

It wasn't that Hugh couldn't stand up, but each time he thought about it, it seemed preferable to stay where he was. It was quite pleasant on the stairs, with the streetlight coming in through the hall door and his warm thoughts of Margaret. They didn't always comfort him, but tonight he thought of her simply. Sensible Margaret, wearing headscarves and the tweed coat that she somehow made graceful. If he stood up, would the dizziness come again? It wasn't nice when it came on the way downstairs. Then he felt he might topple forward, and in spite of the lightness of his head, he knew he was pretty heavy.

Hannah sat through the morning trying to pretend she wasn't there. It had been easy to get up: she pretended she was someone else all the way to work. She was quite an interesting person—someone nothing worried. Pretty flamboyant. Careless. Towards ten o'clock, the illusion began to wear thin. Her head felt dull as a brick. She made herself some coffee in the canteen and for a few moments the hot mug was the centre of the world. Then the office closed in again and she sank into a torpor trying not to feel the time inching towards lunch. Beyond lunch, the afternoon, intolerably long and dull. Just before lunch, Mo came down from her floor and gave Hannah a big smile which cheered her up greatly. She had a few words with the editor in his office and then came by Hannah's desk.

'I'm taking you out to lunch,' she announced. Hannah felt grateful, warm, almost like crying.

'That'd be so nice,' she said fervently. She watched Mo going back down the long room to the swing doors at the end. *You know,* she told herself, *Mo's the best friend I could have.* But at the same time, she could see herself from the outside, clutching at this friendship as though it made everything normal. Observing herself like this, she felt cold and cynical. *That's the real me,* she thought, *the cold one. I care for no one except him. Other people are just satellites.*

Ten minutes before lunchtime she went into the upstairs bathrooms where there were more cubicles and shut herself in the one at the end. Leaning against the wall, she opened the letter.

Dear Sparrow,

I have been studying hard and this is our favourite time of day, just as the light is going. They say it's the time there are most accidents, with people's eyes adjusting. I have to say the sunsets have been spectacular this last couple of weeks. Or perhaps I am more susceptible to them. I have been reading so much I find it hard to get back into the world. I wish I could start to put down some of the things I have thought. Levi-Strauss writes about the transition from nature to culture. It's a thin line, as you know, and many have discussed what separates us from the animals. Everyone seems to come up with a conclusive answer. 'Social forms'—but are we merely accustomed to them, or are they deeply rooted in our make-up, the rituals, the customs, the taboos. Taboo. Now there's an interesting word. Did you know it originates in the Tonga Polynesian word 'tabu', meaning 'consecrated to a special purpose, restricted to the use of a god, king, or chiefs, while forbidden to general use.'? The link with kings and chiefs is interesting: in many ancient civilizations, it was permitted, even encouraged, for royalty to do things that were expressly forbidden to the common man. This was so for the royalty of ancient Egypt, Thailand, Incan Peru, and sub-Saharan Africa. Hence Cleopatra in Egypt with her loose way of life—shocking, I can tell you! Royalty saw intermarriage as a 'fitness maximising strategy'—they'd lose their rank in society by marrying beneath them, thin the blood. And nothing, so it seems, is thicker than blood, Sparrow. You know that, don't you?

I try to imagine you in your job, but I can't. An office, Hannah? I hope you'll start to feel restless with it, and hungry. Don't you feel you're blocking off a lot of yourself? Think of all you've learned, all the things you were learning in college. Have faith in yourself: you're a smart girl.

I miss my smart girl.

I want to tell you a story about a tribe of Africans called the Lovedu's (an apt name, as you will hear). These people have a myth that their state was founded by the son of a marriage between a brother and sister. (Don't fold the paper up in fright—I know your sparrow heart flutters under your thin dress.) This son fled to a new land, so great was the burden of his beginnings to him. As soon as he had gone, the state was plagued by disasters. The King of Time stepped in, and married the sister of the boy, because he thought that by generating a new society he could prevent further disasters. The King of Time and his new wife had a son, but he died, so their second child came to the throne—and this was a daughter! The state became a matriarchy, the disasters ended, the new Queen was hailed as the end to chaos. She took 'wives', virginal females who were brought before her. She was allowed to have children by her younger brother. A fascinating story, but still I think the study of Kings more interesting. They are always so alone, so necessary, and therefore always alienated. Imagine being the centre of society, the epitome of man, neither all God nor all man, but perhaps a little of both. The King may flaunt in public what is forbidden to commoners even in private.

But I've been rambling. It's late. Time for the last word of the day and I think you'll like it. It's not rude, I hurry to say, though it sounds it. That's why I like it: hornipilation. Look it up, dear Sparrow.

 Finch

 P.S. Am I getting any better at these damn letters?

'Any idea what hornipilation is?'

 'The state of my legs when I don't shave for two days?'

 Hannah laughed. She was feeling much better; sort of light-headed and careless again. She felt like she didn't have a care in the world.

 'This is just what I needed,' she told Mo, spooning up some thick potato soup.

 'Yep. I saw that empty bottle and I thought of lunch here at once. It's the only way to get through the afternoon.'

 'I want to quit the job,' said Hannah. Mo raised her eyebrows.

 'Do you. Well, I suppose you can't sit opening letters for the rest of your life. But if you hung around, something else might come up. Can you write?'

 'What, copy? Those stories for the magazine? God, no.'

 'Hannah,' Mo leaned forward, shaking her head slowly, 'a dodo could write those stories while maintaining a state of extinction. You could write those stories while swimming the Channel. You just need to want to.'

 'That's the hard part. All those poor people with nothing better to do than read how to prevent cracks in their china. I just can't invent their reading material. It's too silly.'

 'Good,' said Mo. 'That is the correct observation. You've passed the test. You hate working on the magazine. So where to now?'

'Back to your place?'

'Can't, Sweetie. I've got important things to do. I'm a big wheel in there,' she winked exaggeratedly. 'You know, they've begged me to take Editor-in-Chief several times. But I'm too artistic.' She wiped her mouth generously with a napkin. 'I'd simply overflow the position. Too much talent. And I wouldn't toddle off home two days in a row if I were you, because you won't get a reference and the agency won't touch you again.'

They walked back by the canal.

'That's what I'd like, one of those.' Hannah nodded towards the houseboats moored along the edge.

'Oh no, I'd get seasick,' Mo said, 'or capsize.'

'We took a holiday once in a boat.'

'Where was that then?'

'Norfolk. I was really small. Three, I think. Christian wasn't born.'

A dog came loping down the towpath and clambered clumsily into the canal after a stick its owner had thrown. They watched it paddle out, snapping the stick neatly and turning for the bank.

'Just you and your Mum and Dad?'

'And René.'

'He's a lot older than you, didn't you say.'

'Only three years. Feels like more.'

'And he likes writing letters.'

'I suppose he does.'

The dog scrabbled up the bank and trotted past them with his stick.

'And what age is Christian then?'

'Fifteen. That feels like a big gap too. He's still a real kid.'

'So's my brother, and he's only a year younger than me. They mature slower. Sometimes not at all. Ever wonder when your older brother's going to catch up with you?'

'Not really,' Hannah said.

'Did his girlfriends always mother you?'

'He never really...had girlfriends.'

'What, never?'

'No.'

'Is he gay?'

'No. Not that. He's...well...he's, you know, just one of those people who never really has girlfriends. You know the type.'

Mo didn't know the type.

'There's nothing wrong with him, is there?'

'He's lame.' Hannah felt herself blush. 'Walks funny,' she added quickly. Mo glanced at her, caught her expression.

'I think your uncle's cute,' she said. 'That's what I think.'

The idea of anyone describing Hugh as cute amused even Hannah. They were both laughing as they passed through the swing doors into the office.

When they told stories about Jesus at school, she thought of him. She knew it was wrong; but it was him she pictured on the donkey riding between the palms. The holy pictures around the school, a thin-faced man with a beard, that wasn't what he really looked like. She knew. Sometimes she wondered, when they spoke of the Second Coming: 'He will come amongst us. No one knows where or when.' She wondered. She lay awake in the dark, wondering. She told herself it was a crazy idea. Years later, she told him and they laughed about it. 'But you know,' he said, sobering up, 'there was that time I laid my hands upon the geraniums, and lo! They were with flower!' They laughed again.

'Do you believe in God?' she asked him then, 'and the Bible stories, and all that stuff.'

'All that stuff,' he'd repeated. 'Do you?'

'I asked you first.'

'Well,' he'd tipped his chair back then, dangerously, until it touched the wall. 'I believe in something that created us,' he began, 'and in the human need to attach great importance to this power, worship it, even fear it. I believe in right and wrong.' He paused there for a long time. 'But I think it's up to us to figure out what right is, and what things aren't right and why. I don't think the nuns have any superior authority in the matter. It's up to you. And me,' he added.

'I see,' said Hannah. 'Did you ever wonder if you are Jesus?' she asked then, but she didn't smile.

'If there ever was a Jesus and if he came back,' he said, 'he would probably come back as a punk on the Tottenham Court Road; or a rice-farmer in China; or a member of an Indian tribe in the Brazilian rainforest. He wouldn't be sitting here discussing "all this stuff" with his kid sister.'

Hannah loved it when he called her his kid sister. It made her feel they were in a film together.

'He might be,' she said.

'Go and do your homework.'

She turned in the doorway. 'In case you turn out to be,' she said, 'will you put a swimming pool in the back garden?'

'If I turn out to be,' he said, 'I'll be horribly busy with world peace. But I'll see what I can do.'

'And a waterslide?'

'Lessons!' he said loudly and she shut the door in a hurry.

Five

March was terrible. The weather hurt. Hannah asked herself what the whole stupid thing meant, being in London; where she should go, why she had left Uncle Hugh's house with the comfortable silences and the cups of milky tea. But when she went back on Sundays, he seemed unusually quiet. Occasionally, he was even irritable. For a man of his shyness, this went against his nature. They called her father on his birthday and he was alone. At first he didn't realize why they were calling. When she said 'Happy birthday Dad', he said 'Ah.' Christian was in trouble at school again, he said. Complained he was being bullied. René was out. He was always out. Hannah's father didn't know quite where he was always going.

'Things are falling apart,' Hannah said to Mo. They were in the sitting room on Leighton Road, facing each other across the table there. She pushed her hair back from her forehead and sat back in the chair with her hands deep in the pockets of her jacket. She didn't want to take it off.

'Your uncle needs some love in his life,' Mo said.

'You mean sex,' Hannah said bitterly. Not even talking to Mo was good anymore.

'I meant love.'

'And what about everyone else?'

'Everyone else needs sex.'

Hannah was about to say something ugly but she gave in to a wave of sadness instead. 'Sex isn't all that bloody great, is it?' she said quietly.

'You mustn't be doing it with the right girl,' said Mo. Then she said more seriously, 'What *was* it like then?'

I'm not drunk, Hannah thought. *I feel very calm. I know what I'm saying. This will be alright, if I'm careful as hell, it'll be okay.* 'I think it was the suit,' she said eventually.

Mo went very still. She was all ears. 'The suit?'

'I mean, after we did it, when he put on his suit...'

'He wore a suit?' Mo repeated in surprise.

'Sometimes. He worked in an office.' She lied easily. It was so simple.

'Wow. For some reason, I'd have said he'd have had to be a student. Or—I dunno, not a suit though.'

'Yes I know: People Who Work In Suits, by Mo Royce, I know. When I was fourteen I swore with a friend I'd never work in an office. Now look at me. I sold out.'

'You left college. Why did you leave college? Was it him?'

'Yep.'

'Was that why you left Ireland?'

'Yep.'

'Was he married?'

'No.'

'What then? Come on—tell me.'

Hannah scraped her chair back, but Mo raised her hand. 'Wait, wait, wait. We're nearly there! Tell me about the *suit*.' She smiled at Hannah, the smile that transformed her face so she looked open, animated, almost radiant. 'I won't tell anyone,' she said, and laughter lay just below her voice. 'Go on. Where did you do it?'

Hannah ignored the question. She began slowly but Mo saw that she warmed to the story. 'When he put his suit back on,' she said, looking carefully at her hands, turning them over as though inspecting them, 'and I saw him as he was, before, when I just knew him, I was so excited I made him...I...we did it again. There. With our clothes on. We often did it with our clothes on. It saved time, it saved a lot, it focused everything,' she laughed, an odd kind of laugh. She looked faintly puzzled through her laughter.

'You were always in a hurry then,' Mo said.

'Yes,' said Hannah, 'Always a hurry.' She tipped her chair back then and looked at the ceiling as though she saw a film projected there. 'We didn't do it many times,' she added thoughtfully. Mo lit a cigarette, played with the match till it went out.

At last she said 'You know, if your heart's not completely broken, there's someone I know wouldn't mind—' she stopped abruptly. Hannah was staring at her. 'I'm thinking about Jeremy,' Mo finished quietly. 'And he'd put my head in a brick oven and stuff it with forty garlic cloves if he thought I'd told you.'

Isn't that how it always goes, Hannah thought dully. *Sex and betrayal. Promises and lies.* Jeremy. She remembered his boisterous appearance the morning after he'd slept with Mo. Despite herself, she couldn't help feeling shocked at the liberty they all took with one another. She still felt on the outside, like a schoolgirl at the railings.

'Doesn't he do the rounds,' she said flatly. *So Mo thinks I'm not gay*, she was thinking. *So I must be straight. A boring old two-dimensional hetero at the railings looking in.*

'You mean didn't he spend the night with Mo the Lesbian after the party?' Mo smiled ruefully. 'You think either of us was sleeping with the other? We were sharing a bed, Hannah. Haven't you ever done that?'

'No.'

'You should. It's nice. I'd invite you, but I know you wouldn't relax. Maybe sometime.'

'Maybe sometime,' Hannah smiled.

'It'll be nice. I promise. I've got a big bed. You could have a gathering in my bed. A tea-party. A disco.'

'Pre-marriage guidance classes.'

'River-rafting. We could film a soap in it. He's a really sweet guy, you know, Bit.'

'Why's he called that?'

'Who knows? Bit of a mystery. Bit of a gentleman. Bit of everything really. You should think about it.'

'Think about what? He hasn't exactly asked me out, you know.'

'No. But he asked me to get you to call him.'

'Oh Mo, you—'

'Now wait a minute. It's not what you think. He heard you were chucking the job and he said there might be something going at the studio. Here's his number.' She wrote something on the newspaper and tore it off. 'Just phone him. It's easy. You put your lips together and blow.' Hannah took the piece of newspaper and put it in her jacket pocket.

'I'm cold,' she announced. 'I'm always cold. It's Sunday and there's nothing to do.'

'There's a phone in the hall.'

'I'm too cold to phone anyone. I think I've got frostbite.'

'Why didn't you go and cook din-dins for your uncle today.'

'Just because.' She huddled down further in her jacket. 'He's being kind of cranky.' She sat lost in thought then, while

Mo did a bit of the crossword, and after she went out to do her laundry, Hannah went upstairs and kicked her shoes off, and lay in her jacket under the quilt, staring at the ceiling. *I didn't say very much*, she thought, *I hardly said anything.* But she felt a coldness that crept out from inside. It seemed there would be no safe place now. She had taken a single careless step and though she may retreat, she could never undo it. She pulled the quilt closer up to her chin and closed her eyes. *She'll never know*, she thought. Mo would never make the leap of imagination that even to Hannah, even still, seemed vast. Why should she make such a leap? Who would ever jump to such a conclusion unbidden? The house was silent. *There aren't enough blankets*, she thought. *Why haven't they given me enough blankets when they know I'm cold?* She got up and opened her door, but the landing was gone and instead there was an unfamiliar corridor that curved menacingly round to the left. She followed the wall cautiously with her hands. There were rooms down corridors everywhere. How come she'd never been in all these unfamiliar rooms? She tried the handle of one, jerking the door open and stepping back as though she expected a great black monster to flap out in her face. The room had a mirror over a high fireplace, too high to reflect if there was anyone there. She could hear the screeching of big birds—buzzards, she thought. Birds of prey, circling a courtyard below. She stepped inside. *I am awake*, she thought, *but why should he be here?* René was sitting upright in a stiff formal wooden chair with a high back. 'I thought you'd change your mind,' he said, and his tone was not kind. Fear gripped her. 'What do you mean?' she asked, but he just stared at her. He made her go and stand in front of him, looking at her that way, though she didn't want to. He was feeling in his pocket and she dreaded what he would produce. 'I have something for you,' he said and she was too full of dread to protest. His voice was hard. She'd never heard him like this, never once. *I must have done something really awful*, she thought, and she racked her brains. He was drawing his hand slowly out. *Don't touch me*, she thought. *If you touch me I'll scream*. But he was no longer before her, she wasn't in the room any more, she was in an alley somewhere behind a church. There was rubbish everywhere, broken bottles, piss-stains streaking the walls, and she didn't know what to do with the baby she held in her hands. It certainly wasn't hers. Had it come from someone who left it behind the church? It was a hideous thing, she was forced to examine it, and as her horror grew she began to wrap around its neck the cord that dangled ropelike from its belly. It reached almost to the ground and she'd wrapped it tightly three times before it appeared to get any shorter. Then, as she stared, the face changed to a cat face, lips drawn over a row of piranha teeth, mouth wide in a feral howl. It lunged forward, for her eyes. She tightened the cord till she thought the head must surely be severed.

She woke in panic and a hot flush of sweat prickled over her whole body.

'That one again,' she said aloud. Her jaw ached from being clenched. Her heart was racing. 'That old dream.'

The sound of her own voice was a stabilizer, the horror of the dream began to retreat. The cat-face flashed before her once, and she sat up. It was gone. She took off her jacket, wrestling with a sleeve, and curled up tightly under the quilt. It was gloomy in her room, turning dark. The darkness would be large, inhabited, unpleasant.

What's love anyway, she thought, *someone's sick idea of a joke? I love you. I hate you. What's the difference?*

She was shocked to discover that, thinking over the first part of the dream, she felt a familiar ache of desire. She groaned aloud. Intense desire, intense hatred, within so short a time. Could she distinguish one from the other? Were they entirely separate? She tried to separate herself from the emotions, look at the facts, tell herself the story.

I entered the room in dread, and it was a shock to see him. Or was it? Somehow I knew he'd be there. Of course I did, who else makes me feel like that? But he never did make me feel like that. He made me feel...

She turned over restlessly to lie on her other side and gathered the quilt round her. It was no longer possible to know how he made her feel. She put herself back in the room, before the straight-backed chair and his rigid figure gripping her in the vice of authority and dread. Did she wish he was dead? Would she like to kill him? Kiss him? Do it again?

All of them. She wanted all four.

She laughed aloud, then she sat bolt upright, horrified by the sound she'd just made, the sudden, lewd image that caused her to make it. Snuff movie. That's what they could do together. She lay down again. *Come on, René, a snuff movie of You and Me. Oh God, I'm really losing hold. Who am I anymore? Look what you've done to me. Do it again, do it again, please, do it—*

It took her three attempts to call Jeremy, and it annoyed her. *I don't give a damn,* she thought, *and here I am acting like a schoolgirl.* But she couldn't quite get the level of nonchalance she wanted. 'Oh hi, this is Mo's roommate Hannah.' This was what she had rehearsed, but she felt that instead she might say 'this is Mo's Hannamate Roo.' She thought she might giggle. She slammed the phone down after the second time, then picked it up at once and dialed. She got straight through.

'Hello?'

'Hi. This is—is that? um—I'm looking for Jeremy.'

'This is Jeremy.'

'Oh hi. I'm—Mo's friend.'

'Which friend is that?'

'Hannah. Calling about the job.'

'Hannah-Calling-About-The-Job? That's a jolly strange name, if you don't mind my saying so.'

There was a brief pause, and then he gave a little laugh. It was sort of like a sharp intake of breath and Hannah felt herself tighten her grip on the phone. She turned to the wall and studied the wallpaper intensely.

'Yeah, well Mo said there was a job going at the studio.' She picked at the telephone chord, pulling out the spirals and letting them spring back.

'There is a job at the studio,' Jeremy said. 'But I'm not sure you'd want to work there.'

'Why not?'

'Well, cos I'll be there. And you don't want to work with me.'

This chap's a pillock, thought Hannah, and she relaxed a bit.

'Probably not,' she said, 'but I could always ignore you. And I need a job.'

'Ignore me. Hmm. It's been tried. Many times in fact. You'd probably get quite a lot of practice at ignoring me, but I'm also very good at being really really distracting. It's kind of like that all the time in the studio. Everyone's distracting—or distracted—and no one gets much work done. That's what it's like.'

'Then I've got exactly the right experience,' said Hannah.

'When can you start?' he asked.

'Now,' she said.

'Then you probably just have. Look—' his tone changed, 'I'll have to talk to my boss. I think they're looking for someone to type in lyrics and things, maybe you'd even end up doing some layout work. Know Quark Express?'

'A little,' she lied.

'Good. I'll have a word with Jonathan. I'll tell him you can start right away.'

'I might have that job in the studio,' Hannah told Mo later. 'I rang Jeremy.'

'Good,' Mo said, shortly.

I don't care, Hannah thought. *If she wants to think I'm getting involved with him, she can. But she's wrong, cos I'm not, he's a dickhead. He's a dickhead*, she repeated to herself, and she was telling René.

Six

The evening Hannah arrived to tell Hugh she had quit her job and would be starting at the studio the following Monday, she found him sitting on the stairs. He was recovering from an attack of dizziness, and although he started to his feet at the sound of the key in the door, he wasn't quick enough. Hannah gave a small cry as she saw him clambering up from his sitting position on the darkened stairs. She switched the hall light on, shutting the door behind her, and they both stood, blinking in the harsh light. 'I got a fright,' she said, feeling foolish.

'I was a little dizzy,' he explained, embarrassed. 'I'm alright now.'

'You sure?' She moved to the foot of the stairs.

'Yes, yes, quite sure.' He began to come down, wheezing heavily. She stood aside, afraid to seem solicitous.

'Well I'll make some cocoa, shall I?' She was nervous, looking to him for reassurance, for the return of his usual self. His lapse made her feel suddenly vulnerable. He seemed shaken. Had he been sitting long on the stairs, dizzy and alone? She felt a flush of shame. The good news died on her lips. 'I'll dig out some biscuits,' she said. 'I forgot to bring some. I've come for the night, if it's okay, see, I've finished my job. I mean, I quit.' She was talking fast, to cover the awkwardness. Hugh followed her into the kitchen and sat heavily at the table. 'Lovely,' he said, when she paused.

'But I have another one. In a studio. A friend of Mo's got it for me.' She filled a pan with milk, spilling some.

'You can take your coat off you know,' said Hugh, 'before commencing to wait on your old uncle.'

'I don't have any old uncles,' she said cheerfully.

'This one feels pretty advanced,' he replied, 'in terms of wear and tear. The biscuits are in the bread bin.'

'Of course they are. Don't you have a biscuit tin for the bread?'

'Precisely.'

They carried their cocoa into the back room, and settled in the armchairs. 'Backgammon?' she said, and they played a game, but she felt his heart wasn't in it. He beat her roundly and sat back in his chair. The television was on low, the electric heater ticked and twanged quietly. It was too hot in the room.

'Shall I turn the heater off?' she asked.

'If you like, dear girl.'

She felt uncomfortable. Hugh didn't seem himself, and she didn't know what to say. She'd been planning to stay for a couple of days, cook him some nice dinners, perhaps do some housework for him. She'd felt a bit guilty about the couple of weekends she hadn't gone to see him at all. She wasn't sure if he expected her, or was disappointed when she didn't come. Now he didn't seem to be very well and she wasn't sure what she should do. She wanted to be back in Leighton Road, where everything was easy.

'Heard from home at all?' said Hugh.

'Nope. Well, a letter from René, a couple of weeks ago,' she lied, watching the television. There was a program on about reformed alcoholics. 'I was drinking because I hated myself,' said a man in jeans. 'I needed to blot out parts of my life,' said another man. 'Every time those memories come back at me, I started drinking to blot them out again.' *No*, thought Hannah, and she set her jaw to stop the tears suddenly filling her eyes. *No, that's not like me. I have only happy memories. What could other people have to blot out? A divorce? A murder?*

'Did you think we were wild kids?' she asked Hugh suddenly. He looked blank. 'You know, when we were small?'

'No,' he said, 'No, I looked forward to visiting you.'

She thought back to the Hugh she had known then: a giant, a shambling man who sat heavily in chairs and beckoned her to his knee, and never seemed sure what to do with her when she got there. He always had odd toys with him. A cricket bat. A lasso. Skates, when skates had gone out of fashion. She warmed to the subject.

'But did you think we were well-behaved.'

'Yes. All of you. René especially. He was a good boy, with both of you.' This was what she wanted, she realized, to hear him talk of René. A private warmth crept in her. She felt as if she were watching someone when they didn't know.

'He's always doing things for people,' she said.

'Yes.'

'He sort of looked after me, really. Definitely after Mum died, you know?'

'Yes.'

She sighed and stood up. 'I'm going to borrow a book and go to bed.' She glanced at Hugh before going over to the bookshelf. He was watching the television, but he looked distant. She felt for the first time as though she were intruding. She hurriedly chose a book and made to leave the room, taking his cocoa mug as she passed his chair.

'Night, Hugh.'

'Goodnight. Shall you be staying tomorrow?'

'I'm not sure. I'll go into town and I'll ring you in the afternoon. Had you any plans?'

'No. No plans.'

How dreary, she thought, *coming home here alone every night. How does he stand it? Maybe he doesn't. Maybe he can't always stand it, the loneliness.* She screwed up her courage.

'Hugh—are you really alright?'

He turned in the chair, blinking through his thick glasses. 'Yes, dear girl, I'm fine. Just a little dizzy spell. I think I stood too suddenly.' He smiled briefly and she nodded.

'Okay. I just got worried.' She left the room quickly. Stood too suddenly from where? It looked as though he was coming *downstairs.*

In fact, Hugh had been experiencing dizzy spells for some time. He felt them to be unusual constrictions around the chest, quite unlike the onset of his asthma, and he suffered a dizzy giddy feeling, so he thought he might be sick. Sometimes there were shooting pains in his arms, and once in his left leg, but these, he told himself, were small flashes of rheumatic pain. 'I've been having them for some time now,' he muttered aloud one evening, when dizziness had driven him back to the armchair he had just stood from. 'It's nothing, really, Margaret. Just a little shortness of breath.' He passed a hand across his forehead, wiping away the sweat, and struggled against himself to breathe shallowly. 'Don't think anything of it,' he muttered. 'A good night's sleep will do the trick.'

But he hadn't been sleeping very well. Awake at night, he would turn this way and that, searching for a comfortable position. Sometimes he would say 'Margaret' hoarsely into the speckled darkness, but there was never any response. Sometimes the bedclothes seemed unbearably heavy, pressing down on him like the weighted blanket the medics lay across an X-ray patient. He would ease the pressure with his hand, but the heaviness remained, and his throat hurt and made it difficult to swallow.

Upstairs the rooms were freezing. She shivered, rummaging in the wardrobe for more blankets. *Not staying here tomorrow*, she decided grimly, *it's too fucking bleak. It's like the arctic wastes in this house. I'll spend the day in town and then I'll go home and cook something nice for the girls.* Maybe some people would come over, now that Julia had finished her exams. Maybe Jeremy'd come over.

March 25th.

Dear Sparrow,

It's cold and miserable here. I tried to shake the mood off before writing to you, but I don't seem to be able to, I'm sorry. Things have been in upheaval at work: I'm being moved to a new department where I won't have much privacy or time to myself. This is distressing. I may be able to work at home one day a week, though, which will be good. I can work when I wish and do my own work too. There's never enough time. Sometimes it's so oppressive, working all day, set hours. I miss your sparkling conversation, coming home, telling me what you did all day. I never imagined we would lose each other in this manner—with me pushing you away. I never thought I'd have the strength. I miss you terribly, dear Sparrow.

Later

As you see, I tried to destroy this letter. It has spent some time in the bin in my room. But I didn't destroy it entirely, and that felt like some sign. Perhaps it's wrong of me to burden you with my own longings. Perhaps you will feel caught, learning how vulnerable I am without you. I hope you always felt that I was strong, there when you needed me—I tried to be—and now that we are free, we mustn't trap one another in a different way, that would be just as bad. If you were here I know I could not leave you alone. It's very hard for me to write this. Please understand the absolute necessity to burn it once you've read it. Perhaps you want to burn it before you finish; in the last weeks I've no longer felt able to know you like I did, and that is what was meant to happen, it's alright. But I want you to know that what we did was not wrong. I know we discussed this, and I know you understood, and I think you believed everything I told you. You must hold on to this belief, dear Sparrow. I feel it is the most important thing we have. The only thing no one can take from us. I don't know what your life is like now, I just know I can't protect you from what you might learn, what you might hear, who you will meet. I hope you meet people who will be good to you. Don't let the others bring you down, you smart girl. Don't let the hard lessons hurt too much. People will try to use you, to take you for their own, because you are lovely, and because you lack guile. Don't let them do this, dear heart, keep yourself for yourself. Right now you need to build your strength, remember the things you have learned, they are not trivial. Bring your knowledge into play. Think. Then act. If I don't post this now, I never will. I have tried to understand if Mother knows what we did. She doesn't respond. It may be that, as Ernest Dowson thought, there's nothing, nothing, after we pass the gate.

Crying on the tube, she thought. *What next?* She bit her lip hard and tasted the warm salt water. Stuffing the crumpled sheet back into its envelope, she glanced at the postal date on the other letter. It was the same, March 25th. Could he have written two letters on the same day? And what might this new, black mood have pushed him to write in the second? Shoving both letters in her bag, she got up hurriedly and stood by the doors. The carriage was nowhere near full but there were still too many people for her. What would they think if they saw her crying? The train rumbled into a station. She kept her eyes on the crack where the doors would roll apart, and when they did, she got off and stood looking up and down the platform for the Way Out sign. Way Out and British Rail, she saw. Paddington. She followed the signs, climbing the gusty stairs, standing tensed on the escalator. The station was massive and cold. She stood, temporarily awed by the giant arched roofs, three of them, and the blackened trelliswork, and the grimy glass, high up where she could see the flapping of trapped pigeons. Then the concourse seemed too huge, a waste, no shelter anywhere. She walked up the ramp to Praed Street, where the black cabs swung treacherously round a roundabout and down to the station. *I need a café,* she thought, *somewhere warm, where I can just sit.* She had to open the second letter. A fascinated dread needled her; she had to see how bad it could get, what he was feeling, what he said. There didn't seem to be any cafés, only money exchanges and restaurants. It started to spatter rain. She hurried along the pavement. Everyone had their head down against the weather. She saw a bus and screwed up her eyes to read the destination. It was Camden! A 27. *How bloody marvellous,* she thought through her tears as the doors hissed open and she fished about for her purse. Upstairs was empty and she went up to the front seat and sat with her feet on the bar below the window. She watched Praed Street go by, until they swung out and up on to the Marylebone Road. Then she slowly opened the second letter.

'Dear Sparrow,' she read,
I hope I don't alarm you with the letter I wrote yesterday. I know you understand what loneliness means, and how it can submerge everything else, everything good and hopeful. Today was an odd string of things, and I will try to put them together for you. To start with I had a discussion with Father at breakfast, about you. It gives me mingled happiness and pain to speak of you like this to someone else who knows you well. But by the end of the conversation I had come to the odd conclusion that Father doesn't really know you well at all. You puzzle him. But that apart, he lives so much in his own world now that outside concerns seem to make only the faintest impression on him. He wanted to know what we should 'do' about you. I told him I didn't think there was anything we could do about you, that you were doing very well by yourself. 'She's going to make a success of whatever she does,' I told him, because that is what I believe. My conviction seemed to reassure him. He would be better to be anxious about his other son, who continues to interpret the rules of life as loosely as he pleases. He hasn't been going to school all the time I feel sure, but I can't prove it. Maybe Dad will have to contact the school. Again. Christian spends all his time locked in his room. He says I am down on him all the time. I worry about him.

After breakfast I worked on some work I am doing. Just before lunch I was interrupted by a call from an old friend I hadn't seen or heard from for a long time. He invited me to a party. I said I'd try to make it, but you know me, I'm not much at parties.

All afternoon I was able to work without interruption. Came across some interesting things: did you know that the Church of England used to have a law specifying a list of thirty relatives one could not marry? Thirty! That would include quite a few layers of cousins. The Roman Catholic church in the Middle Ages would not allow marriage within the 4th degree of kinship. This was not for moral reasons, but to keep the wealth from being concentrated in a narrow band of families. Spreading the wealth out through intermarriage helped to ensure the growth of the Church. Wily devils, eh? But in fact the Catholic Church has a rich and colorful history of such things. In 1414 Pope Balthasar Cossa confessed to adultery and being with family members. Less than a hundred years later, Rodrigo Borgia announced fatherhood of his own daughter's child! According to belief, Moses was the son of a nephew and his aunt. Abraham married his half-sister. Lot's daughters made him drink wine and then conceived by him! Then you have the Church turning to the other extreme—becoming paranoid. To the Church of England, marrying a deceased wife's sister is not unlawful...but it is a sin! I find the myths and superstitions surrounding this subject even more fascinating (I hope I'm not boring you). French peasants used to think that the marriage of first cousins brought about crop failure and disease in their animals. The Irish themselves had a tendency to blame crop failure on similar things. And marriage to a relative certainly brought no joy to Claudius. He was poisoned by his niece/wife Agrippa. But she didn't fare too well either: she met a grisly end at the hands of her own son...also her lover...the Emperor Nero. Here Endeth The History Lesson. Here Endeth This Letter. I have to be up early. Write soon, Sparrow, and tell me what you're doing.

She folded the letter and sat staring out at the driving rain. The tears came unchecked now and she didn't feel they would ever stop. She watched the traffic below, an endless procession of cars in either direction. *I wonder where they're all going,* she thought, *at lunchtime on a Thursday.* They swung round onto Hampstead Road. What was he working on, this work of his he kept referring to, that he seemed to be doing all the reading for? And what kind of books was he reading? And why? She didn't want to hear all this stuff about...that. She began to busy herself, folding the letters away in her bag, sorting through the odd scraps of paper she found in there, looking for a hanky: bus tickets, bank machine receipts, gum wrappers. They passed the National Temperance Hospital, and she remembered the man in jeans on the telly, who drank to forget. *I have tried to understand if Mother knows what we did. She doesn't respond.* She got up suddenly from her seat. The bus was fuller now. Everyone was wet. The windows were steamed over. She scrambled down the aisle, hanging on to the stair rail as the bus took a corner, and stood waiting for the doors to open. There were too many people now, they crowded the filthy, stinking space of the bus. If she walked for twenty miles in any direction, she couldn't get away from them. Old people, shuffling along in misery, old men hunched in their macs, the homeless, crouching on sodden cardboard, their scrawny dogs nosing in rubbish bins for scraps to survive. *Does Mother know what we did? Could she...?*

The doors shuddered open and she stepped down into a puddle by the stop. They were on the High Street and the narrow pavements were crowded with shoppers. They milled about her, hundreds of them, women with prams, girls her own age with dyed hair and Docs. She shouldered her way towards the tube station, wishing the rain would stop. What could they all be doing here, these people, what were they all talking about? They passed her talking, quick and slow, mumbles and animation, five, ten different accents and languages. She let herself slip into a numbed half-dream, waiting to cross at the lights, letting the feeling of being suspended raise her up off the scalding earth. Things were mounting. She felt on the edge of breaking down. *I can't stop crying*, she thought, as the tears sprang up again, *not even on the street. Life's too short. You're meant to be happy.*

By the time she got home she was soaked to the skin. The house was empty, soothingly quiet. She ran herself a hot bath. As she lay soaking, she talked herself down from the ledge of panic.

You're not a bad person, she told herself. *You'll remember again how to be the person who can cope. You'll enjoy being Hannah again. This will happen soon. With your new job and your new friends, you can put behind you anything you want to put behind you. Why don't you try to follow his advice, keep yourself for yourself, remember what he taught you, remember all you've learned. It is true that almost everything I know I learned from him. It is true that almost every opinion I have I got through his opinions, perhaps adding just a little of my own self to them, to keep my self-respect. But it's not true what he said: that I have no guile. He doesn't know, he doesn't know about all those thoughts and dreams. I dreamed he was hanging and I was glad.*

She drew her legs up and watched the water run off her knees, turning the last thought over in her mind.

Was I glad? In the dream, when I saw him hanging there, what was it I felt just before I woke so horribly? Could it really have been pleasure? Oh Hannah, she thought, *you're in trouble now. You're sick. You need help.*

But she was already feeling the return of herself as she dressed. 'I don't need help from *anyone*,' she said aloud, angrily, as she shrugged on a jersey. 'They can all fuck off, that's what they can do.' She felt better now, and she sang to herself as she made a sandwich for lunch. But when the front door slammed, she jumped as though she'd been slapped. Whoever it was went straight upstairs, and soon Hannah was settled in an armchair in the front room, deep in the book she'd borrowed from Hugh. Towards evening, the front door slammed again and Julia came in. She slung a red leather duffle bag onto an armchair and collapsed on the couch. Hannah looked at her, coming slowly out of the story she'd been reading, waiting, hoping for Julia to fill the emptiness she felt as the story drained away.

'I'm in love,' said Julia solemnly. She looked intently at Hannah, and then broke into laughter. 'You look so *sorry* to hear I'm in love, Hannah!' She laughed. 'You look as if that's the worst thing that could possibly have happened to me!'

'It is,' said Hannah.

Julia stopped laughing for a moment. 'God! You mean it!' she said. Then she laughed again, threw her head back on a cushion and swung her long legs over the back of the couch. She was wearing bright striped tights. There were two thuds as she kicked off her shoes. Hannah closed her book and put it aside. *Nothing means anything,* she thought. *It doesn't matter.*

'Who are you in love with,' she asked.

'Well you don't know him,' said Julia, staring at the ceiling and fingering the beads round her neck. 'And when you do, you'll probably wonder why I'm in love with him. He's completely ordinary.' She turned her head and smiled beatifically. *How nice,* thought Hannah, *to be completely ordinary.* 'His name's Payton,' said Julia. 'That's P-a-y-t-o-n. Want to know what it means?'

'What?'

'Well I asked him. I said, Payton, that's an unusual name—because that's the kind of stupid, boring, uninspired thing you end up saying to people you've just decided you're crazy about—I said, what does it mean? And he said, it means my parents couldn't get it together to think of a name for me, so they let the nurse who delivered me choose. She must have been mentally deranged, he said. But that was only her second choice. And he asked me to guess what her first was. Want to know?'

'What?'

Julia sat up, to summon full effect for the delivery. '*Tarquin!*' she bellowed, and fell back on the couch, laughing till she had to wipe her eyes. Suddenly, she scrambled up and hung over the back of the couch, rummaging for her shoes.

'Come on,' she said, 'we're going to a party. There's a party, and we—' she straightened with a shoe in either hand, 'are *going.*'

Mo and Julia made her dress up. They sat on Julia's bed while Julia transferred the contents of her wardrobe from its hangers and drawers to the bed, the floor, the chairs, and to Hannah. Mo advised.

'Try this! Try this!' She held up an impossibly small blue linen blouse. 'Or this!' She waved a black, lacy, strapless thing.

'Which bit does that go on?' said Hannah.

'Look—' Mo was unhooking a dozen tiny hooks. 'Lift yer arms up luvvie.' Hannah turned obediently and raised her arms.

'And I think…these.' Julia was holding a pair of pea-green flares critically up to the light.

'Flares,' said Hannah in disbelief.

'They're coming back in,' Julia said reprovingly. 'Another year and they'll be passé. They'll be on Oxford Street. In Top Shop.'

'I thought Top Shop was—' began Hannah, but Mo had finished hooking her up and was propelling her to Julia's full-length mirror. 'Look at that!' she crowed. 'Look at yourself girl!'

Hannah looked. She saw the reflection of her own body, laced in the black camisole. She saw the thinness of her arms, and the hollows of her shoulderblade where he had kissed her. She saw the neck she had arched in the final moments.

'No thanks,' she said briskly, turning from the mirror, pushing aside the jeans that Julia held out. She went back and sat on the bed.

'Oh really,' Julia said complainingly, 'I can't please you. Mo, you dress her. I have to take a shower.' She threw the jeans on a chair. 'You can wear anything you like,' she said as she left the room, 'except the dress on the door, cos I'm wearing that. Have fun!' she called, and shut the door.

'Hannah, Hannah, Hannah,' Mo stood by the mirror, shaking her head. Hannah stared back at her defiantly. 'That's no way to look in the mirror, girl. Really,' she added in a kinder tone, 'let me tell you about mirrors.'

'*Looking In Mirrors*, by Mo Royce,' said Hannah, and she folded her arms, hugging her elbows.

'Even Mo Royce knows how to look in a mirror,' said Mo, 'and you have to confess, she doesn't have much to look at. But it hurts me to see a looker who's mirror-shy. You're supposed to enjoy mirrors if they're kind to you. Look,' she went to the bed and Hannah allowed herself to be gently led till they were both standing before the mirror, Hannah in front, Mo behind, addressing their reflections. 'See?' With her right hand she tipped Hannah's chin, till she couldn't but look at herself. They stood in silence for a moment. Hannah's eyes held Mo's in the mirror.

'You're supposed to look at yourself, darling,' Mo whispered. 'Go on. Take it in.'

So Hannah stared at herself, full in the face. *This is who I am*, she thought. She began to cry then, big tears that she let run down her face unchecked, but when Mo reached an arm around her, she jerked it away as though she'd been slapped.

They sat on Julia's bed smoking cigarettes.

'The smoking's just an affectation really,' Hannah said carelessly, flicking ash into the tray. 'I don't have to smoke, I just like to smoke.' She was still crying. Mo watched her. Then she stooped and picked up a cardigan from the floor. 'Here,' she held it out, 'put this on.' She was hurt by the way Hannah had moved away from her, but she wasn't going to show it.

'Want to tell me what's wrong?' she asked.

'No,' said Hannah. She sniffed. 'What happened to Morgan?'

'What's meant to have happened to him?' said Mo. 'Oh, you mean Payton. Well Morgan's not going to the party tonight. Payton is. That's what happened to Morgan.'

When Julia came back from her shower, she found them both giggling. Hannah was wearing the green flares. They were inches too long for her. She was standing on the bed, playing air guitar, a second cigarette between her teeth. 'I-can't-get-no', she sang hoarsely, 'Payton-Action.' She and Mo shouted with laughter and Julia stood in the doorway, shaking out her wet hair.

'Oh yeah, jealous of my conquest,' she nodded sagely. 'I know—wait till you see this guy, you two, you'll be *crying* because I got there first.'

'He isn't conquered yet, though,' said Mo.

'Payton. Still waitin',' said Hannah, and she played some more guitar, 'No datin', just baitin'.'

'Just you wait,' said Julia, and a big smile crept across her face. 'Tonight's the night, ladies. Julia the Jezebel.' She reached up and unhooked the hanger from the back of the door. She held the dress against her and, holding one sleeve outstretched, began to walk slowly around the room. 'I'm going to be witty,' she crooned, 'and poised, and full of an irresistible—' she spun around, making the dress twirl, '*Je ne sais quoi*! And I shall stoop to conquer.'

'You'll stoop to throw up if you start dancing like that after the gin slings I'm going to prepare for us,' said Mo.

'Gin sling!' said Julia, her eyes lighting up. 'What an *insanely* good idea.'

'But you have to dress the girl first,' said Mo and she turned at the door. 'What do you want to look like tonight, Hannah?'

Hannah looked from Mo to Julia and back to Mo. 'A boy,' she said.

'I give up on that child!' Mo called as she went downstairs.

'I don't look at all like a boy!' protested Hannah fifteen minutes later as she came downstairs to help make gin slings. 'You can see my middle,' she finished lamely.

'We're meant to,' said Mo.

'You can see the tops of my stockings,' she complained.

'Hannah,' Mo held up the quart of gin she was preparing to pour into an empty lemonade bottle, 'Bit's not a homosexual you know.'

'Bit!' exclaimed Hannah, and her hand went instinctively to where her lace bodice and her skirt failed to meet. 'You didn't say anything about him being there.'

'That's right,' said Mo, grinning broadly at Julia, who grinned delightedly back. 'We didn't.'

'I'm changing,' Hannah announced and left the kitchen. Mo and Julia exchanged looks.

'Go after her,' said Mo in a tired voice.

Five minutes later they were all testing the gin sling, Hannah at the table, with her legs self-consciously crossed.

'Tastes a bit bland,' said Mo, 'I'd better put some more grenadine in it.'

Hannah fingered the lacy pattern that ran in a line up the side of her stockings. It was pretty.

'Ooh, look at that!' said Mo, watching lovingly as the colour swam in the bottle. 'It's a pity you can't keep it like that.'

They were all a little drunk by the time they got on the tube. Julia and Hannah sat on one side, Mo faced them with the gin sling poking conspicuously out of her handbag. They giggled a lot, and Julia explained how she was going to impress Payton. 'I'll walk straight up to him and say: "Look, my boyfriend's not here tonight. What do you say?"'

'No, wait,' Mo waved her hands, 'you say "Hi Payton. Is that a gun in your pocket or is it a really obvious hard-on?"'

'Is that a gun in your pocket, Payton?' practised Julia in a mock serious voice, 'because you know, it's illegal to carry guns in this country. So why don't you hand it over, and I'll massage it with Ponds hand cream.'

People were giving them looks. Hannah shivered. She had decided she was going to completely ignore Jeremy.

If he comes up to me, I'll pretend I'm in love with Mo.

She glanced across at Mo and saw that she'd been watching her. She smiled guiltily.

She's envious of my body, she thought, and she felt criminally glad. She let her eyes rest on Mo's thighs. *They jiggle when she walks, and the back of her bum, it's huge, she can't disguise it no matter what she wears. But she's sexy! How come?*

She caught Mo's eye again and this time flashed her a big grin. *I must be drunk,* she thought, and she gestured to the bottle. Mo handed it over without smiling.

The party was out near the end of the tube line. It was in a large flat on two floors above some shops. They clattered down the street, Julia's heels loud on the pavement. As they drew near, they could hear the music. Hannah shivered and didn't want to go on. A knot of panic tightened in her stomach. All those nights out in college came back: leaving early, slipping away, running from pubs and parties for a bus back to safety, back to the sanctuary he always gave.

If I go now, where will I go?

They could see people moving about in the upstairs rooms, and as they reached the front door, Julia put her arm around Hannah. It felt protective and nice, and they entered the party in a little procession, with Mo behind. Hannah was glad she couldn't see her friend's face.

There were people everywhere—dancing in the tiny rooms, blocking the stairs, crushing past each other to the fridge in the kitchen. Julia began greeting people she knew—hugs and kisses—Hannah recognized some of them too, but she hung back. She turned to find Mo and her bottle, but Mo had gone. Now she felt really exposed, standing in the hallway, neither in nor out of the kitchen, horribly conscious of her borrowed clothes, nothing to do with her hands...She looked about her uneasily. What could she do? All these people, she'd have to leave, she'd—

'Hey!'

She looked up. Jeremy was hanging perilously over the bannisters with a beer in either hand. He didn't appear to be holding onto anything, just hanging there, grinning at her. 'I didn't know you were coming,' he bellowed. Some music had started thumping in the room behind her, and she had to shout to be heard too.

'Hi!' She felt her face breaking into a huge smile. The relief of knowing someone! Someone to look at, talk to, be distracted by.

'Are you coming up or will I let go and join you?' shouted Jeremy, and he swayed dangerously. 'Whoah! Here—' he held one beer out a little further so she could reach it, then, with apparent ease, he vaulted right over the bannister and landed in a heap beside her. Someone screamed and there was clapping. 'Asshole,' said a girl beside Hannah. He stood up shakily, but grinning triumphantly.

'Are you OK?' shouted Hannah, incredulously.

'Couple of broken legs, nothing serious. Come on, let's dance.' He steered her into the back room. The lights were down, and she let him guide her into a far corner where there was space, stumbling over couples kissing on a low couch. It was very hot. She pulled the ring on her beer.

'Cheers!'

They started to dance. She felt alright, she felt she could move any way she wanted and not look stupid. She held her beer and accepted the cigarette he offered, and bent close to his hands as he lit it. 'Why don't you take your jacket off?' he said in her ear, and she let him take her can and lift the jacket from her shoulders, and touch her shoulders, and touch her waist lightly with one hand and they danced on and the music got louder and more people were dancing and in between he told her she was looking great and she shook her head and said 'Julia gave me everything' in his ear; he pretended not to hear so she repeated it, and then it was a slow song and they were dancing close and she let his hand play up and down her back; she let him say the things he said. She felt fine, and it seemed suddenly clear to her that René had been right. This was how it was meant to turn out. He'd prepared her, like he said; he'd just been readying her, and now she was ready and it was all falling into place.

I have tried to understand if Mother knows what we did; she doesn't respond.

She closed her eyes, trying to let the music blank her mind. There would never be enough time to understand what had happened, she just had to go on, stop trying to make sense of it, when there wasn't any sense.

Got to start now, she thought. *This is the part he told me about — when I was older, he said, it would all start happening, and now I am older and it is happening.*

Jeremy had let her go and was miming drinking with his empty can. She nodded and followed him through the smoky crowd, out into the kitchen.

'Mo has some gin sling,' she told him.

'Ugh. Mo would have,' he said, and she laughed. He passed her back a beer from the fridge and they stood against the sink and lit up.

'Whose party is this?' she said.

'Fuck knows,' he replied, and blew a smoke ring. 'Julia told me about it.'

'Did she,' said Hannah, and smiled to herself. She was feeling so good now; she watched the party move and she felt part of it. Jeremy talked; she listened and laughed at his jokes and anecdotes, and much later when Mo came in to find her and see if she was ready to go, she left again quickly and Hannah didn't see her.

I must be drunk, thought Hannah when Jeremy released her and stopped whispering in her ear. *I'll wonder tomorrow if this really happened.* Then he asked her to share a taxi back to his place, and she shook her head. He said he promised nothing would happen, and if she'd prefer, he'd go back to Leighton Road. 'We could just sit up and talk,' he said, and he fondled the hair at the back of her neck, and bent to kiss her again.

She couldn't find Mo, but Julia was in a room upstairs, smoking with a group of girls.

'Well hello,' she said when she saw Hannah and Jeremy, 'lovebirds,' she added, and laughed. Hannah laughed too. In fact, they laughed most of the rest of the night, until the party broke up and they were all out in the cold night, looking for taxis. Hannah made Jeremy say goodnight when a taxi came.

'Go home,' she told him, 'like a good dog. Go sleep in your own basket.' Julia held the taxi while they kissed; finally, she called out the window, 'Come on darlings, that's enough! It's nearly the day after tomorrow.'

'See you the day after tomorrow,' Jeremy said, squeezing her hand.

On the way home, Julia wanted to know what had happened. Hannah sat back in the seat and watched double versions of the streetlights go by. 'I think I drank rather a lot,' she said. 'Could that be so?'

'I expect it could,' said Julia, 'but you haven't told me what happened yet.'

'I thought it was obvious,' said Hannah.

'Not at all,' said Julia. 'There are a hundred million variations on the theme. Did he kiss you first?'

'What happened to Payton?'

'Oh, him,' said Julia. 'He missed his chance. He blew it. He's a no-hoper, I'm afraid. Didn't you see him? Arrived on a bike with two girls—absolute dolls—great bodies, nothing upstairs. It was sad. What a waste of great loins.' She sighed and crossed her legs, smoothing her dress. 'And to think I actually waxed my legs on his account. What a fool.'

Hannah watched out of the corner of her eye. Julia stared moodily out the window, her fingers idly tucking back some strands of hair that had come loose. In the passing lights, her features looked sculpted, sort of regal. *She's like some kind of royal figure,* thought Hannah. *The way she carries herself, and the way she never seems to lose control. I wonder what it's like getting your legs waxed.*

'When did Mo leave?' she asked, as the taxi dropped them off.

'Don't you worry about Mo,' Julia said.

'Well, I just wondered why she didn't come and tell me she was going.'

'She did,' said Julia quietly, as she put her key in the door. Hannah followed her in and shut the door.

'How come—' she said, and then she realised what must have happened. She felt lost suddenly, standing in the dark hall with Julia, whose eyes she felt on her in the darkness. They just stood for a minute, letting their vision adjust.

'Is Mo—' Hannah stopped, and finished in the quietest voice she could, 'in love with me?'

Julia put her head on one side and smiled as she would at a small child. 'Don't you worry about Mo,' she said. 'You'll be alright Hannah. You're a good girl.'

But what did it mean, Hannah wondered, as she undressed in the dimness of her own room. Good? Be a good girl. Be good. Are you good? he had asked in a letter. She no longer understood this question. It frightened her. It wasn't how he used to talk. When she was a child, she had known about good and bad, right and wrong. That was what mothers told you about: what to do, what you shouldn't do, and why. Don't hit your brother, he's just a baby. Don't stick your tongue out, it isn't nice. *I have tried to understand if Mother knows what we did. She doesn't respond.* What if her mother had never died? What if she'd grown up like normal people, with a Mum and Dad, and there hadn't been that awful moment when time opened up and swallowed her Mum, and left her and Daddy and René and Christian on the edge, looking down and not knowing what to do? Would it have happened? Would she and René ever have spent those long languid afternoons together? Would they ever have slipped into the easy habits that suited them both so happily? Would he ever have made the first gentle move that slid them both into a moment of catatonic bliss? She sat down slowly at her dressing table and leaned towards her own reflection in the spotted mirror. The lamp threw long shadows. Her eyes looked darker than usual. She stared intently at her face. She parted her lips and tipped her upper lip very gently with her tongue. She whispered his name, and whispered it again. 'If ever we meet in a glass house,' she whispered slowly to her reflection, 'with stones for hands; or crossed talk/ I'd like it heard that I know how it feels/ to be charmed, I'd like our love/ to let us leave that place unharmed.' The incantatory beat of the poem made her feel safer. There was rhythm in the world. There were lines that ran out like those and gave her comfort because she could repeat them at any time, in any place, to give herself the reassurance that things were as they always had been; that there was nothing wrong; that there was nothing wrong at all.

Seven

5 April 1991.

Dear Finch,

It's Sparrow, from inside her P. O. Box. It's a little squashed in here, and I can barely see out the letter slot. Actually, that's a lie. I can see very well, out the window of my new office to the playground across the road. It's lunchtime but there are no kids today. They're all on their Easter holidays. I'm sorry I've left it a whole week to write. I started my new job on Tuesday, and the weekend was Easter, so there was lots going on. You weren't at home when I phoned. Daddy said he didn't know where you were. Tonight there's a film on the TV of *The Heart of the Matter*, because Graham Greene died on Wednesday. I was so sad. I'd just finished reading *Our Man In Havana*. I'd like to see Trevor Howard as Scobie, I think he'll do him justice. 'If one knew, he wondered, the facts, would one have to feel pity even for the planets? If one reached what they called the heart of the matter?' Finch, your Sparrow misses you so much. I ache for you. I miss your guidance, the way you know what's going on with me better than I do myself. The way you care only that I'm alright. I think what I'm trying to say is that I miss being close to someone who loves me like you do. There is no one else loves me like that. Your two letters came together. I took a few days off because I quit my job. I got a new one, working in an art studio. It's still just typing, but it's much more interesting than that crappy stupid magazine, and there's the possibility of some different work later, maybe doing some design stuff. I have to get the hang of Quark Express. I'll be glad when I can use it at all, never mind as well as I told them I could. I didn't have to go through the agency for this one: a friend of Mo's works here and helped me get it. It's in a really nice place. I think I'm going to like it. Everyone's kind to me. What type of book are you writing? It sounds funny. I don't understand what you really care about all that stuff for. Cleopatra and the Catholic church with its laws about marriage. It's all confusing to me and it's not very nice. I want to hear about what you're doing, what life is like in the house now, who you're meeting. I think you should get out more, that's what I think.

<u>Sunday 7 April:</u> Hundreds of thousands of Kurds have crossed the mountains of Iraq to Turkey and Iran. An international relief operation's been launched. They are dying of hunger and cold. They'll die: we have everything. It's horrible. This is the news. I'm in Hugh's—cooked him his Sunday lunch. He's acting a bit funny these days. He says he's getting dizzy spells. Maybe I'll try and persuade him to go to a doctor, but I'm afraid to bring the subject up really. The other day I arrived and found him sitting on the stairs. He said he had a dizzy spell. But he's so dismissive then, I think he was embarrassed, and so was I a bit. I hate illness, you know?

I remember once when I cried. It was like a small volcano. Some dread, some excitement, a sense of doom as forces moved beyond my control, moved deep inside me. I cried, because the two mingled, love and sadness, as they must have for every human being all through the centuries. I couldn't explain it to you. I didn't know if we were like anyone else, and you told me it would never be like this again, that it would always be different, not better or worse, but just completely different, and you kissed away my tears.

The sky outside is washed. Spring wet and windy and sudden sun. Shifting weather, you can never be sure. Maybe we needed the shake-up, the shifting ground, to settle back more ourselves, more sure of what to do. I always thought, if I let it go a couple more days, it will calm down, it will even out and we'll settle back and be normal again. We *did* do that for spells, didn't we: held back, pretended we felt nothing but the ordinary love, the love that's allowed.

I like working in the new place a lot. The people and the atmosphere are very different from the other jobs I had. Lots of joking goes on, and lots of nonsense talk, which I don't join in yet but I will soon. There's a sense that people are creative, artistic, and have to work in their own way. People come and go at odd times of the day; everyone dresses as they like. The people are nice too. There's Anna, she's pregnant—I can't stop looking at her bump! And Jonathan and Jeremy and Robyn (she's a girl) and Tim. My boss is Jonathan. Well, it's hard to draw character sketches of them; they're all kind of offhand and friendly in a funny kind of distant way. You wouldn't want to get too close to any of them, I don't think.

I'm reading *The Golden Notebook*. It's the kind of book you read when you start to live with girls like Mo and Julia. I was half-starved for a good girlfriend, though I never realized the need until it was filled. You always filled everything. In a way, girls threaten me the same way they always did. I always thought it was easier to be the only girl. But the funny thing is—when I'm feeling downright ugly, a frump, and gauche, it helps if there's a good-looking girl there. Julia is like this, because she's so conscious of how good she looks but somehow it just doesn't get in the way. She makes you accept it and then chuck it aside because it's not important any longer. I can't describe to you how bound up in women's matters I feel reading the GN. Anna in her flat with the lodgers and the affairs and her notebooks and her friendship with Molly. That's what's most interesting—the friendship between the two women. But I can't even explain to you what I mean by 'women's matters'. Can't put it into words, how women think, the things that are important.

Write soon. Sparrow.

For a moment she thought the letter was a mistake—that he'd forgotten about the P. O. box and sent one to Leighton Road again. But he'd promised to do as she wished! Then she saw it wasn't his handwriting at all. Relieved, she frowned at the childish letters, strangely familiar, then she ripped it open.

'Who's it from?' Mo asked through a mouthful of toast. Julia looked up from the textbook beside her plate.

'My kid brother—oh *God*!'

'What's the matter?'

Hannah was clutching her forehead with one hand, and scanning the oversize writing. She turned the page impatiently and swore softly as she came to the end.

'I don't believe it,' she looked up. The girls were staring at her. 'He's coming over! On the boat,' she checked the clock on the cooker, 'he's on the boat right now!'

There was a moment's silence, and then she started to laugh. 'He's running away,' she giggled and then bit her lip. 'What'll my Dad say?'

Mo began to laugh then too. 'Good for him!' she crowed. Julia was smiling and shaking her head.

'Let's see,' she held out her hand for the letter. 'I always wanted to run away when I was a kid. Dear Hannah,' she began, 'I'm coming over to see you next Wednesday. There's nothing much going on at school and they won't hardly miss me. If you get this letter before Wednesday don't tell Dad it's a surprise. Where do you live. I get in at Y-u-s-tan,' she spelled, and then laughed, 'Euston station in the evening. Come and meet me or I could as well stay in a hotel. Don't tell Dad or René, he is being dead heavy on me, Christian.'

'How old is he?' she said to Hannah.

'Fifteen.' Hannah seemed immobilised. 'I've got to ring Dad, but he'll have left the house, he's on his way to work—Christian's on the boat—Hugh! I've got to ring Hugh!'

Hugh had left for work too. Everyone was on their way, out of contact. *There could be an emergency*, thought Hannah, *and everyone I know is on a train somewhere. There IS an emergency.* But sitting on a bus down the Camden Road she began to feel it would be alright.

We'll meet him off the train and Hugh will talk to him. Hugh will sort him out. Maybe he could even stay a few days. She smiled to herself, and felt a pang, imagining Christian sitting on his own at a ferry window, staring out to sea. *Bit of an adventure*, she thought, but it troubled her too. He was still a real child, he hadn't made the leap. *Maybe he has now, since I left.* She felt a sudden constriction in her throat. Bullying, her Dad had said. He was such a quiet kid, and his features and fair hair somehow made him look like a girl. *I bet that helps,* she thought grimly, and then whispered 'Never mind kid, you'll be okay', so her breath clouded the bus window.

Hugh accepted the news implacably. 'Dear me,' he said, on a very bad line from the City. 'Well we can't have him arrive without a welcoming party. The boat train's in at six-thirty, if I'm not mistaken. Shall we meet at the station?'

'We'll have to ring Dad.' She hoped Hugh would do this. She didn't want to be the one to tell her Dad, hear the confusion in his voice, start the unravelling of her brother's trouble. She wished the whole thing wasn't happening. 'He'll be upset,' she added cautiously.

'Yes, I expect so. I'll give him a ring.'

Good old Hugh. He and Dad can have one of their brusque conversations and it'll be alright. It's their business, she thought, but she knew it wasn't. It was up to her now. If Christian was in trouble, he had turned to her.

I shouldn't have left, she thought. *I should have realised that with Mummy gone, Christian needs me. I should be better to him, I should've written and stuff*, asked him what was going on at school. But he can't stay. We'll have to send him back there, to whatever drove him away.

A thought struck her then and she clenched her teeth. *I'm not bringing him back*, she resolved fiercely. *I'll not go back. René sent me away and now I've made the break, I'll not go back. Not if he begs.*

She was nervous, she realised, because Christian had come from home only that morning. He'd probably had breakfast with René. She tried to believe it was only three months since she had left. It meant nothing, the arbitrary measurement of time. Those months had gone on and on and on. The time before was another world, another Hannah. *Not me*, she thought, *I don't think that could really have been me.*

Hugh cooked exactly the same meal he'd cooked for her on his first night in London: giant salmon steaks, giant floury potatoes boiled in their jackets, peas. 'A no-frills meal,' he said and brought their three plates to the table with a flourish, like a waiter.

Once he was sure they weren't going to scold him, Christian had relaxed a little. He stopped swaggering, pretending he was used to arriving alone off the boat train in a strange city. He began to look around him, his intelligent eyes lighting on people, on the unfamiliar things Hannah remembered seeing vividly with new eyes too. 'I thought it would be just you,' he said to her while Hugh was buying their tube tickets, but he didn't seem perturbed. She imagined how strange it must all seem to him—the intensity of making this first, early break from all that was familiar. *Fifteen*, she thought, watching him, trying to measure him by her own memories of that age. That was different, her childhood gone, all innocence and simplicity over. *But still, I'd never have done what he's done*, she thought, and she felt like hugging him tightly like she used to when he was small. She wondered how they were going to deal with him, and decided to leave it to Hugh to broach the subject. *Funny*, she thought, *I used to think Hugh was no good at stuff like this.*

'Was there much weather on the crossing?' Hugh was asking. 'Much side-to-side and up-and-down?'

'No,' said Christian, eyeing his uncle cautiously.

'A pity,' Hugh said, taking a large forkful of potato. 'I'm always entertained by the histrionics of the unwell when they see my Sealink breakfast. I always eat a handsome breakfast on a ferry crossing,' he confided, 'because it's the sole pleasure of an otherwise tedious journey. Sealink used to serve breakfast all day. I think they have discontinued this commendable service.'

'You can get chips,' Christian ventured.

'Chips,' Hugh put down his knife and fork, and concentrated on his nephew, 'are a very poor substitute for bacon, eggs, pudding, toast, and a lightly grilled tomato.'

'Ugh,' said Christian.

'But I deduce that you like chips nevertheless.'

Christian glanced at Hannah and she smiled. 'They're okay,' he said.

'Before we put you on the boat home,' Hugh continued amiably, 'we shall have to make sure you taste the best chips in London.'

Christian looked down at his plate. He pushed his fork through his peas but he didn't catch any of them. He was just moving them round the plate.

'Islington,' said Hugh. 'That is where the best chips in London are to be found. In the Upper Street Fish Shop.'

There was silence, while he finished his meal. Christian wasn't eating any more and Hannah didn't feel hungry either. She was waiting for an announcement from her brother. 'I'm not going home,' he would say any minute now. Or 'You can't make me do anything.' But he said nothing. He just pushed peas around on his plate, this way and that. She was afraid to look at him. When Hugh was almost done, she got up and filled the kettle.

'I hope you've prepared for the unexpected, Hugh,' she said.

'I am always prepared,' said her uncle, and he sighed and sat back in his chair. 'In fact tonight, by a stroke of good fortune, I am even better prepared than usual. I must have sensed you were coming.' This last he addressed to Christian, who, Hannah noticed with amusement, continued to stare blankly at his plate.

'What have you got?'

Hugh fixed his eyes on the ceiling. 'Rum and butter, toffee chip, and plain wholesome blueberry cheesecake. And...' he tilted his head to look at his nephew, 'chocolate chocolate chip cookies.'

Christian ventured a weak smile.

'Do you want them in succession, or all at once in a glorious overdose?' asked Hugh.

'At once,' said Christian, and he sounded more like the boy he was.

After the ice-cream, he asked to be excused.

'You're in the front room,' Hugh said. 'You'll stay tonight?' he asked Hannah, when Christian had left the room. She nodded.

'Your father's waiting for a call.'

'What'll I tell him?'

Hugh folded his hands across his stomach. 'I think you'll have to ask Christian that. I'll call to tell him he's arrived, but after that—' he shook his head, 'it's up to him.'

Christian was sitting on the bed, his knees drawn up defensively, but he let Hannah speak first. She sat on the bed too. 'I'm not going to be very good at this,' she began, not meeting his eye, 'I'm not going to force you to go home at once.' It's only a white lie, she told herself. 'But I've got to know what's going on.' She looked at him. His expression was a heart-breaking mix of fear and defiance.

'It's not going on,' he said, and she heard tears in his voice, 'nothing's going on, that's just it. I just came,' he finished blankly. She took him in her arms then and let him cry without saying anything. Then she let him go and he sat back, sniffling, but already looking around him again. She shook her head. 'Is it school?' she said.

He scowled. 'I hate school, I've always hated school, I always will hate school.' He sniffed. 'That's not going to change. But now it's home as well.'

'What's at home?'

'Since you went, Hannah, it's just—there's no fun any more. Dad's always off in his study, and René—' he made a gesture of disgust, and swung his legs off the bed. She watched him picking over the bedspread, then picking sulkily at a rip in the knee of his jeans. 'René's just a weirdo now,' he mumbled at last.

'What do you mean?' She felt almost dizzy, this close to the dreams.

'He just—he's always shouting at me now. He picks on me, and he's cool for a while, and then he loses it—for no reason! I'm not doing anything! And then he just—' he stopped uncomfortably.

'What?'

'I dunno. I just can't stand it there any more. I wish I could stay here.' He looked around at Hannah and her heart went to him. His fair curls, his incorruptible face, those eyes. Where did he get this expression from? Certainly not their Dad, and her mother's had been a darker beauty.

'You can't,' she said softly, knowing there was no help for him. *It's so bitterly ironic*, she thought: *you have to go back, and I've got no choice but to stay.* They heard Hugh calling from downstairs, and she went out to the landing.

'A gentleman on the phone,' said Hugh.

She went down, readying herself to make light of everything, but it was Jeremy. 'Was that your uncle?' he said.

'It sounded like some kind of butler. I'll just fetch the young lady for you right away Sir—'

'What are you ringing me here for?' She glanced across at Hugh, who was watching telly and sipping from a large mug of tea. 'How did you get the number?'

'I promised Mo a packet of Smarties.'

'Oh Jeremy, that's cruel,' she giggled in spite of herself. She thought of his generous mouth, pressed close to the phone. She wanted to hear him say certain things, the way he said them that could turn her insides over. But she thought of her brother upstairs in the front room, and the link he formed between her and home and René, all the things so impossibly far away from her and Jeremy. Since it had started, the thing with him, she had been separating the two even more carefully: home and here. René and Jeremy. They couldn't be far enough apart.

'So what's this about your brother running away? Did he come to London with a spotted hankie on a stick?'

'Oh, he just…came over. He shouldn't be here really.' She glanced at Hugh again. 'We're trying to make him go home.'

'How mean and unimaginative of you.'

'I have to ring my father now.'

'Is that a polite "Get off the line Bit, old chap, there's a dear?"'

'No. It's sort of "If you don't say goodbye I'll cut you off now."'

'How subtle. You know I believe you would? Shall I see you tomorrow then, my little grog blossom?'

'What's a grog blossom?'

'It's a rather wonderful off-license in Notting Hill. But it's also an endearing term for a little girl like you.'

'Oh.' Hannah changed the receiver from one hand to the other. She didn't really want the conversation to end. 'Yes, I'll be in work. I just have to travel in from Harrow, so I might be a bit late.'

'Never fear, that's not as serious as being early. I shall watch for you up the road with your satchel and your lunch pail. Be good to your brother now.'

She put the phone down and felt suffused with happiness. She turned to Hugh, half wanting to tell him, but she stopped herself in time. Christian mustn't find out! He would surely mention it when he got home. She took the stairs in twos and found him examining the contents of the wardrobes. There were old suits in there, old dresses that must have belonged to their grandmother. On the shelves were hats, old photographs, framed prints of the English countryside. Christian blew the dust off a photograph and held it up for her to see.

'Gramma and Grandpa,' he said matter-of-factly. 'Daddy says I look like Grandpa Johnson did when he was young.' He screwed up his eyes and held the photo against his chest, standing in front of her like a soldier. 'See it?' There was a resemblance. Their grandfather had been fair, and Christian had the same delicate, doe-like features, the same old-world dreaminess. The rest of the family were dark: their father, tall and gaunt; René, small-boned, compact, sallow-skinned. Hannah wondered should she cut her hair short like Julia had said. Cropped close to her head. It would show off her bones, Julia'd said. Would Jeremy be surprised? Would he like it?

'Let's go down to Uncle Hugh now,' she said, taking the photo. As often before, she felt obscurely ashamed, witnessing the hoarded relics of the past in her uncle's house. There was nothing ordered about them, nothing that spoke of loving memories, things too dear to be parted with. She got the feeling they simply hadn't been thrown out, and Hugh lived among them as he had when her grandparents were alive and the house was clean, lived-in, organised; without being touched by them, without really noticing they were there. She wondered if he ever came into this room any more. Yet the beds were made up. She wondered if there had once been a cleaning lady or a housekeeper. It seemed unlikely. Her mother had married and left, her grandparents had died, and then there had just been Hugh.

He'd phoned their father and he had instructions.

'Father says back on a plane tomorrow, dear boy,' he said to Christian. 'He was quite sure about this, I'm afraid. He wants you in school on Friday.'

Christian didn't answer. He sat on a straight-backed chair and stared at the floor. Hugh seemed to feel he ought somehow to make up for being the bearer of such news. 'Care for some tea, old chap?' he said, and when Christian shook his head, 'Shall we embark on a backgammon tournament?'

Christian didn't want to play backgammon, but he watched the game between Hugh and Hannah with guarded interest. When it was over and Hugh was out of the room, he said to Hannah: 'I thought Dad might let me stay till the weekend. I thought maybe I could stay with you, in your place.'

Hannah gathered the backgammon pieces and stacked them slowly in their rack.

'You've got to do what Dad says,' she said. 'You've got to go home and finish up school for the year. I won't say "it's only two months" because I know how long that seems, and then exams and all, but Christian, you can't just pack it in.

Surely it's not that bad, is it? I mean, what's getting you down most of all, huh?'

Christian looked away, his chin jutting out aggressively, and then he said, 'René.'

Her heart sank. Some kind of warning signal went off. She tried to sound neutral. 'Why?'

'Just is.'

'Why?' she insisted. She hoped that Hugh wouldn't come in, that Christian wouldn't clam up; yet she hoped he wouldn't spill beans, say something that would echo with too much truth. She sat perfectly still, holding the last backgammon piece.

'Well,' her brother struggled for words, 'he's just gone really funny. He's got all these books in his room and he spends loads of time in there writing something and when I asked him what it was he told me it was none of my business. Fine, that's fine, but then when Dad's out and I have to ask him can I go out or for money or something, he sometimes gets in a real snot, if I just walk into his room and there's all papers there and stuff, he gets really pissed off, and he shouts at me. He's always getting angry now, and he never used to.'

'No, he didn't,' said Hannah. René the peacemaker. That was how it had always been. René the arbiter. People went to him for advice, turned to him for things, he was always calm, always rational, full of good humour and patient as a judge. People relied on him. He was full of good sense, he always had solutions, never lost his temper or made a snide remark. He was a rock. 'That doesn't sound like him,' she said carefully.

'And then he gets all nice again,' said Christian. 'You know, he comes to me and says he's sorry and that. Sort of freaks me out, I mean—one time he was crying.'

Hannah didn't speak for a minute. 'Was he?' she said then.

'Yeah, he came down one night, and I was doing my homework, and he's just standing there, saying he's sorry, and he's *crying*. I mean he only shouted at me to get out or something. That's okay. I don't care. But I didn't know what to say, y'know? I don't know what he was crying about. And then he did it again.'

'When.'

'Just the other day. Sunday, or Monday, I can't remember. We were in the kitchen, and Dad was there too. And we were talking about something, I can't even remember what, and suddenly he started to cry. It was horrible, Hannah, what's wrong with him? I *hate* stuff like that.'

'What did Dad do?'

'He just pats him on the shoulder or something. He didn't know what to do either. He's just looking at me and looking at René, and then he tells me to do my homework. So I got out of there.' He paused. 'That's when I decided to come over.'

'Where did you get the money?'

'I took it from René. He keeps all this cash in his room. I'll pay him back. I don't want his money, I just wanted to get out of there. Fucking weirdo.' His voice had a sullen edge, and Hannah thought he was trying out the swear word to see if it would shock her. She closed and locked the backgammon game. She was sorry, she said, that things were not the best at home. She was sorry they had to do as Dad said and send him back there. She knew it probably wasn't the most exciting place to be right now, but he had to give it time. He shouldn't worry about René, she said, he was probably just depressed about something and that would pass. Everyone got depressed sometimes, she said, and running away from it didn't help. He could have a hundred pounds and pay René back, and he was to consider it a gift.

'Was that your boyfriend?' said Christian.

'What?'

'On the phone. Was it your boyfriend?'

'No. I haven't got a boyfriend.' She saw him grinning at her, the first time he'd smiled since he arrived.

'I bet you do,' he said.

'Well you can bet all you like,' she said.

Hugh came in then with his paper. 'Hannah says she doesn't have a boyfriend,' Christian said to him.

'Well I expect she doesn't then,' said Hugh mildly, but he winked at Christian.

'What's his name then?' Christian poked her across the table.

'There is no boyfriend,' she insisted. Christian seemed suddenly to lose interest. He grew sullen again and slouched back moodily in the chair. 'I don't care anyway,' he said and began to pull a thread in the table cloth. Hannah wished he'd stayed in his lighter mood; she hated to see him lose interest so quickly, return to his hopeless look, withdraw. 'What's it to you anyway?' she teased. Christian just shrugged. 'Dunno,' he said.

She watched him for a while, staring darkly at the television, his jaw moving as though he were clenching and unclenching his teeth. Her thoughts touched gingerly on the scenes he had described, and winced away again. She began to imagine Jeremy at work, watching out the window for her to come up the road. *I'm his grog blossom,* she thought. Stupid name, but it felt kind of special, the way he said it. He seemed genuinely excited by being with her, by the things she said—she still found it hard to believe. Of course, she was only really going to let him go so far, it wasn't love or anything. He was probably just playing around with her. The first love is always the best, you never forget your first love, René had told her. She knew who her first love was. It would always be the strongest. *I promise you,* she thought, brushing the other thoughts guiltily from her mind. She was glad now that she only had the same clothes to wear the next day; that she wouldn't dress up specially for him.

It doesn't matter that much, she told herself. *We're just flirting. He'll get tired of me soon and there'll be no harm done. I told Christian the truth, there isn't really a boyfriend, just a sort of interest.*

When Christian got up to go to bed, she followed him upstairs to show him where everything was. On the landing, he turned to her in the gloom.

'Can I come over here in the summer?'

'How do you mean?'

'When school's over, could I come over here and work and stay with you? Could I?'

She hesitated. 'I promise,' she said, 'that I'll think about it, and talk to Dad if you like. I don't know if you could stay with me, or maybe you could stay here. But you've *got* to go to school between now and then. You've *got* to do your exams. Promise me?'

'Ok.'

She gave him a quick hug and whispered 'Sleep well.'

Saturday April 13th.

Dear Sparrow,

Christian's actions came as a shock to me and Daddy. I don't think he's really happy at school. I've tried to talk to him about it but he won't talk to me.

Oh yeah? thought Hannah. *What am I not hearing here? Come on René, what's going on?*

> We were relieved he came back without a struggle. Maybe he just needed to try it out, like trying his wings. He's promising to go back to school and do well in his exams now. But he's also talking about going to London this summer, getting some job and staying with you. I'm not sure of the wisdom of this. I'd prefer to see him go to work for Uncle Jack again, like last summer. I think he's more comfortable there. It's where he did a lot of his growing up, after all, and they're so good to him. I think it's better for him there. We don't always have enough time for him, Dad or I. Dad's playing golf more and more. And I am always working hard. Sometimes I forget how much time Christian needs. So I partly blame myself for what happened.

But what else? thought Hannah. *Aren't you going to tell me? Are you keeping secrets now?* Then she thought of Jeremy and bit her lip.
I'm sorry Finch, it's only so you won't be hurt.
Would he be hurt? Yes. He would.
I can't, I mustn't let him know.

> 'Now he's back I'll try to give him more time, maybe take him out sometimes. I'm not going out myself much these days, I'm working so hard. The weather has been terrible. They've laid off some more people at work, which means we all have to work harder. But I think I'm fairly safe. They wanted me to move into management, but I'm reluctant. It would mean I'd get to do less of my real work, and spend more time moving people round like pieces. I don't think I'm as good working with people as I am working on

my own; but I agreed to take charge of a project while they find someone to do it permanently. It means a lot of meetings. I have to do presentations. I get terribly nervous, you wouldn't believe, Hannah, you wouldn't know me. I don't like it. I hate standing up in front of a crowd of people to talk to them. I'm just not cut out for it. But things are so bad in the company that everyone has to do the work of two people. I think of you just before I get up to speak and it gives me courage. However, I will admit to feeling a little bleak on certain mornings when I get up and there's no Hannah at breakfast to start the day off well. Do you think you might be coming home in the summer for a holiday? I have held off asking because I certainly don't want to put any pressure on you. Please don't think I'm doing that. It would just be nice to see you again.

Love always,

Finch.

Hannah didn't know what tone he'd ended on. It seemed strangely stiff and formal. It would be *nice* to see her again? In all, she was disquieted by the letter. It seemed to have been written over a period of time during which his mood shifted from a kind of cheeriness to a bleakness he didn't even try to hide. Her heart felt heavy at the thought of him waking in the morning, thinking of her, evoking her image before he stood, trembling, to give a talk at work. It just wasn't like him to admit to such weakness. She felt an obscure shame for him. Was he losing something?

Eight

Hugh felt the pain come on as he left the street and started down the stairs to the station. He hesitated, but the flow of people jostled against him, forcing him down towards the ticket barriers and the escalators. He broke out in a sweat and felt suddenly sick and troubled. The pain worsened, jabbing him as he retrieved his ticket from the barrier. He panicked, turning towards the escalators to the Central line. He wouldn't make it! A wave of giddiness swept over him, and he almost stumbled as he reached the escalator. Then he stood, leaning heavily on the rubber rail, wishing greatly to sit down, but temporarily better and able to wait until he reached the platform. There was a train in and he sank gratefully into a seat, not caring that he left some young girls standing. He closed his eyes so he wouldn't feel so bad. Maybe they would see that he was sick. But that felt worse! He reached for his handkerchief and surreptitiously wiped the sweat from his forehead. He could feel it trickling inside his shirt collar; his whole body felt clammy and uncomfortable, but the pain, at least the pain was gone. And he didn't feel so dizzy now he was able to sit down. It would be much better if he didn't have to change lines at Oxford Circus. It was always so busy, he dreaded the crowded platforms, the bustle of the windy passages. Slowly, he began to feel a little better. He felt the giddiness subside. He opened his eyes and kept them locked on the ads. As the train slowed, the effort to read the station name on the circular wall signs as they flashed by made him feel bad again, and he shut his eyes. As they approached Oxford Circus, he began to prepare himself for the route he had to take from the Central Line platform to the Bakerloo. The Bakerloo trains would be coming frequently and because many people alighted at Oxford Circus, he had a good chance of getting a seat. He got up cautiously when the train stopped. No pain. He made his way off the train and down the platform. His briefcase felt very heavy. Much heavier than usual. The attack hit him just as he reached the Bakerloo line platform. A tremendous wave of nausea and then the sickening pain. He grunted and half-fell a couple of steps, reaching blindly for the wall. There were seats ahead, but all he wanted was to alleviate the terrible pain in his chest. He let his briefcase fall and leaned against the wall, fighting the urge to be sick, to lie down and curl up to beat off the pain. A little boy nearby said 'Mummy, look at that man' in his high-pitched, innocent voice. The pain came again, and he gasped, clutching at his shirt; his head felt as though it would burst. He wanted to be sick again, the saliva swilled into his mouth. He swallowed, breathing in short grunts. When he looked up, he saw the little boy watching him, but the mother was looking away. He tried to smile at the boy but instead he felt his face contort in a grimace of pain. He stood there for a few moments, listening to the sounds of the station coming to him through the waves of pain. Slowly, it became easier to breathe, and he felt able to straighten, to try to look more normal. He caught sight of the digital display. **TRAIN APPROACHING** It was almost over. Everything would be alright if he could just get a seat on the train. The great pain was gone, he'd passed through it, and he hadn't fallen down or been sick. He'd make it home now, he told himself, and then everything would be alright. He reached for his briefcase. No one around seemed to be taking the slightest bit of notice. No one appeared to have seen him, doubled up in his humiliating few moments by the wall. It was hard to tell, but the whole thing had probably lasted less than a minute. As he walked towards the tube doors, his legs felt as though they were made of jelly and would never support him to a seat. He grabbed hold of the rail at the end of the row of seats and sank gratefully down. He felt his shirt cling wetly to his back. As the doors shut, the relief at being seated on the train, at having got through the worst moments, was enormous. He had a momentary vision of himself, stumbling in pain along the platform, doubled-up against the wall. A hot flush prickled at his hairline. 'Margaret,' he muttered to himself as the train gathered speed. 'Margaret, I'm alright.' He watched a few stations go by, quite happy here on the train, quite at ease, even blissful in the absence of pain. He kept his body quite still so he wouldn't feel how wet his shirt was at the back. He sat up as straight as he could, but after a while his eyes closed and when he came to himself, they were pulling into North Wembley station. He felt great relief. It had been almost pleasant, sitting there in a dream, just feeling glad that there was no pain any more, and the stations passing like that, without him noticing. He had been high above everything, unaware of everything around him. He'd been hidden inside something, a place where there was nothing to fear.

It was difficult to walk home from the station. He felt terribly weak. Once he had to sit down, on the plastic seats by the bus-stop. He took out his handkerchief, and tried to look as though he were waiting for a bus. None came, and when he felt a little better, he got up and walked on. When he reached the house, he noticed for the first time in months how shabby the garden was. The weeds were knee-high; the bush by the door was dead. There used to be flowers there, he was almost sure, but it was just twigs now. He wondered what the pain had been, tried to stop himself thinking about it in words, and what he might have to do about it. A good meal would set him right. But he didn't feel hungry: the memory of his sickness in the station overpowered him. He didn't bother turning the lights on, but sat in his armchair in the back room to collect himself before making some tea. Somehow, the fact that he wasn't hungry made him feel most miserable. If only he could have come in and cooked himself a large meal and sat down to it with relish like he did every night, things would seem alright. But now everything was out of joint. He felt off balance, and thought the best thing to do might be to go to bed with some paracetamol and try to sleep it off. He could wake early and have a large breakfast. Or perhaps he could allow himself a doze in the chair, dreaming his dream and when he woke, he'd feel better.

Hannah hadn't written to René for a week. Every night there was a reason. Jeremy came round, Jeremy phoned, there were people in the house. She felt guilty, and angry then. Why did it have to be like this? Every time she thought of writing, she remembered what Christian had told her, and she let it torture her. She went over in her mind what he could be feeling. What did he really think? She knew what they felt for each other, that was not hard to remember, but it was becoming all mixed up in her mind. Once again, she found herself thinking of him as somehow thwarted. She wanted to think: *Poor René, things are not going well for him, he's losing that wonderful control he always had.* Sometimes she almost wished that Christian *had* found out about Jeremy. She imagined how he'd mention this casually at the dinner table. She thought of René choking down the knowledge with his food. *Am I a savage?* she asked herself, and she found that she'd dug her nails deep into the flesh of her palms. She took out her notepad and wrote the shortest letter she ever had. It was cool and factual and she signed it with her name.

No more of this stupid codename stuff, she thought. *This can be one he can keep, to remind him how normal things can be. Work, the weather, the girls. That's my life now. I'm not his scared little bird any more. And who's going to see these letters anyway?*

She stuffed it in an envelope and walked quickly down the road to post it before she could change her mind. *He has to realise,* she thought grimly. But back in the house, curled up on the couch with the sound of music coming from next door, she began to feel awful dread. What if he was angry when he opened it and found she'd broken their strict rule and signed her name? What if he was so angry he phoned her, or got on a plane and came over? She pictured him coming into the room, his white shirtsleeves showing up eerily in the dusk, his wrists and forearms strong, grabbing her arms as she tried to get away, twisting them behind her back, forcing her down, forcing her there on the couch, *This is how we are, this is like no other love—*

The memories broke inside her then and she closed her eyes and let them rise. One day, near the end of October when she was thirteen. They were at the airport. René was coming home from school for mid-term. It was hot, it shouldn't have been hot, and she had worn a short summer dress, blue with many daisies, and tied her hair back. People kept saying how hot it was. She felt sick with fear. What if he didn't look at her that way anymore? What if the new year at school had changed him? She hadn't changed, but she felt a dull certainty he would have. That note he'd written her when he left, she'd been stupid to keep it, reading it every night under the covers, slipping it back under the pillows—he'd never remember what he had said. School would have come between them. She couldn't remember him arriving, the hugs, bags being loaded. She remembered being in the carpark, running her finger through the dust on their father's car, and him taking her finger when their father wasn't looking, taking her hand, crushing it briefly, that look of intense agony on his face. Nothing. He'd said nothing. But she knew then.

That was how it began, again and again through the years. So many endings, so many serious talks about how they had to stop. He would come to her room when they were alone. Tell her he'd decided they had to stop. But she always knew: she only had to touch him, say a word, look at him that way. Those times when he wanted to end it were always the best, the most intense.

The telephone was ringing. She got up slowly from the couch. She was shaking so much it was hard to pick the receiver up.

'Hello sweet thing.'
'Jeremy.'
'What's wrong?'
'Nothing. I'm—just on my own here.'
'All the better to visit you, little hood. I was going to come over anyway.'
'No, please don't.'
'What's up Hannah? You sound weird.'

'I'm fine. I just want to go to bed early.' She hated how normal she was able to make herself sound. The thought of Jeremy kissing her now revolted her. It would be so disgusting. She couldn't let him touch her. She could certainly never never *never* go to bed with him.

'Aw please?' he was turning on his little boy act. 'Couldn't I just come and tuck you in?'

'No.' She felt her flesh crawl. How could she get him off the phone? 'I just want to go to bed, on my own, now. Alright?'

He rang off, petulant, and she put the phone down and stood for a moment with her hands against her hot cheeks. All she could think of was a stupid joke she'd heard once. *Doctor doctor, I feel like a bridge. What's come over you? Oh, cars, buses, taxis...*She stared at the phone and wondered for a moment could she phone and explain about the letter, that she hadn't meant to make it so abrupt. But the thought of his voice, of actually talking to him, made her feel such dread again that she went upstairs and lay on her bed, rocking from side to side, her head in the pillow. 'Cars...buses...trains' she chanted softly in time to the rocking, 'cars...buses...trains... cars...buses...trains...'

Dear Sparrow,

I have been in bed for a couple of days with a temperature and some kind of flu and now I'm feeling much better. In fact I feel sort of renewed and clean and ready to begin again. You know that feeling of convalescence? As though some kind of evil has been washed out, sweated out of you. I had been reading a book about horror in 19th century art before I fell sick and I certainly suffered for it when I was in the middle of delirious dreams! Goyan figures featured prominently. 'The sleep of reason produces monsters' Goya said and they were monsters who assailed me Monday and Tuesday nights. But now it is Wednesday morning, I feel weak as a baby and I've gone back to the book. The horrors just seem ludicrous now. Do you know where the word 'horror' comes from? It's from the Latin 'horrere', meaning to bristle, the way hairs bristle on the nape of your neck when you're frightened. That's because the skin constricts, pulling the hair follicles, and making the hair stand up. The creeps. The moment between flight and fight. Our most alert, our most vulnerable moment. Horror is also the word used to describe the foam that boils on the crest of a wave in a really violent sea. In the 19th century, I would have been diagnosed by a good doctor as having had the horrors, as my temperature dropped and the sweat evaporating made me tremble. Just as well you and I know it was only a chill I caught by getting soaked on Sunday.

To complement my diet of Victorian shivers I am re-reading *Dracula*—the great and dreadful myth. I feel a reluctant affinity with the daemon, though I am completely immune to wolfsbane, mirrors, and garlic. A daemon used to be a neutral spirit, until Christianity appropriated the term and infused it with evil. The whole idea behind the Gothic era at the end of the 18th century was this dreadful apprehension of impending disaster that somehow thrilled people too—the line became blurred between the excitement of the awful and thrilling fear of the unknown, the hinted at. Did you know there were female vampires too? Lamias, they are called. Lamias were staked when they died, Dracula had to be decapitated; happy to die, freed from his burden.

When the Count attacked his victim (and they were not violent, these attacks, his victims were passive, they even invited him), he would suck their blood until they weakened and fainted; but instead of dying, they became the 'Doppelganger' or Lamia, whose punishment for incautiousness is eternal damnation. You have to admit that, aside from the horror, it is a truly beautiful story. 'Even the priest can't help you now,' he told his victim. And the world reinforces the story so perfectly—the castle, the cliffs, the storm, the secret towers, the darkness and wolves howling. Even the priest can't help you now. What was the matter with me? It was just a high temperature and ugly dreams. I'm out the other side now. If I'm not quite right tomorrow I think I'll take the rest of the week off work. It's better if people don't see me. I'm glad Christian came back. You know, he was good to me: brought me tea and the paper. I couldn't read, but it was kind of him. He's a good little brother. Take care, dear Sparrow, I dare not look into the future.

 Finch.

'René was a thin, anxious boy,' wrote Hannah. 'He had sallow skin and dark hair. He was small-boned, small for his age always. He never excelled at sport.' She stopped and tapped the J key gently with her forefinger a few times. 'Sometimes he was bullied, but only by the really vicious bullies in the school. Usually he was liked. He was intelligent. He excelled at Mathematics and English. His essays were held up as an example, and he helped other, weaker boys. His teachers described him as "sensitive". "A loner", they sometimes wrote, "René does not mix with the other boys by choice."'

She let her hands rest again and gazed out the window to the schoolyard across the road. No reaction. There'd been absolutely no reaction to the cool little letter she had signed with her name. It was as if she'd never sent it. The kids were out on their lunch break and she watched them running and dodging, the boys hitting out at each other with ill-aimed punches and kicks, the girls huddled close in bunches, giggling and telling tales.
She typed:

'In the April before he sat his entrance exams for Harrow, his mother died suddenly. His masters spoke to his father. They would understand if René wished to wait, they said, and sit his exams the following summer. There were two other children, younger: an eight-year-old girl, a boy of four; naturally things would be difficult at home. René, consulted, said he wanted to sit the exams. He passed with straight A grades. After Harrow, he told his father, he wanted to go to Oxford. All that summer he spent with his small brother and sister. In the Autumn, the little boy went to live with an aunt and uncle in another city. The girl stayed at home and René went away to school. Every weekend he came home, instead of just at holidays like the other boys. Every Sunday night he got the train back to school. He didn't go out much at the weekends. He studied and watched over his sister as she did her lessons or played. At 9 o'clock she went to bed. He would follow her up to tuck her in. He read her stories. Sometimes she read to him. Before he turned out her light, she said aloud the prayers she'd learned at school. At the end she said God bless Daddy, and Christian, and René. God bless Mummy. "Who's my favourite girl?" he'd say as he stood in her bedroom doorway. "I am," she'd reply.'

She hit Return and saved the piece as *Article1*. She put it in her own directory and returned to the file she'd been working on. Twice during the afternoon when no one was around she opened *Article1* and read what she'd written. She didn't change anything or add to it.

At 5 o'clock, Jeremy passed by her desk and asked her out to dinner. 'I know a charming little place,' he said and smiled coquettishly at her. She hesitated. She had planned to drop by her post-office box to see if there was a letter. It was a full week since she'd sent the short signed missive and she hadn't heard back. Today was the first day she could really expect to, but she felt a nagging curiosity, an urgency greater than usual to open the box and find a letter there, to unseal the letter somewhere quiet and private and unfold the tissuey paper that he always used, and to read his response flat and hollow on the page.

'I've got the car,' Jeremy leaned against a chair back.

'Okay,' she said. 'Let's go then.'

They stopped and started in rush-hour traffic and she put her feet on the dashboard. Jeremy lit her a cigarette and passed it over. It was like the scene in *Brideshead Revisited*, she thought, where Charles lit Julia's cigarette as she drove him from the station to Brideshead—only the roles were reversed. She pulled her hair up so it was short, like flapper hair, and flipped down the visor mirror. 'Think I should cut my hair?' she said. 'Look like Julia Flyte?'

Jeremy glanced across. 'I think you should shave it off,' he said. 'Forget Julia whatsername. You'd look astonishing.'

She flipped the mirror up again. 'Why don't you turn down here,' she said, 'and I can pick up my post.'

'You want to go home?'

'No. Just the post office.'

'The post office?'

'I have a box.' She watched a black cab snake round the corner in front of them, they pulled up behind a Royal Mail van, and she got out. When she got back in, Jeremy said: 'You want to stop in your place for a spliff before we go?'

'Alright.' She put her hand on the letter, crackling in her jacket pocket.

'Why do you have a box then?' he asked. 'Why not just get your letters sent to the house?'

'It's just easier. In case I move again.'

'Planning to move again?'

'Is that a look you're giving me?'

'I'll give you something else, darling.' They drew up outside the house and he turned the engine off and pulled her down till she was lying across his lap. She giggled as his hand went under her t-shirt.

'Get any letters then?' He slipped his hand into her jacket pocket, pulled the letter deftly out, and held it up against the light. 'Hm, no return address.'

She sat up slowly and pulled her shirt back down. She snapped down the visor and looked at herself briefly in the mirror. Then, as Jeremy was sliding his hand around her and getting ready to nuzzle her neck, she plucked the letter from his other hand and swung the car door open. 'Let's go in,' she said.

'It's just a vast uncontrolled fucking experiment,' he was saying. 'The whole of drug research. Try it out on the animals, it they don't die, test it on humans. Nobody has a fucking clue what any of the stuff'll do. Look at coke—Freud was doling it out like aspirin for Chrissake.'

'Yeah, bet his patients were surprised,' Jeremy said.

'Even I'd have made friends with the old geyser,' said a tall skinny guy who was rolling a joint on an album cover balanced precariously on his knees.

'Bloke was telling me the other night how he came off heroin,' Mo said. 'Twenty years ago and he still gets cravings.'

'Operant conditioning,' the first boy said. He said it quietly, like he didn't want anyone to think he was showing off. 'Triggers. They can still work after all that time because you're programmed right down, probably to the single cell level, though they haven't proved that yet. So you kick the habit—fifteen years later you're in a room and you smell matches or you see a needle or something. Of course you're going to get a fucking craving.' He leaned across and took the proffered joint from the skinny guy.

'They call it protracted abstinence syndrome,' he said, and then he took a long sharp toke and handed it on.

'Never seems to trouble you, darling,' said Julia coolly. 'Anyway, have you been reading my schoolbooks again you greedy boy? Why don't you read your own?'

Her brother exhaled slowly and then sat back in the armchair and closed his eyes.

'Plenty of time for that,' he said. 'There's weeks to the exams yet.'

'Two,' said Julia.

'Oi, shut up!' said the skinny guy. 'Have a bit of sensitivity, would you?'

Jeremy began to chuckle in a humourless kind of way. 'Oh college days,' he said, as though remembering them fondly. 'All that studying in the library. All those fun things like exams.'

'Oh run away and play, Jeremy,' said Julia.

'That's just what I was planning, actually.' He looked at Hannah. 'Ready?'

Hannah was sitting on a wooden chair by the door. She hadn't said anything since they'd come in and Julia had introduced them to the boys sprawling on the couch and to her brother, lounging in the biggest armchair. Nobody had paid her any attention. Now, to her surprise, Julia's brother opened his eyes and said 'Why don't you stay and get drunk with us?' He turned to his sister. 'We're getting drunk, aren't we, Ju?'

Julia looked at her watch and sighed. 'It is that time, isn't it?'

'Got any beer?' asked the skinny boy.

'Yes we have rather,' said Julia. 'We've got some Guinness somewhere, haven't we, Mo?'

'Hannah's nearest the door,' said Mo. 'She looks like she's in the mood for fetching beers, aren't you darling?' She gave Hannah one of her wide, innocent smiles.

'I could be persuaded,' said Hannah, 'for a small fee.' She turned to Jeremy. 'Let's stay and get drunk.'

'I thought we were going to dinner,' he said and she could sense the displeasure in his voice.

'Well we can go after, can't we?'

'I'm getting *extremely* thirsty,' Julia's brother announced in a loud voice.

'Can't we?' Hannah said again. Jeremy looked as though he were about to sulk. Beyond him, she saw Mo make a pouting face and cock her head to one side. For a split second she thought she'd laugh aloud. Then she felt unaccountably decisive. Dinner with Jeremy would be dull. Staying here and getting drunk with all these people, even if none of them took any notice of her, would be excellent.

'Well I'm having a beer,' she said quickly, and she stood up. 'Anyone else?'

She came to think of that night as the first real night in her new life. Everything else from the moment she left Ireland was just a sort of in-between time, a preparation, a limbo. She had, she realized, been waiting for this to begin. From that night, she dated her acceptance in a group of people she admired without reserve. But it didn't stop surprising her, that she was part of this group. She never stopped doubting the motives of her new friends—did they only tolerate her because she lived with Mo and Julia?—but she began to grow accustomed to a constant feeling of excitement, of busyness, euphoria. There just wasn't enough time to do everything she wanted to do.

Jeremy left at midnight, Mo told her later. He must have walked or found a taxi because the car was still there when Hannah left for work the next day. She didn't see him at the office. The car was gone when she got home.

Mo told her she shouldn't worry. He wasn't worth it, she said. Sweet boy as he was, and here she'd paused and raised her eyebrows, he'd made a pass at Julia in the kitchen. He must have seen things with Hannah were on the decline and decided to cut his losses. 'That's my assessment,' Mo said. 'Either that or he's incomparably stupid. I mean, he must know Julia thinks he's a pratt. Perhaps it was the large number of beers he'd consumed,' she went on ruminatively, 'or perhaps some kind of bizarre combination of all of the above. Who knows? Anyway, I should think you have more pressing things to think about just now.' She grinned.

'Such as?' said Hannah.

'Oh you dark horse. Go on then—' she added when Hannah didn't answer, 'tell me you didn't kiss Mr. H. E. Alton last night.'

'I didn't kiss him,' Hannah said. She felt older, calm, as though she had found some new way of being. 'He kissed me.'

Everyone seemed to have advice for her. Julia warned her of the hazards of being involved with her younger brother. 'He won't be faithful Hannah,' she said matter-of-factly. 'You might as well know that from the start. Harry has many talents. One of them is for enjoying life.' Hannah nodded, as though she'd known this all along. 'But should an old girlfriend appear on the scene, you won't see Harry for a few days. You just won't see him. Do you understand, Hannah?' Hannah nodded again. Julia was plainly trying to tell her something very important. It was only for her own good. 'And don't expect to be a couple in public with him. Harry's not like that. He won't sit with his arm around you. He probably won't even kiss you in public. He's just not like that. Everything's a game to him. He means well, poor darling, but things are only interesting for the amount of fun you can have, the laughs. He's a good-time boy, my baby brother. I personally don't know why you'd want anything to do with him, but if you do, I just want you to go in with your eyes open. I just want to warn you, alright?' She raised her voice, like a mother scolding her children. 'I don't want any broken hearts.' She might have been telling her not to reach across the dinner table.

'Alright,' said Hannah.

'Don't let him break your heart, Hannah,' Julia said quietly. 'Because he's gifted that way. He really doesn't mean it, but he just takes people—' she looked away sadly, trying to think how to put it, 'and uses them up.'

'He only kissed me,' said Hannah.

Nine

She could feel herself change. It was like when she was little and could feel herself grow. Soon everything she used to wear seemed wrong; everything she used to like was childish and she was a little ashamed of it all. There were new kinds of music, new bands, new clothes she would never have worn before. Harry's college friends spoke a new language, a tight, in-crowd shorthand. They quoted from films she'd never seen and books she'd never heard of. They seemed to know all the same people at the university. Someone was either cool or not worth mentioning except to get a laugh. She fought her sense of inferiority like a net that kept threatening to catch her and trap her. Harry brought her to the house where he lived with six or seven others. She never knew exactly who lived there and who was visiting or just sort of permanently hanging around. Some of them shared rooms but Harry had a bedroom to himself, on the third storey, at the back of the house. It was bleak and untidy—a poster of Marilyn on the wall above the bed, the floor strewn with paper, lecture notes, binders, shoes, rumpled t-shirts. She loved it. Harry called her Baby when he took her to bed. He said it was okay she didn't want sex just yet, they could still have lots of fun. His body was solid, his movements assured, but there was still something boyish about him that made her feel, in her private thoughts, like she protected him. They laughed all the time.

He laughed at the things she said, made her feel funny. When they were in a crowd and he barely treated her differently to the other girls there, she didn't mind. *It's not love,* she told herself, *we're just having fun.* When she thought of René, as she often did when Harry kissed her in bed, kissed her everywhere, she thought of him coolly, without identifiable emotion. She never minded any more that sometimes the presence of Harry fused with the memory of her brother. She just left it alone and didn't wonder about it. For the first ten days she was with Harry, she didn't write any letters. There wasn't time. Although she told herself firmly there really wasn't much going on, she began to arrange her life so she would always be around Harry, or available should he call. She stopped going for walks down to Camden in the evenings, in case the phone would start to ring when she was halfway down the road. She thought about Harry almost all the time.

It was an exhilerating time of year, May, everything a lush green, the rain warm, the evenings long. She seemed to feel everything ten times more keenly than ever before. When Harry called or showed up at the house, she was ecstatic. Pure pleasure would hit her like a wave. When he made no contact for a couple of days, she felt an icy dread steal over everything. She knew what Julia said was true, but she didn't feel she had to think about it. Somewhere in her subconscious she realized that at all those college parties he went to without her, he was with other girls. It didn't ride close enough to the surface to matter. From the beginning, she understood instinctively that to Harry, the present was the only thing there was.

As his exams drew near, he locked himself away more and more to study, and his hours became more erratic. He'd arrive at Leighton Road at three a.m., letting himself in, and she'd wake to a flood of joy as he stumbled round her room, giggling and undressing in the dark. One night he arrived with a crutch. 'Are you hurt?' She sat up suddenly. 'Nah,' he said, stacking it in a corner and jumping onto the bed. 'Found it at a party at the Middlesex. Bunch of nurses and their patients. Jesus, there was one guy there with gallstones. Every fucking detail of how he has to piss them out. And he *wouldn't* shut up.'

'Middlesex,' said Hannah in a sleepy voice, 'is that this bit or this bit?'

'Fucked if I know,' he squirmed down beside her, holding her too tightly, the way that made her hold her breath and never want to be let go. 'I'm telling you Hannah, I can't sleep without you any more. I have to be up at eight to study. Will you come with me?'

'Where?'

'To the library. I'll sit you up on the desk. They'll think you're a lucky charm.'

'I am a lucky charm. So you don't need to go to the library. No need to study—just take me into the exams.'

'Great! So I can stay in bed till eleven, and then we can get drunk!'

They got drunk almost every night; and still, it always seemed like a new idea, a bright solution to a dull moment. 'I know!' she'd say suddenly. 'Let's get drunk!'

Or they'd go to the Pembroke on Malet Street 'for one' before he went off to study in the library. Later, they'd stumble out into the surprisingly balmy evening and she'd walk him to the university and catch a 29 at the top of Tottenham Court Road, smiling hugely to herself, still glowing from his goodbye, gazing from the top of the bus on a London that looked sunny and young and full of promise.

At the studio, Jeremy was cool with her for a week or two, then asked her out to lunch 'for old times' sake'. She went because he seemed so cheerful and because she herself was treading so weightlessly on her cushion of air that not even a petulant or hurt Jeremy could have brought her down. Everything that happened seemed right, part of some enormous plan.

They went to a new place, expensive, full of yuppies. Jeremy acted as though he knew all the waiters and most of the clientele.

'So how are things?' he said when they'd put the menus away. 'Hitched up with that chap, Julia's brother, what's his name?'

'Oh that,' she said. 'Nah. We just had a bit of fun. It was nothing really.'

'I've fallen myself,' he said, catching the waiter's eye and then turning back to Hannah with a look of concentration, 'rather foolishly in love with an Oxford girl. Her Dad's a professor there, geology or something. Got a flat in the docklands—one of those done-up warehouses. Amazing place.'

'What's her name?' asked Hannah politely. She could tell he didn't feel a bit foolish about being in love with somebody rich.

The waiter arrived and the rest of the lunch was taken up with Fiona. Her horses, her Dad's time-share villa on the Italian riviera, her hopes of landing a job at Sothebys. He said, on the way back to the office: 'I say Hannah, no hard feelings, eh? You know, about that night at your place, and Fiona and all that?'

'No,' she said, suppressing a smile. 'No hard feelings at all.'

That afternoon, she typed up a quick letter.

> R—Too long since I wrote, I know, and it burns me. Life has sped up, that's all, and there is too much of it to get through every day to have time to tell you about it, though I do want to very much. You know I used to feel that nothing had been properly experienced until I told you about it. I guess that makes you a cipher. I like that word. It makes me think of something sculpted out of translucent paper. Japanese. I have a new group of friends. I met them through Julia. They're all students at UCL—mostly engineers and mathematicians. (Are you a mathematician when you're just studying maths or not until you do something noteworthy, like discover a new number or something?) They live in a couple of houses near the university, big old draughty London houses with giant high ceilings and those little, useless wrought-iron balconies with dead flowers in window boxes. Harry, that's Julia's brother—"

She stopped typing, then erased that sentence and continued.

> The thing is, they're all coming up to exams right now and it's reminded me how much I liked exam time. It was the best time in college—everything feverish and intense, time running away from you, friendships suddenly becoming like blood bonds. Well it didn't quite happen that way for me, but I saw that it could have and maybe if I'd given it more time … I'm sort of half-thinking of trying again over here. I'd have to get some A-levels but I don't think that should be a problem. I could study at night. The job,

as you so rightly surmised, is a big empty train going nowhere. Julia thinks I should go ahead and so does Mo. And I know all of you (Dad, Hugh…) would be delighted as I know exactly how you all felt about me quitting, not that you went on and on endlessly about it until I had to run away with a spotted hankie on a stick and start a new life overseas or anything. Now you're all throwing wobblers because Christian's turning out to have a personality. I thought he was quite funny when he was over here, I have to admit. He watched Hugh as though he were a gaoler. What are you *doing* to him, you and Dad? Now you'll be angry. Well that's alright: you don't exercise that particular emotion enough. I think I only saw you angry about three times in my whole entire life. Now when I dream about you, you are often angry. You just act furious with me, you never say anything, so I don't know what I've done. What have I done? You grab me and you're always in shirtsleeves and you hold me in a vice grip. I expect there's something going on there. Then again, maybe not.

I am getting enough sunlight. London is getting warm. I sit in the sun on top of the bus. Water alone does not sustain so I'm drinking rather a lot of beer and hanging round with a fast crowd some of the time. I like it: don't advise me against it. Everything is a funny story to these people and I like laughing. We didn't laugh enough, you and I.

Well don't let your library books get overdue. What are you reading these days? I'm getting some awfully funny letters from you. Love always—Sparrow.

As the exams drew close, Hannah felt everything rising to a fever pitch. Her whole world became the house where Harry lived and studied and smoked and drank into the night with the others. Her job, the studio, seemed laughably pointless. She became inured to getting in at nine-thirty, riding out hangovers till lunchtime, sitting at her computer trying to ignore the dull pounding of a sick headache. In the afternoons, she scrambled to get the work done so she could leave on the dot of five and run for the tube. Ironically, she turned out flawless work on those warm May afternoons. Jonathan glanced approvingly over her shoulder as he passed one day and said she was doing well. She was pleased, but increasingly the job chafed. As she hung around Harry and his student friends, listening to their conversations—even wildly drunk they could all hold their own on a huge array of topics—she felt dull and lame-brained. Harry told her she should apply for UCL. Get a couple of A-levels. She could cram for them at night, do them in a few months. She probably knew most of the stuff backwards anyway. 'You're not stupid,' he told her over and over when she hinted of her fears. She thought about college, the excitement of learning, the heady lifestyle. She called the UCL admissions office one day from work, told them about her year of college in Ireland, asked what she'd have to do to apply. When she put the phone down, she looked round the studio and knew it was time to move on.

She took the bus home that evening, reluctant to go underground with the weather warm and the sunlight filled with particles streaming through the bus-stop glass. Dust, pollen, seeds, everything everywhere bursting into leaf; buds on the trees, the gardens rich and green after the night's rain. It occurred to her that there ought to be some way she could gather to herself all the things that would make her fight against losing this life she had found. Things like the way kids piled out of a car, or the way a song she loved would suddenly come on the radio in a shop and she'd stay there fiddling with the racks and smiling to herself until it was over; or the way the bus was stopped at traffic lights now and a carpenter putting up shelves in a shop window looked out at her and winked, and she'd never see him again but she smiled back and thought that, when you looked closely, people were great and the world was full of trees just coming into leaf; and somewhere white snow-slopes were glistening and a snow-leopard was standing, frozen for a moment, his eyes fixed on a twig that had moved, and by the time the bus was pulling away from the lights and going into second, he was running over the snow with more grace that she could ever imagine.

That night, Harry begged her again to make love to him.

'It'll be different,' he promised her, 'different between us. Honestly. There's a bond. Once you make love to someone there's always this bond between you, even if you meet years afterwards, it's still there. It's really special.'

She wondered how many girls he'd said that to, and if it really happened that way. If he met her, years later when she wasn't with him any more, would they exchange that look like he said? Would there be something special that had never died? *But it's not love*, she thought as she lay awake after he'd given up and fallen into his solid sleep. *I won't even say I love him.* She had refused, surprised at herself, a few days before when he'd entreated her to say it. Surprised at her own sad little 'I can't. Not yet.' Not because she couldn't say it but because she wouldn't.

At other times, she felt herself hanging on his every word. In company, her stomach tightened when he came close, the world was sublime if he touched her or winked at her. At home in Leighton Road, she danced on a knife-edge waiting for the telephone or his quick step up the path; the very sight of his jacket, dark with the white streak of the hood, sent her blood racing. And still, that quiet moment when they lay together on the couch and he said in his open, boyish way that she loved so much, 'Tell me you love me', she said 'No'. This was *her* strength, coming up all unexpected in her bones like a cold fire. 'I'll say it when I mean it,' she'd said, and he'd nodded. Once again she felt drawn along by events, through something that was so right; she seemed charmed. Everything she said, everything she did, was part of a bigger picture. *It's alright*, she said to herself over and over. *This is what's meant to be happening. Life is meant to be this good.*

The night before Harry's first exam, they went out to a pub they'd never been in before; a quiet bar near the British Museum, full of old men watching the telly; a dartboard, pictures of huntsmen decked out in their faded last-century scarlet.

'Two pints of Newcie,' Harry told the barman without even asking Hannah. She felt proud that he didn't ask. She was one of the lads now. They sat in a dark corner away from the incongruous sunlight pouring through the frosted pub windows.

'Are you scared?' she asked.

'Shitless,' he said. 'But I know I'll get an A. That's the weird thing. Seems like if I'm not scared enough, it won't happen. So I'm terrified.'

'I used to love exams,' she confessed.

'Yeah—what was it with you and college then?' he sat back and looked at her quizzically. She felt herself blush. The beer was already making her fuzzy.

'I got bored,' she said. 'All those intellectual types. I read that book by Milan Kundera, *Life Is Elsewhere*. Y'know?'

'Well you were right babe,' he said, and taking up his beer, he drained it and banged the glass down as though this should automatically signal the barman they were ready for another. 'Life is right here.'

She smiled happily and took a long swallow of her own beer. 'I'll get this one,' she said, and slid adroitly out from the table. Carrying the brimming pints back, she caught his eye and they grinned hugely at each other. 'This is what college is all about,' he announced, holding up his pint to hers. 'A couple of swift ones the night before exams.'

'What about the summer,' she said lightly.

'What about it? I'll probably go home for a while and then Dad will fix me up with some fucking awful job with his cronies in the city; I'll come back up, and we can have a merry old time making packets of cash and getting drunk every night.'

'Well, not every night. I mean, what about Tuesdays? You can't really get drunk on Tuesdays, it's not...' she searched for the word, 'polite.'

'No,' he agreed. 'Tuesdays we could stay sober, do laundry, call home, pay the bills. And Glastonbury! We have to go to Glastonbury. Rumour is, the Pixies are going to be the Sunday mainstage surprise.'

'You have to help me buy a stereo,' she said. 'It's embarrassing me that I only have that crappy cassette deck thing.'

'Julia's got a stereo,' Harry said, as though that should, as a matter of course, be enough.

'Yeah but,' she said, 'I dunno. I sometimes feel funny about using Julia's things. They're very good.' She thought for a moment. 'I used to be scared of her.' She half-laughed, but she felt self-conscious too.

'You're scared of everybody,' he said.

'When she was going out with Morgan, I used to think they were, like, society people, like in the '20s, flappers, all those people who smoked cigarettes in holders and drove those lovely old cars.'

'Have you been reading F. Scott Fitzgerald again? "Gatsby believed in the green light",' he began, holding up his beer as though it were the green light, "the orgiastic future that year by year recedes from us. It eluded us then, but that's no matter—tomorrow we will run faster, stretch out our arms farther..." Fitzgerald was only forty-four when he died,' he finished matter-of-factly, as though he didn't want her to think of the quoting as some kind of boast. She recognized this, but nevertheless, she felt the familiar creeping humiliation. Harry, Julia, their friends, these people really belonged in the world. They knew so much: it was as though they were born knowing what they should know, and just added to it throughout their charmed lives, lives they deserved. She was a fraud. She knew nothing. Everything she'd learned she had forgotten. A whole year of English literature at college and nothing to show for it. She didn't know F. Scott Fitzgerald died at forty-four, and here was Harry, a science student, quoting from a book he'd probably read once, years ago. She took a gulp of her beer. She knew it wasn't really important, knowing these things. She thought of the things René said. An orchid, he'd called her. It was pathetic—kind but pitiful—the way he tried to build up her confidence. He must have known all along that she really wasn't anything special. She'd read *The Great Gatsby* twice in her last year at school. She couldn't even remember the story.

'Gosh, you're pretty.' Harry was looking at her in a way that seemed to make his eyes go darker and darker. She finished her beer in one go, swallowing too much too quickly. The warmth in her head coated everything with a kind of blankness through which it was surprisingly easy to say 'I love you Harry'.

They kissed, squashed together in the dark leather booth, not caring what anyone thought.

'Say it again,' he said. She said it. *Who knows what love is anymore*, she thought. She could already feel him slipping away from her, into a nervous kind of mood, the pressure of his exams always just under the surface, governing how they spent their time. She felt panicky, badly wanting him to agree to stay in the bar for another pint, knowing he wouldn't, that he'd refuse, say he had to go and study, break the mood. And from tomorrow, once the great train of the exams got started, it would roll him away from her. He'd be swept up in events she had no part in. What would happen after the exams, when he left London? What if he didn't come back up to a job? What would the summer do to them?

The mood of anxiety intensified. They parted on a corner of Russell Square, a brief, miserable kiss. 'Good luck in the exam,' she whispered, panic rising in her throat as though it were she and not he who had to sit a paper the next day. 'I'll call you on Friday,' he said. Already he was far away from her, facing four days of exams. He'd pass with his habitual honours. But four days till she'd see him again. 'Fucking years,' she muttered to herself as she walked to the bus-stop, more to convince herself not to cry than anything. Hunched on the top of the bus she thought: *No, I won't make love to you Harry, because you wouldn't care enough about it afterwards and I would care too much.* No matter what he said about always having that lovely bond with someone, she clearly saw that the bond would strangle her as he moved away.

I can't do it, she thought numbly. *Even if you have to turn to someone else, then you will do that and I won't be able to stop it.*

May 20th 1991.

Dear Sparrow,

Sorry I haven't written back for a while, I've been reading voraciously and can't seem to put the books down long enough to pick up a pen. Mostly gothic novels, since you ask, some cultural anthropology and studies of family systems. I know you think I should be out in the world *meeting people* (that is what you advised, isn't it?) but you know that's impossible for me at the moment. Besides, this work is so consuming, I don't feel the need or desire to be around other people. Did you know that Mary Shelley's *Frankenstein* was the result of a challenge? It was a bargain struck between Percy, his sister, his half-sister Clare Claremont, and Byron (who else?) one night in 18-something, to write a 'chiller'. Well Mary (Godwin as she was then—it was before she married P.B.) certainly deserves to have won. But it's a little-known fact that several (at least two) other books arose out of that fateful evening. I have read one of them and it doesn't hold a candle (excuse the weak pun of sorts) to Frankenstein. The first was written by a chap called Polidori, Byron's physician, present on the night of the wager. It's full of the usual pornography so necessary for the gothic shock element. (As the vast majority of the audience was young and female, their phobias and secret fears were exploited for the greatest effect. If you were 18 years old in 1816 and had read your allotted quota of gothic novels, you too would have expected the same.) The fascinating thing about the genre is how strictly it adhered, with minor variations, to the rules:

the characters sinned, they suffered the thorns of guilt, they experienced violent (sometimes) retribution. In general, if the siblings never acted on their love, they would usually both be saved. If they mistakenly consummated the act, the male would as a rule be exiled. If the male carried out the act in full knowledge, he would die or meet with a generally unpleasant fate. Don't you think this is a startling parallel with a story we both know? I think it fitting that, although it is you who has been exiled, I am the one working over and over how I could see you again, how we could make this story come out a different way, yet without harm to you, which I now believe is only possible if we leave this distance between us. There is no way this story can come out. It is a broken story and we are dangling from its two broken ends.

George Eliot saved her child protagonists by drowning them together in the Floss: swept into each other's arms at the final moment. Their tombstone read: 'In their death they were not divided.' Apparently they had to forsake the privilege of living to satisfy their unspoken desires. When I read some of the more scholarly texts on the subject, however, I come away with a strong impression, almost a taste, of the loathing with which society loads the scales. 'An inability to negotiate developmental tasks' I read somewhere about 'victims'. And somewhere else, that studies have shown 23% of them show no ill-effects. You don't tell me how you are. I wonder if you're alright. Ill effects? I don't know what they might be. I try to imagine how you feel about me now and I cannot. The Hannah in London is becoming a stranger now, as she is meant to be. The Hannah of memory—well, though I try to be realistic and figure there must have been times when it was only ordinary to be in one house with you, as it is for others, as it ought to have been, all I can remember was rapturous happiness.

Finch.

Ten

It was her father who called her about Hugh's heart attack. With his few words, he sketched a picture more vividly to her than if he'd described it in detail. It happened at the office, he said. Hugh was conscious through it all. Somehow that made it worse: thinking of him on an office floor somewhere, old grey linoleum, with strangers flocking round him, everyone frightened and curious. All the secretaries talking about him after the ambulance came and they took him away. More strangers. And Hugh, seeing it all through the impossible glare of pain. Or was it like a web, she wondered? Something that entangled you so you couldn't get free? She felt for her own heart. It beat frailly under her jersey.

She thought about Harry, two miles away, finished with his first exam. He wouldn't surprise her tonight. He had his second paper in the morning. There was no hope he would come. How had it been before him? Less than a month, and she couldn't remember. *Oh God, make me like myself,* she thought. *I can't remember who that really is.* She lit a cigarette, sat with her knees drawn up on the couch. It was a hot, heavy night. The street was alive outside, car windows open. She heard a snatch of classical music from a radio. It would be nice to think that in two years, or eight, or ten, she would look back and remember how fine it was to be nineteen, how well she was doing. Getting things done, winning. Instead, it seemed the struggle of getting from minute to minute was what occupied her. Keeping her head above water, not striking boldly out. She looked out on the gardens in the early evening sun. Somewhere on the other side of the city, Hugh was lying, big and still, in a hospital bed. The air was like treacle. He might not be able to get enough. Even with the hospital fans, even though the attack hadn't carried him off, maybe now, nearly twelve hours later, he wouldn't be able to get enough air, and like a huge fish gasping on the boards at the bottom of a boat, he'd die.

She got the telephone book out from under the hall table and phoned the hospital. Her uncle was doing well, the nurse said, he was sleeping. A bit groggy and probably not up to visitors for a day or two. Tell him Hannah called, she said, ashamed of her relief about the visitors. Tell him I'll come in tomorrow. The nurse said yes and put the phone down too quickly.

They haven't time to talk to the patients, thought Hannah. *He won't know I called.*

She was still seated smoking on the couch an hour later when Mo came home.

'Alright?' called her friend, carrying shopping bags down to the kitchen.

'No,' said Hannah. What she felt exactly in need of was a talk with Mo.

'Anything a beer could solve?' she called from the kitchen. Hannah could hear the bottles clinking in the six-pack as they went into the fridge. She didn't answer until Mo came in with a beer in each hand.

'You know I don't drink,' she said then through her cigarette, taking a beer.

Mo spread herself out in the armchair. 'I fail to see,' she said loudly, 'why you should scrunch up teensily there on the couch while I get this narrow receptacle for my ample frame.'

'Hugh's had a heart attack,' said Hannah glumly. 'He's okay. I'm going to see him tomorrow.'

'Golly,' said Mo. 'Poor sweetheart.'

Hannah wasn't sure whether she meant Hannah or Hugh. 'Harry's disappeared into Exam-Land,' she said, 'and I'll probably never see him again. Let's talk about you.'

'Dear me. Well, I've been offered a job in Sheffield.'

'Have you?' *I knew it*, she thought. *The beginning of the end. Everyone's leaving. Big holes, cold wind getting through.*

The summer seemed fragile all of a sudden, leaden with the possibility of great heartache.

'They want to do a Northern edition of the magazine. Want me to set it up.'

'Sheffield. Don't they make cutlery there?'

'Yes. But that's not the only exciting thing about the place. There's a lot more I can't go into right now.'

'Will you go?'

'Good Lord, I don't know.' Mo rested her beer on her chest. 'I might. London's sort of dead in the summer. Horribly muggy. Full of tourists. And Sheffield, as we know, has all the attractions of sun, sea, and sand, without hordes of people.'

'Apart from the sea and sand.'

'Apart from those. But who knows, it might be a burgeoning metropolis with an absolutely screaming gay and lesbian scene!'

'Have you ever been there?'

'I should think not, Darling. I've never been north of Finchley. I don't go into the outlying regions if I can help it. The Midlands. Ugh!' she shuddered. 'Norfolk. Hawtonunder-Scruggy. I shall have to get on the train with a good book and surface somewhere north of Leicester.'

Hugh was in a tiny room with someone else. The curtains were closed around the other bed and every now and then peculiar noises emanated from behind them: long snores, groans, some kind of nasal clearance that made Hannah's stomach turn. She was shocked by the cramped quarters, the bed surrounded by machines and metal arms and pulleys, a chaotic jumble of receptacles and pillows and charts. She had pictured him in a room on his own, plenty of space, sun coming in the window. She couldn't even see the window. And shouldn't he be under more surveillance, the day after a major heart attack? She'd expected nurses to be popping in and out. Certainly not this casual air. Hugh, his hair plastered down, looked grey and sick. He managed a smile when she poked her head round the door and ooh'd when she took out the fruit and books she'd brought, but he soon lapsed into a kind of torpor from which she felt reluctant to rouse him with vapid conversation. The surroundings made her squeamish. She was embarrassed by his body, large and fleshy in the blue hospital gown. She was afraid he would move and the bedclothes would fall away and she'd see something she shouldn't. She was afraid he'd take a sudden turn for the worse while she was there—have another heart-attack, a bout of something. She shied away from his pain and didn't know what to say.

'So Dad's flying down on Friday. They say you can come out Saturday, right?'

'Yes, I think so.' His voice was wheezier than usual. He breathed in quick sighs.

'That's amazing. I mean, so soon,' she said nervously.

'Yes, marvellous.' He shifted a little in the bed and she glanced round the room.

'It's very cramped in here. I thought you'd be in a room of your own. You know, a view. It's very sunny outside.'

He had closed his eyes. She wondered if she should just go. Watching him, she felt a surge of affection and tears sprang to her eyes. He could have died—lying on cold linoleum somewhere, surrounded by secretaries. She leaned down close to him.

'I'm glad you came through it okay, Hugh.' A tear spilled over and soaked into the sheet. He opened his eyes.

'Dear me,' he said, in little more than a whisper, 'it was a narrow squeak, wasn't it.' He reached over and took her hand in his. 'I'll be back beating you at backgammon in no time.' He let her hand fall as though he wasn't sure how long he should keep it for.

'You may have to cut back on those backgammon games,' she said. 'The strain of losing so frequently to a relative beginner can't be good for your heart.'

'Mm.' A pause. 'How are things with you?'

'Oh, fine. I brought you some Thurber,' she picked up the books. 'I thought he'd be good to read in hospital.' He nodded and moved again in the bed. She wondered if he hated her being there, seeing him like this. He looked quite miserable.

'I think I'll go now then. Let you get some sleep.'

He watched her collect her jacket and duffle bag. 'Thanks for coming in. No need to come again, I'll see you when your Dad gets here.'

'Okay. See you then.'

She stood at the door a moment. His eyes were closed already, she wasn't sure if he was still awake. Then he stirred, as she turned to go, and said 'Goodbye Margaret'.

She paused again without turning round, wanting to say something, but she couldn't think what. 'Bye Hugh.' It was a relief to be out in the corridor. *Funny*, she thought, *I wonder if he really thought I was Mum for a minute. He's worse than I thought.*

Hugh was trying to be his old self as they drove home, but she quickly saw it was a front and that underneath, something had faltered. He and her father kept up their usual conversation about economic recession and the stock market; she sat deep in the back seat of the Volvo watching London, unfamiliar from a car, and thinking about Harry. When they reached Harrow, they stopped at Sainsbury's to stock up the fridge. Hugh stayed in the car. She and her father filled a trolley with fruit and vegetables, All Bran, low-fat milk, cans of beans and packets of dried lentils she was sure none of them would know what to do with. At the freezers she pointed ruefully at the array of ice-creams.

'It's their fault,' she said.

'Yes,' said her father doubtfully. 'I'm sure he'll be on a strict diet from now on.'

'I know.' She picked the All Bran out of the trolley and read the nutritional information. 'Let's not go overboard though; I mean he's not going to eat this stuff, and *I'm* certainly not. Are you?'

'Put it back,' said her father, and glancing down the aisle, he took it from her and slid it between two stacks of kitchen roll.

They were in the checkout queue when she remembered Hugh calling her Margaret.

'Hugh thought I was Mum the other day,' she said.

'Hm?'

'Hugh thought I was Mum when I went to visit him in hospital the day after the attack. He called me Margaret.'

'Mum or the other Margaret,' her father said.

'What other Margaret?'

'Hugh's Margaret.' He started stacking food on the semicircular conveyor belt.

'What Hugh's Margaret?'

'Margaret. You remember.'

'I *don't*. Tell me!' She was consumed with curiosity.

'Maybe you were too young.'

'*Tell* me, Dad!' she repeated, exasperated. There would never be time for adequate details before they got back to the car, and she didn't trust her father to be anything but distressingly vague. 'I never remember Hugh and any Margaret. Who was she? What was she like?'

'Oh, nice.' He began the complicated manoeuvring of the trolley to the front of the checkout and then he started packing bags with the checked groceries.

'It was after Mum died?' She joined him bagging groceries.

But he was distracted, trying to figure out how to pay with his credit card. She plucked it out of his hands and turned it so the stripe was the right way. 'You don't need a PIN number, it just goes through and you sign. What was she like?'

'Marvellous,' he said, but she realized he meant the machine. She picked up the bags and glanced impatiently out at the car.

'Was she young? Old? Dad!'

But he was chatting to the checkout girl about automatic payment. She watched a toddler standing by the swing doors, looking open-mouthed as people left the supermarket, the doors swinging abruptly open each time the mechanism was activated. When her father joined her, he was saying, 'It's not necessary to say "PIN number" because "PIN" stands for personal...'

'...identification number,' she chorused with him. 'Yeah yeah, Dad, number number. But tell me more about this Margaret person. I'm feeling left out of a family picture.'

'Well, she was Hugh's only lady friend I ever knew about. There may have been others.' They were approaching the car.

'What happened?' she said, but it was too late, he was fishing for the keys to the boot. She piled a couple of shopping bags in the back seat and climbed in after them. 'We bought you All Bran and non-fat-low-cal-non-sweetened everything else.'

Hugh groaned. 'I'll never see real food again.'

She watched him from the back seat: Hugh in a new light. It was hard to imagine what she might have looked like, this Margaret. She guessed sensible clothes, gently permed hair. Nothing glamorous. It was a sensible name—not one she had ever thought suited her mother, that fragile, pretty young girl in the home movie. Hugh's Margaret wouldn't have been fragile or pretty, but kind and generous. She wondered if there were any photos. She wondered if Margaret had treated him right. When they drew up at the house and her father switched off the engine, they all sat silently for a moment, as though it struck them all at the same time how Hugh might never have come back to his house. She realized for the first time the enormity of what had happened. His heart had stopped! For a few seconds, he might have been dead. No more Hugh! It was impossible to imagine. There he was, getting out—so slowly—of the car. She scrambled out and ahead of him to the front door with her key. 'Welcome home!' she opened the door with a flourish. He smiled, but he leaned against the door-jamb for support and she thought for a moment he would trip on the step. Afraid to seem fussy, she went back out to the car for the groceries. She followed her father indoors and kicked the front door shut behind her. Hugh was in the kitchen sorting through a pile of mail.

'How do you feel?' she said cautiously.

'Oh, fine. A little tired.'

'I'm going to cook us something healthy, I'm afraid.'

'Yes.' He sat down rather heavily in a kitchen chair. She heard her father switch on the TV in the back room. Hugh took his glasses off and wiped them with his sweater. It was warm in the house—she saw sweat standing out in beads on his forehead. She said gently, 'You will have to be careful what you eat, though. I mean, didn't the doctors say so?'

'Yes.' He sighed. 'They had a long talk with me. They gave me a list. Scolded me thoroughly.' He put his glasses back on and began sorting through the letters again, but she saw that he wasn't really looking at them.

'Would you like to go up to bed and I'll bring dinner up on a tray? Then you could have a nap and get up later.'

He put the letters down. 'Lovely idea,' he said. She caught an odd tone in his voice, and a moment later he leaned one elbow on the table with his hand shielding his eyes and she realized to her horror he was weeping. It was awful. He made a sound and she knew he must know she'd heard him. Should she just leave? She was almost sure he'd want her to. Or maybe he didn't care.

'I'll ask Dad what he wants for dinner,' she said, and her voice came out low and calm. She wasn't sure he'd heard. On her way past, she let her hand rest briefly on his shoulder. In the back room, her father was standing close to the telly, watching intently, but looking as though he intended to sit down at any moment. It was something he'd always done. Now she had grown up and moved away and that didn't seem to have changed him. *Dad,* she thought, *all those years and you never really knew me.* It was a peculiar feeling, regarding her father like this, as just a man. She saw him for the first time as he might appear to other people: tall, slightly stooped, a shambler like Hugh was, but without the bulk.

'I have a boyfriend now, Dad,' she said, still standing at the door. He watched the cricket. Her words penetrated slowly, past the innings.

'Hm?' he said, and turned around. 'A boyfriend. Good!'

There didn't seem to be any more to say so she went back to the kitchen. Hugh was still at the table. He wasn't crying any more.

'It must have been scary,' she said, sitting down opposite him and resting the heels of her shoes on the rung of the chair. It wasn't embarrassing that he'd cried after all. It was just part of life, and she wanted him to know that.

'It was,' he said. His eyes looked a little puffy, but otherwise you wouldn't know he'd been crying.

'Does it make life look sweeter now?'

'Yes, I suppose so.' He looked at her without smiling. She fancied he could detect that she was grown up now, she was in control, he could talk to her like an adult. *I'm nearly twenty,* she thought.

'I just feel old and tired and fragile,' he said.

She nodded. 'Vulnerable.'

'That's the word.' He stood. 'I'm up to bed. Get my old vulnerable bones some rest.'

Cooking dinner, she thought about Harry again, about how it would be wrong to mistake his gentleness for real trustworthiness. It wasn't his fault. It just spilled over in him. Sometimes, she knew, he did things he shouldn't. That was why she should just keep on having fun with him while it lasted, and not get in too deep. She didn't even mind that she wasn't going to be with him tonight. It would all begin on Friday, after his last exam. Her heart quickened. Life was too good—it was all ahead of her!

Pausing at the door of Hugh's bedroom with the tray, she realized she'd never been in the room before. She couldn't imagine what it would be like. When he went to bed, he disappeared into a murky region from which he emerged the next morning. She had never imagined him going to bed, and she paused, reluctant now to intrude in his room. He called for her to enter, and she balanced the tray precariously on the doorknob while she opened it. Inside, the business of looking for a place to put the tray down relieved her from actually having to look directly at him in his bed. It was a big, high, old-fashioned bed with lots of pillows and wooden knobs at each corner. She waited while he struggled a moment with the pillows, then she set the tray down on the floor.

'Here: I'll do those.' She reached behind him and stacked the pillows so he could sit up straight. 'Daddy didn't want his dinner yet, so I was wondering if I could have mine up here with you.'

'Of course.'

'It's lots of vegetables with pasta. I don't know what you're allowed to eat.'

'Not much,' he complained. But when she returned he was eating heartily.

'Good,' he said through a mouthful. 'The first good meal I've had. Delicious. Dreadful what they try to feed you in the hospital.' He seemed much brighter, and she smiled happily at him. While she ate, she allowed herself a quick glance around the room. It was immensely spartan. A single kitchen chair with his clothes thrown over it; a wardrobe like the ones in the front bedroom, big and old and dark; a chest of drawers under the window. The wallpaper looked as though it had been there since the house was built. She glanced surreptitiously at the bedside table, wondering if there'd be a picture of Margaret there, but there wasn't.

'So tell me what the doctors said, exactly.'

'Oh,' he finished a mouthful, 'much as you'd imagine. Eat right. Lose some of this—' he patted his stomach. 'Less fat. Cut out this, cut out that.'

'Well, food. I mean, you should probably stop eating altogether, right?'

'Mm. That's the general idea.' They ate in silence for a while.

'I've got a new boyfriend,' she said shyly.

'Really? How exciting. Is he worthy of you?'

'Oh, sometimes. Actually, he'll probably break my heart.' She put her knife and fork together sadly. It was true, wasn't it. He wouldn't mean to, but someone else would come along and the next thing she knew she'd have to let go and fall or the train would run over her hands. She saw it so clearly she couldn't even raise a smile about it.

'Well don't let him do that, dear girl.' Hugh sounded genuinely concerned.

'See he doesn't mean to,' she said, 'but he can't help it. He'll be playing round with other girls, because he thinks life is meant to be that way. The whole thing's just a big story to him. All he wants are funny stories. That's what I love him for, laughter. We just laugh all the time.'

'Perhaps you should just stay that way for a while; then, when it's time to move on, you'll know. If he insists on wasting his energies on other girls when he could bestow them upon you, he may not deserve further attention.'

She'd never heard him talk like this: as though he had a sense of what her life might be like. 'You might be right.' She had to smile now. Then she took the plunge. 'What was Margaret like, Hugh?'

If he was taken aback, he didn't show it. He took the knife and fork off his plate and laid them to the side. Then he lifted the tray off his knees a little and pushed it to his right, on the empty side of the bed.

'She was gentle,' he said, and Hannah thought her heart would break, the way he said it. 'Gentle and honest.'

'Did you love her?' She was half-amazed at her own audacity.

'Oh yes,' he said quietly.

'Did she go away?'

'She went back to her husband.'

'Oh.' She knew she should stop, but she couldn't help it. If he showed the slightest sign, she would stop. But he showed nothing of what he was thinking. 'Was that the right thing for her to do?'

'Yes,' he said. 'He was very ill. He needed her, and she went back to him.'

But you're sick now, she thought. *You could do with someone to nurse you.* 'Where are they now?'

'She's in Edinburgh, I believe.'
'They're not together?'
'He died. Several years ago now.'
'How do you know?'
'She wrote and told me. A year or so after.'
'A year after he died? So how come—' Was this time to stop? His eyes met hers and she couldn't think how to say it. 'You didn't...' She trailed off again. He looked at his plate. Then he said quietly—

'It's not always that simple, dear girl. Years had passed. I'd become used to being alone. Too set in my ways.'

No, she wanted to say, surely not. Surely it *is* that simple. You loved her, didn't she love you? Why couldn't you come together again? What could be so complicated about it? How terrible, to let love pass you by because you'd got used to being alone.

'Hugh—' she shook her head, looking down at her hands, confused. Was that his life? Had she heard it now? That was all? It was so stark, so lonely a sentence.

'You want things to end happily, don't you,' he said. She laughed shortly, shook her head again, as though she gave up.

'I know there's lots I don't understand,' she said. 'I'd just like to have met her.' She met his eyes again, and smiled bashfully. 'That's all.'

'You can see her picture,' he said. 'In the top drawer over there.'

'You don't mind?'

'Go ahead.'

She opened the drawer and took it out reverently—a black-and-white photo in a worked metal frame. She looked just right: kind, serious, looking straight at the camera. She wasn't plain, though. Not pretty exactly, but better than pretty, with fine bones and lovely sympathetic eyes. Hannah said nothing, just looked for a long time, imagining this woman with Hugh, here in the house; and going back to her no-good husband. It wasn't fair. She laid it back and shut the drawer slowly. Out the window, clouds were scudding by. She had a slow vision of herself in a cotton dress, walking through a hot town, to a beach somewhere in the future. She would be with a man who would take great care of her. Someone who loved her quietly, without conditions, without caring who she was or what she had done.

'I hope she deserved you,' she said, and gathered her plate and his tray without looking at him.

'Thank you,' he said when she reached the door. She was afraid to look back.

Hugh sat for a long time without moving. It was quiet in the room. He didn't need to see the picture again, his memories of her were all still so much more alive than that single photograph. He turned them over, one by one by one. And yet, maybe over the years she *had* become somewhat static in his mind. Without knowing how she might have changed in all that time, how could he really picture her? Not now; only as she had been then. That was alright, he didn't want to picture her now. Only then. Margaret, in her Sunday hat with the little veil. As they walked together, he would put a hand under her elbow, just so that by the gentle pressure she would know he was there. Not guiding, not following, just beside her. Odd how the weight of loss could still swing down on him after all these years. It was seldom he allowed himself the bitterness of grief. Such a cold, useless companion. But now, after his brush with destruction, he felt lonelier than ever. She didn't know about the pain that had finally brought him down, gasping and afraid, surrounded by strangers he had known for years. In his most terrifying moments, she had probably been going about her business, cheerful and unconcerned. And she must have had her own moments of agony that he knew nothing about. He took his glasses off and permitted a few hot tears their unfamiliar escape.

'Twice in one day,' he muttered. 'Still, if I can't shed a few tears when I'm in choppy waters, then I'm an old fool.' The thought immediately cheered him a little. He reached for his book, then hesitated and clambered out of bed. He crossed to the chest of drawers, took the photo out, and closed the drawer. He had to clear a space among the books and bottles of pills on the bedside table. Reinstated, Margaret stared across the room unsmilingly. He settled himself down a little on the pillows and took up his book. After ten minutes had passed, he put the book aside and gazed into space for a while. Then he got out of bed again and put his dressing-gown on. He picked the photo up without looking at it and put it back in the drawer as though he were just tidying the room a little. When he came back from the bathroom, he got back into bed and turned on his side so he could go to sleep.

Her father persuaded Hugh that a holiday would do him good. He himself had taken two weeks off work in the hopes that Hugh would be well enough to travel. Somewhere quiet, he thought, like the Cotswolds. They could stay in a B&B for a week. Gentle walks in the hills, lots of reading, perhaps a game or two of golf. After some initial hesitation, Hugh agreed. His doctor warned against over-exertion, something, Hugh confessed, that was not on his agenda; but he thought the country air would do him good. Her father wondered if she'd like to go with them, but Hugh winked broadly at her and aired the opinion that there was probably some compelling reason why the prospect would be less than appealing to her.

'Probably,' she grinned broadly. 'he's doing his last exam on Wednesday.'

'Who?' said her father. She grimaced at Hugh—*Dad! He's so clueless!*

Late Sunday morning the phone rang. She stopped dead. It could be René, it could be Harry. She let Hugh answer it. 'A chap,' he said, when he came back in to the kitchen, 'for Hannah Jane.'

She laughed nervously and skipped out into the hall with her heart doing cartwheels.

'Heartwheels,' she said into the phone. 'Harry?'

'When're you coming in?' he said.

'Shortly. After dinner. D'you miss me?'

'Yep. How's your uncle?'

'Better. Shall I come to your place or will you be at Leighton Road?'

'Leighton Road,' he said. 'We've tickets to see Jane's Addiction at the Brixton Academy.'

As soon as she put the phone down she was impatient to leave. The switch had occurred, over to the other life, and it was agonizing to have to hang around her father and Hugh for a moment while people might be gathering at Leighton Road, ready to head down to Brixton. What could they possibly understand of the excitement that gripped her now. She couldn't even eat, couldn't sit still. When Hugh went upstairs for a nap, she threw her arms around him and hugged him tightly.

'Have a lovely holiday. And remember,' she released him and wagged her finger exaggeratedly, 'don't eat any FOOD.'

'And you be good,' he leaned in close to her conspiratorially, 'but if you can't be good, have fun.' She smiled in answer and sat back down opposite her father. She hoped he wouldn't start to ask questions now, or talk about home. He had scarcely mentioned anything about either of her brothers all weekend, and she couldn't face it now. She was already thinking about the tube back to town, dying to see Harry, ready for a night, a week, a summer of dangerous excitement. And here was her father, solidly planted in the old life, looming out of the past as though nothing had changed.

'What's the new boyfriend like then?'

She shifted in her chair. She didn't want to talk about Harry. Suddenly, she wanted to probe at an old wound, pick at the scab that had begun to itch so persistently.

'He's cool. How are things at home?'

'Well I've left your younger brother in the care of your older.' There was a pause. 'I'm not entirely sure how either of them are.'

'Oh?' she said nonchalantly, 'Is Christian going to school?'

'Far as I know. He knuckled down fairly well after his escapade. I promised him a decent summer if he passed his exams.'

'He wanted to come over here. You're not going to let him, are you?'

'No. He wants to go picking fruit with some friends of his. I can't quite picture it myself, but I expect the money is the draw. He wants a motorbike of course. And of course he's not getting one.'

'Golly no. Mum would've had a fit! He will be a biker, though, later on, Dad. I can see it.'

'You think so?'

'You won't be able to stop him. I wouldn't try if I were you. It's the perfect alienation scenario.'

'My father let me have one, I suppose.'

'Really? What age were you?'

'Eighteen.'

'Hugh told me a bit about Margaret yesterday. Showed me her picture. What happened Dad? Why didn't they get together again after her husband died?'

'Don't know. He never spoke to me much about it, except once, just after she went back to her husband. He said he had to let her go.'

'Did she break his heart?'

'I don't think Hugh thinks in those terms,' he began. Then he sat back and lit a cigarette. She took one from the pack and he frowned but let her. Then he said, 'I expect she did, though, yes. I've always thought so.'

'Poor Hugh.' She would go now, as soon as she could. Nothing about René. Probably better that way. She'd been ready for it a moment ago, but she wasn't now. Leave, quickly, before anything was started.

'Oh, I have a letter for you from your scholarly elder brother. I forgot.' He fished in his trouser pocket and took out an extremely crumpled envelope. She accepted it as though it were a telegram about a death. 'Why scholarly?' she said, reluctantly.

'Well he's writing some sort of book, far as I can make out. You know him—never know quite what's going on behind those closed doors.'

She was sure he meant this in all innocence. What could be going on? A book about what? She knew, she realised. She knew pretty well what it was about. All those letters about the books he was reading that she hadn't wanted to hear anything about, and had tried to put out of her mind. All that talk about myth and taboo and those stories…

'Yeah, well. I'm off now.' Put it out. Put it out of the mind. 'Have a great time in Gloucestershire.' She thought of Mo saying 'the Midlands—ugh!' It did seem interminably dull to be leaving London just now, when so much was happening.

'Off to see what's his name?'

'Yes. Good old whatsisname. I'll never forget him. Take good care of your brother-in-law.'

Who'll take care of your elder son, she thought as she slung her bag on her shoulder and pulled Hugh's gate shut behind her. On the tube, behind the intense excitement of going back into the thick of things, she felt an old lingering sadness. It was almost melancholy, almost pleasant, until the thought struck her that she had *gone away* and she might never be going back. This new life, all the excitement, it wasn't just a holiday, a temporary thing. This was it! The next bit! No going back. Just when did she think she'd see him again? They were pulling apart, who had been so inextricably together for so long. She was doing it, and she didn't even realise it. *We're not together any more. We're apart. It's over.* She took the letter out.

May 26th 1991.

Dear Sparrow,

It'll be quiet here, with Dad in England and Christian studying for his exams at his friend's house. He says he's studying. I've no way of knowing. I wanted to send something over with Dad, a gift of some sort, but as you can see I didn't. Too busy these days. Some days I can't find myself. There's so much to figure out. I stumbled on a book by Chateaubriand the other day in which the hero had a fate similar to mine. 'Go your way,' he was told. 'Happiness can only be found in the common paths.' So that was my mistake. His sister was stuck away in a convent. Amelia. A very poorly drawn character who atones for her sins—

Hannah gripped both her hands into fists, crushing the letter, and clenched her jaws. With her whole body tightened like that she felt stronger, less vulnerable. She could sit here on a train and not be blown away, not shrink down into a husk. If she just sat still for long enough and stared at nothing, the fear would end. It would go away and she'd feel normal again. Blank the mind. Put out memory. Put out grief. Life's but a walking shadow—

She told Julia she was going to bed with a terrible headache.

'Tell Harry I'll see him tomorrow and good luck in the exam,' she said, 'I just want to sleep.' Through the haze of two of Julia's sleeping tablets ('I'm a medical student, sweetie, I can get you to the moon!') she heard people arriving downstairs; Harry's voice, Joe's, Skin's high-pitched laugh, some girls. Then creaking on the stairs and her door cracked open. Harry whispered 'Hannah?' She lay still, afraid she would move, break, give in to the sudden urge to be with him. She had never resisted before. The sight of him was always enough to tip her over, much stronger than any resistance she could pretend. So she kept her eyes tight shut, feeling odd, like somebody else. It was hot behind her eyes. *If I wake up now,* she thought, *I'll tell him everything. I'll blast open and René will come out. That cannot happen.* The door closed. Later, everyone left. She waited till they'd gone to cry in case anyone came in to say goodbye, but she couldn't cry very much anyway. Much later, when Harry slipped into bed beside her, warm and beery, she only half-woke. 'Let's make love sometime,' she mumbled and he held her and called her his baby till she fell back asleep.

Eleven

2 June.

Dear Sparrow,

When I think of you, for some reason, I always think of you in that yellow dress. You were about eleven. It had small blue flowers and straps like dungarees. Cotton print. Swinging down the end of the garden, a quick streak of colour through the apple trees. You were a happy child; I used to love coming home from school on Friday nights, knowing we'd have the weekend together. The boys at school used to pour scorn on their sisters, especially little sisters, if they mentioned them at all. I never mentioned you. God I remember you learning to count by colouring squares in a larger square with crayons. Your first ink pen, the bottle on the kitchen table. I don't think you'll ever come home for good so there are some things I must tell you. We were not wrong. Although almost no society tolerates what we did (in some countries, only murder incurs longer sentences), it is society's stigma that colours us the colours we are. Had we been born into a different time, a different place on earth, there might have been no horror evinced—some embarrassment perhaps—but not the collective horror you and I have come to expect. And yet, had we been born somewhere like in the Jale tribe of New Guinea, and discovered, we would both have been put to death. You and I, swept away in the Floss. We won't be discovered, Sparrow. We need never tell anybody. If you ever need to talk, you know I'm here. I haven't called you because I couldn't bear the loneliness after I put the phone down: but that's my affair and I shall get over it. So here we are, stuck in our natures. Not such a bad place to be. Can I overcome my nature for a moment and allow myself the indulgence of telling you how badly I miss you? I can't explain it, but while I'm feeling that way, I am still glad you left. I know I made you go and I had to and you did the right thing: you went. Things could not have gone on that way. I keep dreaming of you though: real dreams I wake from in an agony of loss. I wonder how long this will go on—how long I can bear it.

<u>3 June.</u> Something I read today: that for love to develop, there needs to be an element of surprise, a certain degree of novelty. But there *was* surprise. I didn't always love you. Not that way. For many years you were just my little sister. Then after Mum died and you were so frail and clinging like a young flower: I felt protective at first. I came to love you slowly. Like any love, forbidden or not. Twelve, thirteen are such magical ages in a girl. I tried to hold you so loosely in my hands, so you wouldn't even feel it, so I could feel your heartbeat but you would know nothing of it. It makes itself into a haiku, what I knew of you then, what I imagine I know of you now: Under your thin dress/strongly beats your/sparrow heart.

My only hope is that now we have stopped it, it never needs to scar you: that we can go on with life, apart, though it's a black idea. That you can go on, without having been damaged. You are not damaged, are you, little sparrow? I am not damaged because I have my memories and they are intact and safe and nobody can enter there, it's a place where I can always be alone. We all need that. Me perhaps more than most, since I don't do too well in the bright light most people take for granted as their day. I prefer the darkness, myself. Not to hide me, but because I feel it is where I belong, where I am best suited. I wait for the day to be over. I open in the night, quietly. I don't disturb anybody. Nobody hears me.

I think this is the last letter I'll write for a while. I shall send it tonight. I think you probably need a break, a rest from me for a while. That's good. It gives me hope that you are able to go on without damage, that I didn't hurt the one I love.

Finch.

Harry said he loved her because she was different from all the college girls. It was such a closed world, he said, and she was outside it. He made her feel like something special. But she felt so inferior to those girls, she told him. The girls who hung around his house all seemed tremendously sophisticated. He told her to stop being scared of everybody, and he undressed her slowly, stopping to admire each part.
'One thing I'll never understand,' he said as they lay still in the darkness when it was over, 'is why all the beautiful girls hate their bodies so much.'
I'm empty now, she thought. *I'm emptied out. There really was nothing to give after all.*
   'I thought you were a virgin,' he said curiously.
   'No.'
   What happened now? Did he feel the special bond like he said? Would anything change?

'It's my birthday on Saturday,' she said. 'I'll be twenty.' He turned to her and pulled her close.

'Who was it?' he whispered.

'Nobody you know,' she said.

What was he talking about, being suited to darkness? What did that mean? He's not making sense any more. Something's going wrong. I don't know who the person writing those letters is. It isn't René, not the René I know. What's happening to him?

She turned over, away from Harry. *I may as well be made of wood,* she thought resolutely. *Oak, birch, mahogany, maple. Willow, supple in the wind, but absolutely no use in an emotional crisis.*

'You OK?' he asked.

The truth was, he'd been very different and yet she'd thought of René anyway. You couldn't say that, though. *I was thinking of someone else all the way through it.*

'Yes. Fine.'

It didn't make any difference, then. She loved Harry the same as she had, still with the great wonder that he'd chosen her, and dread that she wasn't good enough. She wondered if she'd ever have sex that meant anything. It didn't matter. There was now, today, and that's all there was. She wasn't going to hear from René for a while: no more letters. And she didn't have to write to him. Was she damaged? Had he hurt her? She couldn't think. The words seemed to bear no relation to what she remembered. *I love you,* she thought. *I want to be with you and I can't be. So I'll be with Harry. He's fun and lovely and I love him too. He'll get tired of me, but they all will. Only you would never get tired of me. You would be the only constant. The only one. You're the only one.*

She opened *Article1* and read over the last sentence she had written.

'"Who's my favourite girl?" he'd say as he stood in her bedroom doorway. "I am," she'd reply.'

Glancing round the office, she began typing a new paragraph.

'She did well in school, but she hated it.' She erased 'hated it' and typed 'didn't like it'. 'She liked the learning, and the chance to play tennis and swim. What she didn't like were the tight bunches of girls, their cloying friendships and their silliness about boys. She wanted a boyfriend too, but she hated to admit it to any of these girls. She was ten years old, and she thought she would never make it to fourteen: that seemed too grown up, too far away. By the time she was thirteen, she thought there was no more growing up to do. Everyone said she was very grown up for her age. It was because of her Mum dying like that, they said, it made her have to grow up fast. She didn't do the kinds of things the other girls did. She didn't hang out down by the sea-front or by the sweet shop, gossiping about boys and smoking. She stayed at home. She had to look after her little brother, she told people. She had to take care of him because they didn't have a mother. She liked being at home more than anywhere else, especially at the weekends. She never wanted to be anywhere else. In school, she looked at the other girls and thought their lives were empty and dull. It wasn't that she felt superior. She felt...' she paused and saved what she'd written. Then she typed 'lucky. She felt so lucky.'

She stopped again and worked on something else for a while, some layouts. When she'd finished, she brought up *Article1* again.

'One night it began,' she wrote. 'It must have begun one night.' She stopped. 'She was thirteen.' She stopped again and stared at the screen. Then she slowly typed 'He was the only one,' and saved the file, and closed it.

The week went by in a blur of late nights; people finishing up and celebrating wildly; people leaving for the summer. Even though she was only on the periphery, Hannah felt sharply the sense of something ending—the shutting down. Behind the elation of finishing exams, Harry and his friends became morose.

'It's such a fucking shame,' he explained to her. 'You spend the whole year working so *fucking* hard, you forget to enjoy all your friends. Some of these people won't be back next year.'

'What about the summer?' She was increasingly dreading the summer. Harry would go home—would he come back? He was terribly vague about his plans. He talked about a job in the city, a house in Clapham with some others, a job at the airport, a job in the docklands. 'The summer's going to be weird,' he said. Then he caught her expression. 'Hey! It'll be great! Come here you,' he folded her in his arms the way she loved. 'We'll dig up all the people still in London and have a fucking three-month-long *ball!*'

She wasn't convinced. For her birthday, Harry organized a party at his house. She was filled with the usual fears: would people come? Would anyone care? Would they even notice her? She needn't have worried. Everyone came. It was summer and exams were ending. A party anywhere was enough to attract a hundred people. She got the impression most of them didn't even know it was anyone's birthday. There was a cake in the fridge that someone bought but people put their beers on top of it and crushed it. By early in the evening it was ruined, a sticky mess that people picked at with spoons. Eventually she saw it in the sink, surrounded by glasses and cigarette butts. Harry was gloriously drunk by six. At eight, wandering round the house in her own half-drunk haze, she realized he'd disappeared. She fetched another beer and sat out in the garden, wondering if she felt miserable. She tried to imagine if there'd be a card or present waiting in the post-office box. It had been over a week of silence. Surely he wouldn't forget her birthday?

It felt like four in the morning, but it wasn't even midnight when she left the party; picked her way deliberately between the bodies in the hallway, let herself out into the warm night and walked the forty minutes back to Leighton Road. Neither Mo nor Julia were home. The house smelled of cigarette smoke. She made her way slowly upstairs, peeling off her clothes as she went. 'He's with someone else, that's for sure,' she said aloud when she reached her bedroom. 'That's the way, isn't it. I can't say I didn't know. It comes as no surprise.' She lay down without taking off her shoes and fell easily into a deep, untroubled sleep.

She lay on her back. She was naked from the waist up. Her ribs showed, making it look as though she were arching her back. Below the waistband of her jeans, the two hip bones stood out starkly. The denim stretched taut over them, leaving a gap between the flat stomach and the row of metal buttons. He sat beside her. It was warm; the sun had warmed her bare skin and her nipples felt silky. There was no feeling nicer than the feeling of her bare warm skin beneath his hand. Her lips parted. She smiled that smile—go on, it said, keep doing this or I'll get mean. Go on, go on, it said, and I dare you to go further. He slipped his hand between her stomach and the jeans. He felt the elastic waistband of her knickers. His fingers passed over the fabric, felt the prickly roughness underneath. He was breathing heavily and she could feel him straining against her. *I don't care about right and wrong*, she thought. *I don't care.* He leaned over her till his face was inches from hers. They stared at each other, his hand moving rhythmically with her. This was time, this was all, all he ever wanted; he was ready, he was dying, he would take her here, one last time, the final time, and then they'd never do it again.

Something tickled her bare stomach. She flipped it away, but it came back. She opened her eyes. Harry.

'What were you dreaming?'

'Just lying here, drifting. London's so great when it's hot.'

'I know I fucked up last night,' he said. 'I'm sorry.'

'Yeah,' she said and smiled. 'I don't care though. Let's lie here and become bronzed demi-gods.'

'Or we could become demi-gods drinking an ice-cold pint of lager,' he said.

On the way to the pub she told him she was going to do A-levels and go to college. 'History, Math, and Chemistry. I was good at those. Then I can do any science degree I like and come out with something useful. I want to be a professional. Nobel Prize Chemist. Mixing bubbly stuff up in test-tubes. That sort of thing.'

'Drugs,' said Harry. 'You could form a drugs ring. Nobel Prize procurer of illicit substances.' Sitting in the pub she felt the familiar wave of euphoria. It was five on a summer Sunday. They'd have some pints, get some food somewhere, then back to one of the houses: it was all so free, so easy. No responsibilities. Nothing to fear. Even when Harry told her he was going home for a few days, she didn't mind. 'I have to put in an appearance, sort a few things out. Then I'll be back.' He didn't ask her to visit or come with him. She didn't suggest it. In fact, the prospect of a few days alone suddenly seemed appealing. Over the previous few days she had lost the sense of urgency to be in the thick of things. It would be fine to be quiet, on her own, eat healthily, sleep long nights. *I must be growing up,* she thought. *I don't need so much now. I have everything I want.* After a curry in Camden Town she told Harry she'd like to be alone for the night. They kissed briefly at the station. 'See you in a few days then,' he said cheerily. Walking home she felt light and calm as she hadn't felt for weeks. Something was settling. This was how things were meant to be.

In the post office, there was a letter and a birthday card. The card was funny. He had signed his name in his normal hand. She put the letter in her pocket and folded the card in two, held it tightly, fearing it would be caught by a gust of wind coming from nowhere and blown out of her hand. She carried it home that way. For once, anyone could ask her to see and she could show them: a birthday card from her brother—look, nothing to hide. Perfectly normal. For the first time in a long time, when she tried to think of him, she couldn't picture him. What would he be wearing? Had he changed at all to look at since she left? Had he any more grey hair? Some had been starting. She'd made a joke of that. Now he slipped around in her memory. She couldn't quite fix on him. Leaving the new letter in her pocket, she lay down carefully on her bed and folded her hands on her chest, the way she used to lie waiting for him to come up and say goodnight. She glanced at the door. It had never been fear. Excitement, mixed with fear, but not because of him: because some part of her knew it was wrong. She leaned down to the drawer in her bedside table and took out the last letter again. She read it through, trying to pretend it was the first time, that she didn't know the person it was from. What would she think of him? Gingerly, in her mind's compartments, she lowered the bars she'd so carefully raised and let him cross over into her life now. What would Mo think of him? Julia? Harry? She was surprised how completely she had separated past and present. They had really never mixed, had they; she hadn't allowed it. She got up and went downstairs, carrying the birthday card, leaving the letter on her bed. The sitting room was filled with late sunlight. She put the card on the mantlepiece and started tidying the place. She moved slowly; he was in the armchair watching her. She knew the way he would be watching and how that made her feel. The front door slammed and Mo came in. She kept on tidying, stooping down to pick things up, moving round the chair he was in without disturbing anything there. Mo stood in the doorway. He did not leave the chair. They were both there, in the one room. It *was* possible.

'Alright?' said Mo.

'Mm.'

'I brought you something for your birthday. Late, I know.' She put a parcel on the table and handed Hannah a card. Hannah smiled and opened the envelope with care.

The card was a picture of two people kissing through the open window of a train. The girl was leaning down, the boy stretching up to her. Inside, Mo had written 'For my favourite straight girl.' Hannah glanced at her and she smiled ruefully. 'Wish you weren't,' she said simply. 'Go on, open the pressie.' It was a dress, a tiny piece of cloth in Hannah's hands, red, with giant flowers, purple and green, looking painted on with bold strokes. 'It's amazing!' She laughed. 'It's tiny! Are you sure it'll cover anything?'

'Try it on,' said Mo. 'It'll look stunning, I promise you. You don't show off your body enough.' She followed Hannah upstairs. 'Use Julia's mirror.'

'There,' she said, when Hannah had shrugged off her jeans and t-shirt and crept into the dress. It fitted her perfectly. She turned slightly in the mirror, saw how the fabric accentuated the little bumps of her hip bones, her narrow waist, the curves of her shoulders. She turned to Mo. 'Thanks Mo. I feel—different.' She glanced back at the mirror. What would he think if he saw her now? She allowed herself a brief illicit moment of luxury. She knew what he would think.

'I told you, you should wear stuff like this all the time Hannah. Go short and sexy. You look fab.'

She hugged her quickly. 'Wait till Harry sees you in this,' Mo held her out at arm's length and widened her eyes, 'He'll be a happy boy.'

Yeah, thought Hannah. Somehow Harry's delight, compared to the other, seemed light, inconsequential. *I wish*, she thought. *I wish...something.* She scooped up her clothes and took a last look in the mirror. *Tart*, she thought. *Whore. Lovely, long-legged whore.* 'He's gone home till Friday,' she said. 'I'm going out to Hugh's after work tomorrow. He and Dad are back from their holiday and Dad's off on Tuesday. They want to take me out for a birthday dinner. D'you want to come?'

'Can't, Darling. I'm off up to Sheffield tomorrow to see some people about that job.'

'Oh,' said Hannah. 'Is it decided?'

'Not till I've made sure I won't die as soon as I'm more than fifty miles from London. But it's nearly decided. I think I'm going to go.'

In her room, Hannah removed the dress slowly and sat cross-legged on the bed in her underwear. She picked up the letter. Inside was a single sheet of tissuey paper. Across the middle, in writing that was recognizable as his, though a little larger than usual, as though written in a hurry, were the words 'Sim-pua'.

It wasn't in any of the dictionaries she could find at work. At lunchtime, she slipped out to the local library. It wasn't in the largest dictionary she could find there. In desperation, she asked the librarian. 'I think it's Chinese,' she said, 'and I can't find it in any dictionaries.' She showed the woman the words, which she'd written on a slip of paper.

'Mm, does look Chinese. What was the context?'

'It was…an article about Oriental society.' She felt herself blushing.

'I know,' the librarian motioned for her to wait and picked up the telephone. 'I'll call the Soho branch.' She was an oldish lady, comfortable-looking. Hannah liked her instinctively. While she asked questions and jotted something down, Hannah tried to let the familiar smell of the library calm her, convince her that the explanation would be simple, perhaps a joke even, nothing worth the dread she couldn't quench.

'Well,' said the librarian brightly, putting the phone down, 'You were right—it is Chinese. It's a marriage custom: the parents of a boy adopt a one-year-old girl, then raise both of them and marry them after puberty.' She looked down at the notebook she'd been writing on, and shook her head. 'Barbaric really,' she said. 'Poor children. What a strange society. I sometimes—' But Hannah had turned and was making her way between the tables of quiet readers to the doors and the air and the street outside.

Back in the office, she worked for a while and then opened *Article1*.

'Sometimes she won't allow herself remember the details,' she wrote. 'Her memory slips around trying not to remember his hands on her, his body, the things he would say, because without him there, it no longer seems alright, it is no longer bearable and more than bearable, lovely and terrible and terrifying and ecstatic. Without him it is just terrible and confusing.' She erased 'confusing' and wrote 'tormenting. It's tormenting because it is all pain without pleasure, whereas then it was both, in equal measure. She loved him. Let nobody take that away. She really loved him and she doesn't know what has happened.'

She read over the whole paragraph, then deleted everything after 'equal measure.'

'When she was thirteen, in Ireland, they were together,' she wrote. 'He asked her to tell him if she wanted to stop. She didn't. It happened maybe five or six times, when he was home from school in the summer. Then again in the spring when she was nearly fourteen. Ten, fifteen times, she doesn't know, she can't remember. Then he stopped it. It wouldn't happen again, he said. They had been lucky, they had kept their secret and nothing bad had happened and no one had found out. For two years they were never together. He finished school. Everyone expected he would go to college, but he said he wasn't sure. He was brilliant, but he said he might travel for a year before he went to college. She thought about him all the time, dreamed about him taking her with him when he went away. She waited for it to begin again, hoping it wouldn't, hoping it might. They never mentioned it any more, but it was there and she waited for it, dreading it, not able to believe she would never touch him like that again. Then on her sixteenth birthday she did. In his arms, in the quiet hot night, pure pleasure and terror. The fear of being caught was much worse than before. They talked about this. They could prevent it, he said. They must stick to their rules, keep their heads, take no risks. But the risks were what she loved, being with him in the early evenings that summer when he came home from work, scared their father would come home, or Christian. Nobody ever found them. They were lucky. Sometimes for weeks nothing would happen. Then a week of frenzy.' She erased 'frenzy' and typed 'intense closeness'.

'He didn't go away. He got a job in the city, said he was saving to put himself through college. She had to work very hard at school. She wanted to do well, though she couldn't think what would come after. He persuaded her to try for college and she got a place.' She paused. 'That was the beginning of the end. In school it had all seemed possible: she never thought about telling anyone. She never needed to. It was different in college. She felt pushed towards danger. She felt she might tell someone, let it slip, trying to impress or be heard in all the noise. He didn't seem to fit so easily into her life any more. He prevented her from belonging fully at college and she couldn't stand that because she knew that wasn't what he wanted at all. When she asked him why he never went to college he said he could learn all he wanted by reading. He said that life and books could teach him all he wanted to know. He read all the time. But things were too different. He was working, she was a student. It felt wrong. They began to fall apart. It seemed she wanted it to be all or nothing between them. It couldn't be all: there were too many fascinating people at college, though she couldn't get close to any of them. It couldn't be nothing. She had grown and changed and she still loved him and it was no good. He told her it was no good and they would have to stop. He said it was the hardest thing she would ever have to do.'

She stopped and read over the last paragraph. She looked out the window. *Sim-pua,* she thought. *Poor children. Poor stupid barbaric life.*

'Looking back,' she wrote, 'it was how much it hurt him that made it impossible for her to stay.'

Hugh was looking better, but he still seemed to move gingerly, sitting down as though he were afraid of breaking the chair. 'Lovely time,' he said when she asked if they'd had a good time. 'Your father forced me on immensely long walks. One would think I was in training for a marathon.'

'Except you have to run on a marathon.'

'Well yes, there is that. But I'm practically ready for it.'

At dinner, in a quiet local French restaurant, there was a different story.

'Hugh and I have something to tell you,' her father said when they had ordered. Her heart froze. She glanced at Hugh. He was spreading his napkin carefully on his lap.

'The doctors have recommended a bypass.'

'Golly.' Now she was afraid to look at Hugh. She looked instead at her father and they talked almost as if Hugh weren't there. 'Have they said when?'

'End of June. They want him to take things easy till then. No work, try to rest as much as possible.'

'No marathons,' Hugh said. Now that he had spoken, she felt able to look at him.

'I can come and stay, Hugh. Before and…after. If you like.'

'I'll be over for a week or so in early July,' her father said.

'That's very kind dear girl. It won't be necessary before. I expect I'll be in the hospital for a while.'

'The doctor suggested he sell the house, get himself a flat in town. Something manageable and convenient.'

'Will you?' she said.

'I haven't quite decided.' He fiddled with his fork. There was silence.

'Well if you decide to, I can help you clear out the house. And look for places, I love looking at places.'

He nodded, but he didn't smile. He looked different, tired and bewildered. The waiter came with the wine, pouring a splash in her glass. She felt foolish, going through with the tasting ritual as though there were even an outside chance she'd return the wine. But she felt grown up too. When their glasses were full, Hugh raised his to her.

'My favourite niece,' he said. 'Happy birthday and *Salut* to your twentieth year.'

As they walked back to Hugh's after dinner, she said to her father, 'Oh I forgot. I've a letter for René. Will you give it to him?' *If he knew*, she thought, as her father slipped the letter in his inside breast pocket; if he stepped completely out of character and decided he'd like to read a letter from his daughter to his son…but she was completely safe. It would never enter her father's head. And if it did? It would be *René's* fault, for acting weird like this, for turning things. Really, she told herself in a smart, irritable inner voice, if he was going to start behaving foolishly there was nothing she could do. He would have to learn that he couldn't start playing games.

They'd always played games, but never ones where only one of them knew the rules. *Alright,* she thought evenly, *you'll see that I can be honest.* She thought of the letter in her brother's hands and began to imagine it being read. What would he feel. Disappointment? Jealousy? Anger? Of course that was what she wanted: his jealousy. Let him imagine her with Harry for a bit, see how he liked the idea. She'd given him just enough detail to make the picture clear. 'Of course I'm not deeply in love with him, but the sex is wonderful, and he cares for me. He looks after me. We have a huge amount of fun. That's really all I want right now.'

She groaned inside as they turned onto Hugh's road. She would have to think about something else, quick.

'Would you miss this if you sold the house?' she asked Hugh.

'I've lived here for many years,' he replied.

'Lots of memories.'

'Yes.' He laid his hand on the garden gate. The weeds looked dusty, waist-high, forlorn. The windows seemed opaque. A house where the life had burned and sunk back down, nothing but embers.

'I think you should move,' she said warmly. 'A lovely old flat in Hampstead or Highgate. Near the Heath. Near town. You could get to work in less than half the time.'

He was putting the key in the door. How many times? Ten thousand? Four hundred times a year for the last thirty years of his life.

'However would I read the newspaper?' he said. 'I'd have to travel out to the end of the tube line and back every day.'

'I'm off early in the morning,' her father said. 'Don't bother getting up.' He took out his wallet. 'Not terribly exciting,' he counted out five notes onto the hall table, 'but a birthday present in its natural state.'

'Dad!' She gave him a quick hug.

'At least I visited a retail outlet,' said Hugh and he picked up a slim parcel up from the bottom stair. She opened it shyly, excited to see a book he might have lingered over, or picked purposefully from the shelf, knowing it was something he wanted her to read. 'Erich Fromm. *The Art of Loving*. I've heard of him.' She was too touched to think what to say. 'Thanks. I'll read it carefully.' She reached up and gave him a quick kiss on the cheek. He made a move with his arm, but thinking about it afterwards, she couldn't decide if he had been about to embrace her or instinctively to shield himself. *Margaret*, she thought, *I wish I could meet you.*

In the tiny front bedroom she flipped open the title page of the book. 'The affirmation of one's own life,' he had written, 'happiness, growth, freedom is rooted in one's capacity to love.'

You really loved her, didn't you Hugh? she thought. *And now you're going to go through a horrible operation and she's up in Edinburgh and she doesn't even know, and if she knew, she'd want to be here. She'd want you to wake up from the bypass and see her there, sitting by your bed, smiling at you. She'd want to look after you in your convalescence, give you something to get better for. It's just not fair that you lost your Margaret. I want you to have your love beside you again. What a family,* she thought as she undressed and slipped between the cool sheets. *The art of loving, indeed. We're not really up to much, are we?*

When she was leaving the next morning, she promised Hugh she'd be back on Friday night.

'We might have some cleaning to do, right?' She grinned at him. 'I could at least pull some of those weeds out the front. It's like Birnam Wood out there.'

'Some of those weeds and I have been friends for years,' he complained.

'They'd look very cheerful on a bonfire with all the newspapers in the scullery.'

'Not allowed to have bonfires in North London,' he grumbled, 'Clean Air Act. Greenhouse effect. Raises the level of the ocean.'

'And that worthless load of old books in the back room,' she continued, sensing that in spite of his mock reluctance, she might really be winning.

'Burn the lot, Savonarola,' he said, opening the newspaper. 'It'll save on the gas bill.'

'We could toast marshmallows. All crunchy on the outside—oops, I'm not supposed to talk about food, am I.' There was no response from behind the paper. 'Well, I'm off to work. See you Friday. You'll be alright?' He hadn't been alone in the house since the heart attack, she realised.

'Quite,' he said, folding the paper temporarily to look at her.

'Well, I'm not going to be a fidget, but you don't seem entirely fine and I wish you'd take care.' She stood up and waggled her finger at him as she slung her bag on one shoulder. 'No swearing or getting high. And absolutely *no* Jaffa cakes till the weekend.'

He opened the paper again with a chuckle. 'Man Coats Heart With Protective Layer of Jaffa Cakes,' he said. 'It's a breakthrough in cardio-vascular research, say scientists.'

There were no letters Tuesday or Wednesday. Thursday, she decided she'd forego the postbox checking ordeal and treat herself to a movie. Sitting in the dark cinema watching a love film, she thought about Harry's return. He'd called her at the office on Tuesday. He'd be back Saturday lunchtime. He had a surprise. Did she miss him? He really missed her.

She did miss him, but it was a sort of relief that he wasn't around for a few days. When she allowed thought on the matter to fully form, she was deeply disturbed by the Chinese letter. It jarred, like a piece out of place—something was going wrong with the pattern. She tried to put it out of her mind, but the notion of those tiny Chinese girls filled her with despair. After work on Wednesday she had gone to the library, another library, and pored through a dozen books. Eventually she found it. 'Participants' the book called them. Participants loathed each other. There was twice the normal rate of adultery; often divorce after the death of the parents. What was he thinking when he wrote the words? When he licked the envelope down, stamped it, put it in his pocket? He was a stranger to her, walking to the box on the corner. Had he come to loathe her? Did the memory fill him with disgust? Why the sudden change from the letter before? She checked the postmarks at home that night. Ten days between them. And in the meantime, a birthday card signed, perfectly normally, with his name. She decided not to check the postbox again for a while. Not for another week at least. The decision freed her. She tried to put the letter out of her mind.

Hugh was a lot more like his old self when she arrived in Harrow on Friday night. He had cooked dinner and they ate in the back room, plates balanced on their knees, watching TV—like old times, except that when Hugh collected her empty plate he remarked ruefully, 'No biscuits tonight I'm afraid. I forgot to stock up.' On Saturday, over breakfast, he told her they had set the date for the operation. June 28th. Then he announced cheerfully that he had taken to walking. Nothing too strenuous, he added hastily, but there was a park nearby named after the English Lord. Did she know who that was? He would give her a clue. A poet. Died in Greece. Still no suggestions? Wild, flamboyant character. Fell in love with his sister.

'George Gordon Byron,' he pronounced, when she still didn't reply. 'Died in the tiny inconsequential town of Messalongi. I was there once. Odd choice for a great man. Or perhaps not. Perhaps having left a town where he was spat upon in the streets, Messalongi was just the ticket.' She went with him on his walk and they chatted about poets and writers. She thanked him again for the Fromm book and its inscription. He said nothing. She wondered if they were both thinking of Margaret. When they reached the house, the phone was ringing. 'It's probably your father, dear girl, you answer,' he said, so she did. He waited a moment in the hallway after she said 'Hi,' to see if she'd hand the phone to him, but instead she turned away from him and there was silence. 'Can't talk now,' he heard her say, in a small, tight voice as he went into the kitchen. He put the kettle on and dropped a teabag into a mug. From the hall, he could half-hear the rhythm of her conversation, but he wasn't listening consciously enough to make out the words. Just before he got to the door with his mug of tea, her voice came to him quite clearly down the hall. 'Stop it,' she said, then louder, 'Stop it, stop this—stop what you're doing, I don't want to hear.' He was in the doorway, newspaper in one hand, tea in the other when she shouted: 'STOP IT!' and slammed down the phone.

He saw her standing with both hands to her face, then she turned and he saw she was crying. For a moment they stood facing each other. Her hands were still at her face. She looked to him like a small child who, standing from a fall, spends several long seconds gathering herself to bawl. 'Dear girl—' he began, but she gave him no chance to speak, turning and taking the stairs in twos, and then he heard her bedroom door slam shut. He remained standing in the doorway, looking down the hall at where she'd stood, then he moved uncertainly to the foot of the stairs. Halfway, he stopped, listened for a moment, then turned with his tea and paper and went into the back room.

Half an hour later, her room was still like a bruise in the house. He climbed the stairs carefully, trying not to make too much noise. At the top he stopped and looked across the landing at the shut door. Although he had lived in the house since he was a child and knew every room like the back of his hand, he found he had trouble remembering what that particular room looked like. He could not picture the bed, the other furniture, her things in the room. 'Hannah?' he called. The word came out as a croak. He had to clear his throat, he hadn't spoken for so long. 'Hannah?'

Nothing. He made his way slowly back downstairs. As he was washing his mug in the kitchen, the doorbell rang. He could make out several silhouettes through the frosted glass, and they were laughing and horsing around. When he opened the door, a short fat girl said 'You must be Uncle Hugh. Mo Royce.' She held out her hand. 'We've come to whisk Hannah away.'

'In a dreamboat,' added the other girl, and they laughed.

'Come in,' said Hugh, 'she's upstairs' he added, but he hesitated, as if unsure who should call her.

'Mind if I go up myself?' the boy said, gesturing up the stairs.

Hugh did not mind, but he seemed perplexed.

'Haven't seen each other for a few days,' said the tall girl, nodding after the boy, and she held out her hand. 'I'm Julia. It's lovely to meet you. That's my brother Harry.'

'We heard you'd been ill,' said Mo sympathetically. 'Are you on the mend?'

'Yes, yes,' he ushered them down the hall to the kitchen and they were all three laughing at something when Hannah and Harry joined them. She looked as though she'd been crying for a long time. 'Hi,' she said to the girls. She didn't look at Hugh.

'Well that wasn't much of a reunion,' Julia said reprovingly to her brother. 'Reducing the poor girl to tears. Has he told you?' she said to Hannah. She seemed to be taking charge of matters. Hugh watched his niece.

'About the surprise?' said Hannah weakly. 'Yes. He's got a car,' she explained to Hugh.

'A shiny new red car,' Harry said. 'Well—a dirty old red car, but it goes the same speed as shiny new ones. May we abduct your niece and take her on a pleasure trip?'

'Dear me,' said Hugh, 'if I wasn't tottering on my pins and entirely uninvited, I'd go myself.'

'You're invited by default,' said Mo. 'But if we can't get you, we'll take a substitute member of the family.'

'I have my stuff,' Hannah said to no one in particular, and she looked around her as though chilled by a draught. 'I'll drop by next week, Hugh.' She barely made eye contact, then they were all trooping out of the kitchen and down the hall. 'Where are we going?' she asked Harry. Hugh noticed they were holding hands. 'On a picnic,' said Harry. 'Up the A409 to the M1 and out to greenest Hertfordshire.' He looked at her as he held the front door open for her. 'And you're Queen of the Dreamboat.'

She smiled, and as they left, she looked back at Hugh in the doorway and lifted her hand in a hesitant wave. She seemed about to say something, but changed her mind. Hugh watched them pile into the cabriolet, then they were off, shouting and waving goodbye. Closing the door, his eye rested on the telephone. He shook his head and went back to finish the paper.

Harry's father had given him the car for his twenty-first birthday. He told him if he wrote it off, he would be written out of the will.

'Did he mean it?' asked Mo lazily as they sprawled in a field somewhere west of St Albans.

'Daddy always means what he says,' Julia said. There would be a party too, Hannah learned. On the 28th. 'That's the day of Hugh's bypass,' she said, lying on her back, squinting up at the sun through her fingers. Harry rolled over and nuzzled in close to her. 'You're sure you're alright?' he said in her ear.

'Yes' she said. 'Tell me about the party.'

When Harry found her crying in the bedroom, she'd said she had nothing to tell him. There was nothing to say, she was just crying, and he could leave her alone or he could take her somewhere sunny and warm and make her laugh. He'd taken her in his arms, rocked her. He'd told her if she liked, he could move in to Leighton Road. Julia was going to Paris for the summer. Mo was off to Sheffield. They could share the house till she went, then find themselves another housemate or a little flat somewhere, camp out for the summer, driving away for the weekends, and see what the autumn would bring. He would help her get her A-levels, he said. She could register at a cram school at night. It would be a cinch. By Christmas she could be applying to Universities for the following September. All the places where he'd decided to try for his Master's. By the time he graduated, they could both be on their way to Oxford, Cambridge, St Andrews...Hannah listened, her head resting on his shoulder. She smiled. It was so unlike Harry to talk about the future, and she didn't believe a word of it, but she smiled and hugged him and said it would be great. Harry moving in to Leighton Road was something she had never anticipated, but she accepted it as part of the flow of events, the bigger picture of which she was just a tiny part. Oddly enough, although he was more attentive to her than he had ever been, she no longer felt the euphoria of the first weeks. A kind of numbness had taken hold. There were things she couldn't think about. Pain waited down somewhere beneath the surface.

He seemed to have been chastened by his trip home. That night, he told her his father had 'taken him aside'. 'Gave me all that bullshit eldest son bit, laid it on about the car, and my final year, all that. But the old man has a lot to say. He talked to me about you.'

'About me?' said Hannah, astonished.

'Well, he asked me if I was "courting" anyone. I told him a bit about you.' He lit a cigarette and passed it to Hannah, taking another for himself. She remained silent. 'Don't you want to know what I said?'

She smiled and stretched out on her bed. 'Harry, what is all this? Are you trying to scare me?'

'No,' he protested. 'I'm just thinking about stuff my Dad said. He was pretty reasonable about it all. He said he realised

I didn't want to follow him into medicine and he didn't want me to feel that I was disappointing him. He wanted me to continue with the path I've chosen if that's what I want.'

'Is it?'

'Fuck knows. I'm going to do post grad for the pure and simple reason that I can stay a student for another few years. I mean, I like what I'm doing, but I don't want to start working before I have to. Three months this summer will be quite enough to last me a decade. Last summer was boring as concrete.' He stared darkly out the window for a moment, then stubbed out his cigarette and sat up. 'Curry, pints, and a quick roll, or the other way round?'

'Let's go for a curry.' She wondered how she was going to check the post office box with Harry around. So far they'd been together every free moment since he picked her up from Hugh's. Until he got a job, he was at a loose end and no one was around. He drove out to meet her at the studio and take her for lunch; he picked her up after work. She had no time in the mornings to run to the post office, which was in the opposite direction from the tube. Tomorrow, she would leave ten minutes earlier, she decided. She carefully avoided thinking about what she might find waiting. Life was now: eight o'clock on a summer night, and she and Harry were going for a curry at their favourite curryhouse and a few pints after at the Dove, their favourite pub, on the river at Hammersmith. *Live for the moment, Hannah*, she reminded herself as she rooted in the wardrobe for the dress Mo had given her.

'Ooh!' said Harry appreciatively when he saw her in it. 'We might have to reverse the order of the evening's entertainment after all.'

'No,' she said as he put his arms around her. 'Let's go out. I'm starving.'

'You're still upset, aren't you,' he said, as she followed him downstairs. He flipped through the mail on the table. 'Postcard for you.'

'I'm not,' she said, taking it. 'I'm just—' she stared at the card a moment, 'hungry.'

'Who's it from?' he said. She just stood and stared at the card.

'I don't know,' she said. She flipped it back on the table and looked at him. She seemed to be travelling back from a long way away. 'I don't know,' she said again, matter-of-factly. 'It isn't signed.'

'Can I see?' he said curiously. She handed it to him, and called out 'Mo? We're going for a curry.'

'Alright darlings,' Mo appeared at the top of the stairs. 'Going anywhere after?'

'The Dove. Want to join us?'

'I just might. All this packing is engulfing me in a cloud of dust. A pint would go down nicely.'

'Who's Artemisia again?' said Harry as they left the house.

'I don't know,' said Hannah. 'Probably a friend of mine from college. Did classics. He was always translating reality into some Greek myth or other. Pretentious idiot.'

They consumed a good deal of beer with their curry and were on their second pint in the Dove when Mo arrived. 'Did you know "Rule Britannia" was written upstairs?' she said as she set three brimming pints on their table.

'What I don't know about this pub you could write on the head of a pin,' announced Harry. Hannah giggled. 'Don't you mean a gin?' she said.

'Pistols for two and champagne for one!' he said loudly, and drained his half-empty glass.

'Well I'm all packed,' said Mo. 'I'm off on Thursday, so any gifts you've been burning to lavish on me—you've only got tomorrow.'

'Here,' said Hannah, and she took a few coins from her pocket and pushed them across the table to Mo. 'Buy yourself something expensive and keep the rest.'

'Who's Artemisia, Mo? You studied literature,' said Harry.

'Why don't you shut up about Arte-fucking-misia?' said Hannah, annunciating very carefully. 'It's Mo's last night tomorrow. I think we should have a farewell thing. Something small and mean.'

'Let's get drunk,' said Harry. 'That way maybe you can at least blank out Sheffield for the first couple of days by the sheer magnitude of your hangover.'

'Getting drunk would be rather special,' said Hannah. 'I've never tried that. We could get drunk *and* stoned. *And* eat lots of chocolate and fattening subspences.'

'Subspences?' said Mo.

'We could drop a tab,' said Harry in a low voice.

'Artemisia,' said Mo, 'Where did she come from?'

'This postcard Hannah got from somebody.'

'What was the context,' Mo asked Hannah. 'I know she rings a bell.'

'That was Quasimodo,' said Hannah thickly.

'Love like Artemisia,' said Harry.

'Wasn't she the one who built the mausoleum?' said Mo. 'The first mausoleum. Cos she named it after her brother. He was Mausola, or something. Mausolus. That's it. She drank his ashes with water.' They both looked at Hannah.

'Well,' she said. 'That confirms it. He's out to lunch, just like he used to be, this *friend* of mine. In fact, I think he's out to dinner.' She giggled. 'He's probably out to all sorts of meals, if you examine him closely.'

'Who?' said Mo.

'College friend,' said Harry, as Hannah got up unsteadily.

'Another beverage for you chaps?' she asked.

The next morning she was late to work and she didn't make a detour to the post-office. When she got to the studio, she sat quietly at the computer all morning and spoke to almost no one. During lunch, she sat at her desk and read a magazine. When it was nearly time to start work again, she opened *Article1* and read it through from the beginning.

'Years later,' she typed slowly, 'in another life, they met again. Their bodies were in a single room.' What would it be like? The edges of the picture in her mind's eye fuzzed and prickled like vision before fainting. 'It was very calm and peaceful. She fell into memory and how it was to be with him and rocked there gently. All violence was over. All pain was healed and distant. She told him she had never loved anyone else, but he already knew. It couldn't have been any other way.'

She selected all the text from the beginning and italicized it. Then she changed the font a few times, right-justified it, made it double-spaced, then single again. She previewed how it would look on the printed page. Anna came by and left some work on her desk. She took a last look at the paragraph she had just written, then she deleted it and typed 'In the summer of 1991 he went insane and she had to bury him.'

A little after two o'clock, Jeremy passed her desk and dropped an envelope in her tray. 'This was in the office mail for you.' She stared at it dully. The pounding in her head had abated, leaving her in a tearful mood. She slit the envelope and drew out a postcard of the pyramids. There was nothing written on it, but the explanatory text was circled in red. 'The pyramids were built by the first non-legendary brother-sister monarchs,' she read. 'Their outer structure—the sibling pair at the top descending through successive sibling marriages to the base so that all base siblings have two common ancestors—houses an inner chamber representing a womb that unites the siblings in death just as they came from the same mother.' She turned the envelope over. The postmark said *London, 6pm, 15 June*.

'I think I have to go home,' she said to Anna. 'I'm not feeling well.' As she packed her bag, her phone rang. 'Someone for you Hannah,' Robyn called from across the room. 'I'm putting them through.'

'Thanks,' said Hannah and lifted the phone. 'Hello?' She listened for a few moments, then she said, 'Have you got a number where I can reach you? I can't talk here.' She turned her back to the room and moved towards the window. 'Please,' she said, 'please tell me where you are. I can come to you. Hey—' She put her hand up to her forehead. 'Please don't cry. Please don't.'

She put the phone down after a while, finished packing her bag and left the office. At the corner, she phoned Hugh and asked could she come over.

'Everything all right?' he said.

She watched a black cab go by, heard the squeal of a bus slowing. 'Not really,' she said.

Twelve

Malton, Yorkshire. June 15th.

Dear little sparrow,

This is certainly beautiful country! In all England, I do not believe that, in the good words of Ellis Bell, I could have fixed on a situation so completely removed from the stir of society. A perfect misanthropist's Heaven. The spirits of the Bell sisters very much alive, as you see from my stolen words. I am resting. Rest is good. Much sleep, and in the daytime I read *Wuthering Heights*. I have some trouble concentrating. I think I will get better soon. I mean to cause no alarm, so I hope Father understands it was better for me to go away.

 Finch.

Sleights, North Yorkshire. June 16th.

Dear heart, for you are dear as my own heart to me, in spite of the wrongs I have done you. I shall be here for a while. Should you wish to contact me, you can do so through Box 39 at the post office in Sleights. The last few weeks seem very long. I have come part of the way on a journey, but in my clearer moments I can see there is still a long way to go. What I have written, I have saved on disks. I will keep them for you, should you ever want to see them or have them when everything is said and done. I am not living in Sleights, but in a nearby village. Please tell Father I am alright and he shouldn't worry or try to find me. I do not think we should meet, my dear Sparrow. I do not think we should meet.

Thirteen

'It's your father,' Hugh said, coming back into the kitchen. Hannah got up silently from the table and went out. Hugh took the plate of cold dinner she had barely touched and put it in the fridge. Perhaps she'd eat it later.

'Daddy?'

'Hello Hannah. Hugh tells me there was another postcard.'

'Yes. Today.'

'Where from this time?'

'A place called Sleights. He's still in North Yorkshire. He says he's living nearby and not to worry. He says we can write to him at Box 39 at the post office there. I don't have the post code. I'll have to call them.'

'Are you alright?'

'I'm fine.'

'Is there anything…you want to tell me?'

She paused, then said in a tired voice, 'Daddy, I don't know why René disappeared like this. I haven't seen him for six months. Everyone keeps asking me like you all think I was in on the secret. Why don't we just leave him alone? He's a big boy now.'

'Well, we don't think it's that simple, Hannah. Your brother's not been well. He's been…' he trailed off.

'You think he's sick in the head?' she said.

'That's a bit strong. I think he's very unhappy.'

'Do you think he's suicidal, Daddy?'

He sighed. 'No. I don't think so. I think he needs help. I think he really needs some help.'

'So let's write to him and ask him to get help.' Her voice was steady, but she lifted a hand silently to wipe away the tears that wouldn't stop.

'He wouldn't listen to me when I suggested it.'

'And you think he'll listen to me? Maybe. Dad, I don't know. Let me think about this. I don't know what to do. Maybe I can go up there, or maybe it's better to write. He doesn't seem to want to be found. Does he have much money?'

'Enough to last some time, probably. He was always careful with money.' How old he sounded, her father. He sounded like he'd had about enough.

'I love you Dad.' She closed her eyes, fought for her voice. 'This'll work out.'

'Of course it will, Love.'

'I'll call you if I hear anything more. I'll talk to you at the weekend.' She put the phone down and sat on the bottom stair. Through the little window above the telephone, she could see the tiny sliver moon against a dark bluish-yellow sky. Almost the longest day. She hadn't slept more than three or four hours any night for a week. She kept sleeping for half-an-hour in the early evenings, on the couch, and waking in a web of dreams, with the panic rising and the memory of his weeping on the phone.

Hugh came out and stood in the hall. 'Care for some tea?'

'No thanks.' She stood up. 'Harry's coming to fetch me at nine. He should be here any minute.'

Hugh nodded but he still stood there.

'Dad sounded tired,' she said. 'Like he's had enough of us all. Hugh—'

'Yes dear girl.'

She looked out the window, at the tiny moon. 'Do you know what's happened to René?'

There was a long silence. Then he said, 'No, I don't think I do know. Do you think I should know?' He waited for her answer and when it didn't come, he said gently, 'There's always tea if you want it,' and went back into the kitchen.

'You have to love a pair of jeans,' Harry said lazily, and he stretched out on the blanket with his hands behind his head. 'I've had these ones since I was sixteen. Grown to me. A second skin.'

Hannah watched him as he lay smoking, tapping the ash into the grass. He wasn't skinny, like his cousin. But he wasn't fat. She tried to think of the word. Stocky wasn't it. She tried not to look at the cousin's girlfriend, lying near Harry on her side. She'd been trying not to look at her all afternoon, ever since they'd arrived, showing up in leathers on the cousin's motorbike, fresh from a drive up through Europe. Hannah had been feeling numb, as though someone else were taking her over. In spite of this, she found time to be overawed by this girl, who seemed distant and sexy, mysterious. They had come to Kensington Gardens on the tube so they could drink beers in the hot afternoon sun and eat an expensive picnic they'd shopped for on Queensway. Hannah didn't ever want to leave the park. She stretched out one leg, looking at the worn denim of her jeans. It was almost white at the knees. Soon they'd tear.

It is what happened to us, she thought. *Just a story. The whole thing, everything is a story.* It felt better, looking at it that way.

Through the railings, she looked older to him. Maybe her hair was different. Longer. It fell across her face when she turned her head, coming down like a curtain that obscured his view of what he most wanted to see.

'You should take a trip to Greece,' Harry's cousin said. He was the only one of the group who didn't smoke. 'Before Greece, as we know it, disappears.'

'Yeah, bit of a shame about old Greece,' said Harry, who had never been to Greece.

These were the jeans I had on, she thought, *more than once. He touched them.*

'Hannah and I were going to go there,' Harry said. He didn't finish.

She put her hand on the grass beside her, spread her fingers. It was warm, coarse dark green grass. It looked like a plastic lawn.

'We could go to Greece,' she said.

'Prague's about the only place in Europe where you can still get a pint for 15p,' said the cousin.

He wasn't like these people, she thought. He was so kind. Not like these people, cruel, trying to tear things down. Out for a free ride, out to get high. He'd moved beyond all that before she even remembered. He was grown up when she first noticed him properly, when she began to really think about him. Fifteen or sixteen, but he seemed like a twenty-year-old. Had he ever been like these people were? She didn't think so. It wasn't in his nature. There was a calmness about him she didn't remember recognising in anyone else she knew. Slowly, it became possible to remember properly what she had first loved in him: his singularity of purpose. There was always a purpose. If he had nothing to say, he said nothing. Everything he did had a reason. If she waited long enough without asking questions, it would emerge. There was nothing wasted; no wasted movement, no words.

I want to be like you, she had said to him once. What would she have been, ten? Eleven? No, he had said. Don't. The most important thing you can do in your life is to stay you. Be what you be, he had said to her more than once. Do what you do. *Belief in myself,* she thought. *It seemed so easy back then. Every day, another reminder that he thought I was a good person. Now there's only me and I can't remember good any more. I can't remember why it's important to be Hannah Newell. I still want to be like him.*

She pulled out her cigarettes. The sun was going down. Beyond the railings, a figure took his sunglasses off and put them in his pocket. He watched her light the cigarette, saw the boy on the grass lean forward and take one from the pack she held out. They were too far away for him to hear what they were saying. He turned away, crossed the road and walked without glancing back towards Lancaster Gate.

After work that Monday Hannah waited for a bus and when none came after five minutes she began to walk. This made it unexpectedly simple for him to follow her. She walked past the school on St Charles Square, across Ladbroke Grove and onto the Portobello Road. The market was deserted. A few buses passed while she was between stops. One stayed, throbbing at the bus-stop, until she was almost caught up. She didn't run and it moved off just as she reached it. A little farther on it stopped at traffic lights till she caught up to it again. She kept walking.

He stayed maybe a hundred yards behind, sometimes stopping in doorways or at shop windows. While she took money out at an ATM, he stopped by a bus shelter, his heart pounding. He took photographs of her. She looked different, he wasn't familiar with the clothes she was wearing, and yet at certain angles he could catch the old Hannah. He turned the camera and strained to get a good shot. She was so far away. He didn't want her to see him, she mustn't see him. When she moved on, he moved on too.

At Westbourne Grove, she turned east. The buildings were familiar to them both now, long forgotten familiarities from childhood: scenes at once completely remembered and partially strange. Snatches of songs came into his mind, memories of her as a schoolgirl, skipping down this same street. She stopped at a small supermarket and bought two pears. The first one was ripe, too juicy. The juice dribbled down her chin as she walked. She threw the second in a dustbin just before the garden gate of the house where she had lived.

She stopped at the gate as though about to go in. She stared down the path for a while, at the stone steps, the front door, the cracks in the walls. Then she turned and looked up and down the street. He had moved into a doorway and she didn't see him. He stood there with his camera clutched against his chest. His legs were shaking, as though he were about to stand in front of hundreds and give a speech. He couldn't stop them trembling. He leaned against the wall, and then forward a little so he could look down the street. She seemed to be looking for a place to sit down, pausing in front of the hairdressers and then a newsagents. She took a last look at the house and walked on. Near the end of Westbourne Grove she got on a bus and he lost her. He stood on the pavement watching the bus turn the corner and when it disappeared he closed his eyes. His camera was over his shoulder, and his arms hung straight down. He looked like a man who had just been told some very bad news.

He filled out the slip and handed the two films over the counter to the sales clerk.

'Please,' he said, 'take good care of these. They're very important to me.'

She barely nodded and tossed the pack into a flat box behind her. 'That'll be an hour. Twenty-past-twelve.'

'Thank you,' he said.

Outside it was very warm. He took his time getting to her office. She wouldn't take lunch before noon if she took it at all. He didn't necessarily expect to see her again before his train to York, but he sat on a bench near the corner with a newspaper. At five-to-twelve, the same boy he'd seen in the park drove up in a red open-top Volkswagen and sat in it, smoking, until Hannah came out. She was wearing a blue cotton dress with white flowers and a low circular neckline. The newspaper shook very slightly in his hands as he watched. She leaned over in the front seat and kissed the boy briefly. She ran a hand through the short hair at the back of his neck and as he started the engine, he said something that made her throw her head back and laugh. They were both laughing as they turned the corner and disappeared from sight.

René folded the paper and laid it beside him on the bench. He sat for a while without moving. Then he took a small notebook from his pocket, and a pen, and wrote at the end of a page of close notes: 'There is the comfort that he makes her laugh.' He closed the notebook and sat quietly for a while, his eyes on the ground in front of him, and the grass verge, and the grating at the edge of the road.

London, June 19th, 1991.

Dear René,

I wish I were on a ferry, leaving that brilliant foaming trail behind, the sun a brilliant white-yellow, somehow fresher and cleaner than London sun. Old London, dying through rush-hour now. The days are very long, though it's only about 5:30 now. I've made a decision, but first I want to tell you about the corn I saw in a dream—fields of it between London and the coast, ripe June green, one kind a very deep green and stiffer, shorter—I imagined it rustled in the wind. It didn't wave too much in the wind. The other kind was a lighter green, more like thick hair, fronds; it flattened out in long supple waves in the wind. It was exciting to watch. And my decision? Not to be scared. I am often scared, I think. I used to be much more sure of myself. Sometimes now I don't know what to do from hour to hour or day to day. I can't predict my own reactions to things, it could go any way. I don't know myself. Naturally, I felt better when we were together. You protected me. I didn't need to look elsewhere. What we did is in the nature of a secret. We were set apart, and now we have to blend back in. I am learning what it's like to be normal. It is very dull, and repetitive, and sweet. It makes me smile, being normal. It seems in the last few months my brain woke up. I feel more alive now than the first months after I left. I've just begun to read *Zen and the Art of Motorcycle Maintenance* and it's perfect for my mood because it's forcing me to think. I don't want my brain to doze off again. I like this brightness, even if I am frightened and it hurts.

Robert Pirsig asks, instead of 'What's new?' 'What is best?'. I am asking 'What is important?'. I think it is important you get help. I wish you had not hung up that day you were crying on the phone.

This summer I am going to sleep less—go to bed at midnight, get up at 7, be in work early so I can behome again by 6. Behome. I've invented a verb.

The dreams have the uppermost hand. The dreams come first.

Last night, it was on a street, with a crowd of people. Down the street there was a disturbance. A boy was dying. He was doing it in style: screaming, white-faced, writhing. He was getting thinner in front of my eyes, his face an eerie kind of bright white. He was like a puppet, flopping around the place. People scattered before him. And then it was a woman: the same person, but a girl-woman now, in black clothes, we were in a church now, on our knees, each person silently begging death to stay outside on the street, but she came in, screaming, whirling like a dervish. She came right up to my row, crying out in anger and fear and pain. People tried to ignore her. I knew she would choose me. She did.

I may be moving. Both my housemates have left London. It was nothing I said. I am living with the brother of one of them. Harry, the one I told you about. I suppose you could say I'm still his girlfriend. I thought I loved him for a while but I don't. I'm really with him because he makes me laugh and that is the most valuable thing he could do for me now. Often I don't want him to touch me. Since you left home I have asked him not to be with me much. He knows some things but I have told him enough lies that he doesn't suspect the real secret. I think perhaps I should end with him—as time goes on I move deeper into lies and it isn't fair. He is a good person, and he deserves someone who can at least open her heart to him and not spend all her time trying to keep herself locked away. You see what we learned: how to be good at hiding. That's what I'm good at. I want to be out in the light with other folks. Ordinary people. I'm going to stop writing to you, my love; this will be my last letter unless you ask me for help. Unless I can help you by writing to you or visiting you. Please let me know if this is the case. You know I won't hesitate. In the meantime, if I can't help you, and I don't believe in my own heart that I can, I hope you'll find someone who will. I do love you, and I always have.

    Hannah.

North Yorkshire, June 20th.

Hannah,

It is raining hard. The walls are grey carpet and the air feels like it is only pretending. The memories crowd in. They're going to stay here and shorten our lives considerably for a while.

    René.

Fourteen

The Saturday before Harry's 21st birthday, and Hugh's operation, they drove to Winchester. Friday was midsummer's day, and that night they sat outside the Anchor at Southwark with a crowd of people Harry knew from college. Hannah had met some of them before, at the house in Euston, and she wondered how she had ever felt intimidated by them. Harry sat across from her, laughing and cracking jokes. Now and then he caught her eye and winked. As they walked through the back streets up to Southwark Cathedral with the others after closing time, he put his arm lazily around her and said they should take a trip to the country for the weekend, just the two of them. He asked her where she'd like to go and she thought for a bit and said Winchester. Because of the song, she said, the Robyn Hitchcock song about standing in the Talbot in his flares. 'Far-out Phil and Pat were always there,' she sang dreamily, 'and if you go then baby I don't care.'

They climbed the steps up to London Bridge Road.

'This thing with your brother's really upsetting you, isn't it?' he said.

'Yes. It is.'

'But you know where he is. You have to let him sort it out. It's not your responsibility.'

'That's why I haven't gone up there.'

'I'll take you up there if you want to go. You know that, eh?'

'I know. Thanks.'

It was impossible to talk about it with Harry. Maybe if Mo were still here—but what could she have said? There was nothing to say any more, to anyone. René had gone somewhere she couldn't reach. His letters didn't even respond to hers any more, and she didn't know how to make hers respond to him. It wasn't communication, just a sort of fragmented conversation between two people, neither of whom appeared to be able to hear the other. And in London, everything had changed. People were gone. The summer that had stretched out with such promise was cold. She lay awake at night and thought of being far away; of leaving London. Even Hugh seemed distant, immersed in the details of putting the house up for sale, planning his stay at the hospital, his long recuperation. Her father was coming over for a week. They'd pack up the house, help Hugh to move to the flat he'd rented in Islington, see that he didn't do too much while he was recovering. She thought often of Margaret. She had formed a vivid picture in her mind: a woman of strength and good counsel; full of comfort and understanding. Hannah imagined calling her. She held conversations with her in her head, tried to piece together how she would find out that Margaret still loved Hugh after all this time and wanted to meet him again. She would arrive just in time for the operation.

Winchester was cool and damp. They had lunch in a pub.

'It's not the Talbot, but I bet that's far-out Phil,' Harry said, nodding towards a man sitting at the bar, wearing a suit several sizes too large.

'Looks like they just let him out,' said Hannah.

'He dresses really well though. I think it's a look I could benefit from if I practised hard.'

'Heart valves,' said Hannah, 'flex through an angle of sixty degrees or more eighty million times a year.'

'Would that be leap years,' said Harry, 'or non-leap years?'

'It didn't say.' She looked out the window gloomily. 'They're going to be opening up his chest and fiddling round with his heart. I don't think I want them to do that.'

'You know they use tape now to close your chest afterwards?' said Harry, mopping up some mayonnaise with his bread. 'They don't do stitches any more. A giant roll of Sellotape. Seal you up. Put a stamp on your tit and send you home.'

'My Dad's going to be here for a week,' she said.

'You need a rest from your family. Let's go to Greece for a month. Get an Inter-rail. Buy a tent. Sleep on the beach. Let's go island hopping. Greet the locals.'

Hannah finished her cider in silence. 'Something needs to change,' she said at last. 'Let's go, shall we? Back to London. I want to visit Hugh.'

'I'll drop you up to Harrow,' he said when they were back on the M3.

'No Harry, it's alright. Drop me at a tube.'

But he insisted. They drove in silence, with Harry switching impatiently between the radio channels, looking for a good song. She pictured herself opening the gate, walking up the garden path to Hugh's front door, her key in the lock, his mail on the hall floor. She pictured gathering up the mail, calling his name once, afraid of waking him from a nap. She would carry the mail up the hallway, leave it on the table under the mirror beside the kitchen door, push the door to the back room slowly open. He'd be in the chair, his eyes closed, quite dead. She held her breath a moment, blinking back the tears that started at the picture. *Hugh,* she thought, *you're the only steady thing for me now. Don't leave me. I need you.*

She persuaded Harry to drop her at Safeway. She needed groceries to bring to Hugh's and she wanted to walk. Most of all, she wanted to arrive alone at Hugh's, not to have to ask Harry in and sit talking with him and Hugh, waiting for him to leave. She just wanted an evening alone with Hugh.

He was reading the paper in his old armchair. She smiled as she put the groceries away in the kitchen. He was so predictable, so comfortably a creature of habit. *My stability,* she thought, *the still centre in a moving world.* She made him tea and brought it in. She felt like doing small unasked-for favours. Things he would like. He was listening to opera and she picked the record sleeve up from the top of the pile as he folded his newspaper and thanked her for the tea.

'Just what I needed. You *are* good at mind-reading.'

'Tannhauser und der Sangerkrieg auf Wartburg,' she read aloud. 'What does that mean?'

'Tannhauser and the singers' contest at Wartburg. Early thirteenth-century medieval legend. Here, let me be the first to play for you,' he leaned over and picked the needle off the record, 'The Pilgrims' Chorus.' He dropped the needle expertly in place, as though it were a book that opened naturally at an often-read page. She sat in the armchair facing him and drew her knees up, clasping her arms around them. They listened as the Pilgrims' voices sang the opening bars in careful measure. Hugh moved his hand slightly in the air as though conducting. She thought she'd never heard anything so beautiful. Then the violins, throbbing, brought the pilgrims to their exquisite crescendo, the proud Allelujahs, and the steady finish. Hugh reached over and lifted the needle. The speakers fed out the recurring crackle of the turntable. Hannah sighed. 'Lovely,' she murmured, shaking her head.

'There's a letter for you,' he said. 'Now where did I put it.' He moved around the table, picking through the papers there. 'Ah—' he held it out to her. She took it and put it on the armchair. Then she turned it over and read the postmark.

'I got another postcard yesterday,' she said. 'This feels like a letter.' She turned it over so the address was on the front again and spread her hand over it as though to keep it down. Hugh stood uncertainly looking down at her. 'I don't really want to read it.' She started to cry. It was like when she was eight years old, crying at school about her Mum. Something she couldn't help; and no one to hold her. Hugh moved toward her, bothered by her tears, but he didn't know what to do. She took the letter in both hands and sat sobbing, watching the record turn. 'Play "The Pilgrims' Chorus" again,' she sobbed, 'will you?' He dropped the needle in exactly the right place and the pilgrims began their choral chant. When it was over, Hugh left the room and returned with a sheet of kitchen towel. She had stopped crying. She took it from him and blew her nose.

'I'm thinking of breaking up with Harry,' she said.

'Is that a good idea?'

'That's what I want you to tell me. Somebody. I want somebody else to make the decision, and then I'll do it.'

'How about a chat with Mo.'

'God no!' She laughed and then sniffled. 'Mo is possibly the worst person to ask.' She sat back in the armchair and drew her knees up again. 'I miss her though.'

'Why not visit?'

'You know that's an idea! There's not much going on at the studio. I could take a few days. Can I use your phone?'

Mo was enchanted. 'Can't last terribly long without me, can you sweetie?' she said. 'Well of course you can come and visit. We never got a proper goodbye, with that business about your brother. How is he—have you heard from him?'

'Yes. He's alright. Well, he's not alright. Mo, I need to go somewhere I can forget about families and everything to do with them.'

'Sheffield is it, then. They don't allow families here. You have to give up your children at birth to the authorities and you're only allowed to live with complete strangers. It's very refreshing.'

'Can I stay for a few days? I'll come up Tuesday or Wednesday. Have to be back Friday. I'll call you with the train time.'

Back in the dining room, Hugh had laid out the backgammon board.

'Hugh,' she said, sitting down at her side of the board and picking up the dice. 'Do you ever feel lonely? I don't mean loneliness for contained things. I mean when you realize everything stretches the same as far as the light travels and you are on a very small patch of ground.'

'Frequently.'

'How do you put up with it? What do you do?'

He threw the dice and thought about his move.

'Have you ever read the Book of Ecclesiastes?' he said, peering at the board.

'Is that the one they did that song about—The Byrds?'

Hugh moved his pieces and, pushing his glasses up on his nose, got up and went over to the bookshelf. 'A meditation on the utter futility of existence by The Byrds. It sounds just unlikely enough to be so. But I think you mean "to everything there is a season", and that's not the part I meant. Here we are.' He pulled down a leather-bound Bible. It was marked with many slips of newspaper, yellowed and torn.

'Vanity,' he said, leafing through it.

'Vanity of vanities, all is vanity?' said Hannah helpfully.

'That's the one. Now listen carefully.' He looked at her rather severely over his glasses and she wasn't sure if he was joking or not. 'I'll only say this once.'

Then he read. 'The wise man's eyes are in his head, but the fool walks in darkness: and I myself perceived also that one event happens to them all. Then said I in my heart, as it happens to the fool, so it happens even to me; and why was I then more wise? Then I said in my heart, that this also is vanity. For there is no remembrance of the wise more than of the fool for ever; seeing that which now is, in the days to come shall all be forgotten. And how dies the wise man? As the fool.'

He stopped and turned the page, scanning for the verse he wanted next. 'That which has been is now; and that which is to be has already been...For that which befalls the sons of men befalls beasts; even one thing befalls them; as the one dies, so dies the other; yes, they have all one breath: so that a man has no pre-eminence above a beast: for all is vanity. All go unto one place; all are of the dust, and all turn to dust again. Who knows the spirit of man that goes upward, and the spirit of the beast that goes downward to the earth? Wherefore I perceive—' he paused, laid the book down for a moment as though the next words were difficult to read, 'that there is nothing better' he continued slowly, from memory, 'than that a man should rejoice in his own works; for that is his portion.'

'That's it?' said Hannah carefully. 'That's all you get?'

'For some it's a lot. But for the likes of me, my dear, it is not a very bountiful portion. When I feel, as you say, that everything stretches the same to the horizon, I like to remember that whatever has been is now, and what is to be has already been, and that ultimately, we are all consigned to the dust, and this brief span is a flicker of light and it is what we have: no more and no less.'

'So you don't believe in a life after death?'

'Dear girl, if I knew what in God's holy name occurred after death, perhaps I could roll with equanimity towards those theatre doors next Saturday.'

'You're afraid you'll *die*, Hugh? You're not—' she stopped.

He blinked rapidly several times through his thick glasses. 'Well there's always the slightest chance, dear girl.' He smiled. 'You, of course, shall have all my books.'

'Hugh!'

'And the house. To do with as you will.'

'Hugh, stop joking!'

'I'm not joking. I've drawn up a will. Your father is executor. Should anything untoward happen to your poor old uncle, you shall be the proud owner of one small, draughty, and declining domicile, much the worse for wear. Rather like its current owner.'

'But—isn't there someone you'd rather leave it to?'

'Apparently not.' He threw the dice and looked intently at the game. 'Now we have a situation here. If I blot you *there*,' he pointed at the corner of the board, 'and I'm terribly tempted to, I shall leave myself open to ridicule *here*. You won't throw a five will you, Hannah Jane?'

She grimaced as she always did at her full name. He didn't miss it, and smiled.

'If I do, I shall waste no time in making a public laughing-stock of you,' she said.

When they had finished and he was setting up the board again, she picked up the Bible. 'Where's that bit again? About the spirit of man going up?'

'Ecclesiastes, Chapter Three.'

'What does it mean, that bit?'

'Read the Prologue, it may make a little more sense to you. Read it aloud, slowly. Start with verse two.'

'Vanity of vanities, says the Preacher,' she began, 'vanity of vanities; all is vanity. What profit has a man of all his labour which he takes under the sun? One generation passes away, another generation comes; but the earth abides forever. The sun also arises, and the sun goes down, and hastes to his place where he arose. The wind goes toward the south, and turns about unto the north; it whirls about continually; and the wind returns again according to his circuits. All the rivers run into the sea; yet the sea is not full: unto the place from whence the rivers come, there they return again. All things are full of labour; man cannot utter it; the eye is not satisfied with seeing it, nor the ear filled with hearing. The thing that has been, it is that which shall be; and that which is done is that which shall be done; and there is no new thing under the sun.' She stopped. 'Didn't Eliot write about that in "Four Quartets"?'

'Indeed he did. "Time present and time past are both perhaps present in time future."'

'And that makes you feel better?'

'No, dear girl. It makes me feel less alone.'

'But how? I mean, it all sounds pretty hopeless and depressing to me. Nothing new under the sun? I want something new! Don't you think your life is something new?

Don't you think there's never been you before? Nobody ever played backgammon with me just now. Nobody ever loved Margaret just the way you did.'

He sat across from her, fingering a backgammon piece. It was cream-coloured, smooth, like a sweet, or a part from some fine and expensive machine.

'Margaret Skinner,' he said eventually, 'was something new under the sun.' He stopped, as though the sadness needed room to breathe in silence. 'In that you are absolutely right. But me?' He laid the backgammon piece in its place on the board and took up the dice. 'I'm not good for much. The sun rises and the sun goes down. If I don't wake up on Sunday it will be no great catastrophe.' He moved his pieces. 'Now if you were to throw double fours, *that* would be a catastrophe.'

'It would be a catastrophe for me if you didn't wake up,' said Hannah, somewhat hotly. 'You're the only…stable thing in my whole life right now.'

Hugh regarded her thoughtfully. 'Then it would, as you say, be a catastrophe,' he said, and he inclined his head as though accepting a fact he hadn't thought about before.

After midnight, when they called a halt to what they agreed was the lengthiest backgammon tournament in the history of Harrow, she flopped into an armchair and eyed the letter, still on the arm. Hugh went to make cocoa. She picked it up and slit the envelope. Across the top of the page, in careful capitals, was written 'Temptation leads to an increase in prohibition—Sigmund Freud.' And beneath: 'The social forms we are familiar with are just that: forms. They are not the only possible way to be.' Below that, in a very shaky hand: 'You're invisible now/You've no secrets left to conceal.' Bob Dylan. 1965. Before you were born. I love you too; I want you to survive unbroken, my long-stemmed rose. Ninety million species died out before Homo sapiens came along. None mourned. R.

'My uncle thinks there's nothing new under the sun,' said Hannah.

'What about this olive?' said Mo, fishing it out of her martini. 'I think it's rather new-looking.' She popped it in her mouth. 'Mm. Definitely a brand new piece of the universe. But I can understand his point. I mean, how could he have known about the olive when *it's* in a pub in Sheffield and *he's* in Harrow?'

'I told him about it,' said Hannah. 'But he wouldn't change his mind.'

'Pity,' said Mo. 'P'raps it's impending heart surgery that leads him to that somewhat gloomy view of the world.'

'He's not gloomy, exactly,' said Hannah. 'I don't think Hugh knows how to be gloomy. He thinks he might be going to die. He wants to leave me his house.'

'Good Lord. Well there's nothing terribly new under the sun in that little inheritance.'

'No.' Hannah giggled, remembering the newspaper she'd once found in the front bedroom dated May 1977. 'Some of the clothes in the wardrobes would fetch money at Christie's.'

'Does he really still have his parents' clothes there?' said Mo. 'They must be fabulous!'

'I think that's who they belonged to. I've never asked him. We'll know soon enough. I'll be helping him build a bonfire when he moves.'

'Goodness—don't throw anything out without consulting me, will you?' said Mo, concerned. 'You could be sitting on a gold-mine of retro apparel. The London gay community will be hammering on your doors. "Throw out the polyester! We know it's in there!"'

'What are you two having such a good time about? Are you picking on people your own size?'

Mo turned round. 'Darling that would be much too limiting. Robin, this is Hannah. Hannah, this is Robin—landlord, man-about-Sheffield, and cocktail-mixer extraordinaire.'

'Hi.' Hannah shook hands with a tall, fair-haired man wearing a Hawaiian shirt.

'Speaking of which,' he said, moving behind the bar and picking up a shaker, 'I'm in the mood, so I need your orders, girls. What is your pleasure?' He turned to Hannah.

'Stick to drinks, Hannah,' said Mo, 'he's not your type.'

'Quiet you, or I'll raise the rent. Can I make some suggestions?' he said gallantly to Hannah.

'You can,' said Hannah, 'but I'll probably disappoint you because I know exactly what I'd like.'

'And that proves,' said Robin archly to Mo, 'how very little you know about type. What would you like, my darling?'

'A greyhound.'

'Tasteful. Very tasteful.' He began to assemble bottles, pouring and mixing, and in a shorter time than Hannah thought possible, produced her drink with a smile. 'And for the Lady Royce?'

'You know I believe I'll have a Slippery Nipple. More for the thought than the flavour really.'

'Tasteless, but quite in character,' said Robin as he mixed the drink.

'How long have you known *him*?' asked Hannah as they moved to a table with their drinks. Robin watched them go.

'Only since I got here,' said Mo. 'He's a friend of my cousin's. That's sort of how I got the place. He's rather special, actually, is Robin. I want to tell you about him.'

Mo had struck lucky when she got to Sheffield. Her cousin thought his friend Robin might have a flat for rent above his pub. She couldn't resist, she told Hannah, having a pub in her ground floor sitting room. Robin had interviewed her and offered her the place at once. 'I told him I'd worked in the Underground Bar in Camden Town and that he wouldn't have to worry about angry boyfriends in leathers punching holes in his walls. Angry girlfriends in leathers, maybe, but only if I got lucky.'

'He seems cool,' said Hannah.

'He's a sweetheart, and a softie and although you mightn't think it to look at him, a very astute businessman,' said Mo. 'Has another pub in York.'

'Where's that exactly?'

'Oh, I don't know, sort of northeast. Up there somewhere,' Mo grinned. 'I tell you what Hannah, now that I've sprung myself from London Gaol I think I'm going to have a little explore. Trot around the North of England a bit. Learn the lingo.'

'Is this Mo Royce of 96 Leighton Road, Camden Town, London N1?'

'Aha, no. That was a former life.'

She'd bought a car. It was parked behind the pub. She insisted Hannah come and have a look. It was a bright yellow Fiat. 'I'm going to have it custom-painted,' she said, 'soon as I get the money together.'

'What colour?' said Hannah politely.

'Not all over, you pillock!' cried Mo. 'Patterns! Sunflowers! Happy indie-rock hip-hop designs. That sort of thing.'

'Oh,' said Hannah.

After a curry, and several more greyhounds up in Mo's flat, she told her friend she was thinking about leaving Harry.

'Oh dear, is he bounding?' said Mo.

'No, it's not that. Actually, he's being...extremely monogamous now that we're living in Leighton Road,' said Hannah. 'He wants us to get a flat together somewhere. Get me through my A-levels, and then he thinks we could both trot off to the same college somewhere. He keeps talking about it.'

'But you're not sure.' Mo lit a cigarette and eyed her friend through the smoke.

'Can I've one? I've run out. Thanks.' Hannah eased off her shoes without undoing the laces, and stretched out on Mo's couch, holding her drink with both hands on her stomach. She felt at the same time quite drunk and quite lucid. 'Yes I am sure. I'm sure it's not going to happen. I mean, can you see a plan like that actually coming to fruition in the life of Harry Alton? No,' she tipped her ash, 'I do love Harry—I still get butterflies, I still, you know—' she smiled and Mo nodded. 'But he's not...' she searched for words.

'He's not exactly the chap in the suit,' said Mo quietly. Hannah looked at her. 'You remember the chap in the suit, don't you?'

'Yes,' said Hannah.

'I know it's none of my business,' said Mo, 'but I do want to check you're not wasting your gorgeous young life holding out for someone, Hannah.'

'No,' said Hannah. 'It's not like that.'

They smoked in silence for a while, then Mo sighed and picked up the vodka bottle.

'Well darling, I wrote tomorrow off the moment you called, so let's not fall short of expectations.'

Later they went back down to the bar for a drink before closing time. Robin wasn't around but he'd left a note for Mo. 'Says he'd be happy to show you round Sheffield tomorrow if you've no other plans,' she said, 'drop you off with me for lunch.' She crumpled the note. 'What a sweetheart.'

'It's alright?' said Hannah doubtfully.

'Oh don't worry about Robin,' said Mo. 'He may be a ladykiller behind the bar but he's really a total gentleman. Plus he has a very lovely girlfriend called Sandy and they're sweet together. You can trust Robin.'

'I've to call my uncle tomorrow,' Hannah said as they stumbled giggling back up the two flights of stairs. 'Check he's okay. His surgery's Saturday, and he's scared, I can tell.'

'What about your brother then,' said Mo, as they made tea in her miniscule kitchen.

'Oh,' said Hannah, 'not a lot to report. He's been sending cards from North Yorkshire.' She pushed her hair back off her face and looked around the kitchen. Already it looked entirely lived-in, like Mo's bedroom in Leighton Road—comfortable, cluttered, lots of stuff on the walls. 'He's...well, he's not doing too well it seems.'

'Finding himself, is he?' Mo swirled hot water around in the teapot and emptied it down the sink. The kettle began to whistle.

'Something like that,' said Hannah, sitting down unsteadily on a kitchen chair. The kitchen was starting to seem too small.

'Hannah, can I ask you an awfully personal question?'

'Hm?'

'It's really awfully personal, and if you don't want to answer, just tell me to sod off.' The two girls stared at each other across the room. Mo reached over and unplugged the kettle and the whistle died down to a sigh. 'Was your brother the chap in the suit?'

Hannah blinked. 'God, no,' she said, with a small laugh. She swallowed. 'Though I can see how you might come to that conclusion.'

'I'm sorry,' Mo came over, put her hands on Hannah's shoulders. 'I'm so sorry. That was out of line.'

'No,' said Hannah, looking up at her seriously, 'No, it wasn't. It was just a hunch, and it was wrong. That's okay.'

They stayed that way for a moment, then Mo leaned down and kissed her friend on the forehead. 'Yeah well, whoever he was, the suit, he shouldn't have messed you up,' she said.

'No,' said Hannah. 'He shouldn't have done that.' She took her tea from Mo and held it in both hands as though it were freezing in the room. 'But maybe he's paying a price now.'

'Who knows,' said Mo. 'Good things happen.'

Robin showed up just after eleven a.m. in a silver Jaguar X16.

'Oo-ee,' said Hannah, as she sat in and closed the passenger door. 'I should have worn my furs.'

Robin smiled broadly. 'I know that pride and greed will send me to hell, but I do love this car.'

He pronounced himself famished and they drove straight to a small café in the centre of town.

'So Mo tells me you came to London from Ireland not so long ago,' he said, tucking into a large plate of eggs and bacon.

'February. January. I don't know. Years ago, seems like.'

'You like it then.'

'Well I lived there till I was twelve, so it felt more like coming home, though I don't live in my old neighbourhood, and I've made all new friends.'

'She said you're temping.'

'Well I have a job at a studio. I'm trying to sort things out. Whether to go back to college.'

'Back?'

'I did a year in Ireland. Packed it in.' She saw him looking at her quizzically. 'It just didn't amount to much. I wasn't having fun and I wasn't learning much.'

'I like your priority there. Would you consider leaving London?'

She looked at him over the rim of her coffee cup.

'I'll explain. I've bought a pub in California. It's going to be an English pub. I'm planning to do it up like The Blacksmith. May even call it that. But properly—I've been over there quite a bit, lived there for a couple of years actually, and I've seen their English pubs. They're not right, they don't work and the Americans love 'em! I haven't seen one that gets it right, and still the Californians, and ex-pats, flock there to drink Newcie and watch the soccer. I'm going to do it right. Proper wood panelling, the wooden bar with the mirrors, the real thing.'

'Frosted windows with big bunches of grapes,' said Hannah.

'Exactly! Old Singer sewing machine tables, heavy wooden benches, a snug with a private bar, and all the paraphernalia. It'll be great!'

They both laughed at his enthusiasm.

'See the thing about Americans,' he said animatedly, 'is that they love all things European. They think we're cultured.

But a lot of them, particularly if they haven't been here, can be bought off with cheap imitations. The customer I'm going after, Yank or ex-pat Brit, knows the real thing when they see it. When I lived there I kept trying to bring American friends to an English pub, give them a taste of a pasty, and I kept being disappointed. So,' he pushed his plate away and leaned a little closer to Hannah, resting his arms on the table, 'this is my proposal. It comes out of the blue—' he held up a warning hand, 'and I'll want you to think about it before saying a word. But here's the deal: you get a work visa,' he counted off on his fingers, 'accommodation while you look for your own, and a full-time job from day one. I'll even help out with an interest-free loan for the flight if you need it.'

Hannah stared. He smiled at her. 'You're a good girl Hannah. Mo says so, and I trust Mo's judgement in girls. She tells me you've waitressed but not done bar work. That's okay, you could start off on the tables—it'll be table service for lunch and dinner—move into bar work if you wanted. You're wondering,' he held up his hand again, though she hadn't been about to speak, 'why on earth I think you want to go back to waitressing when you've set your sights on Oxford or Cambridge and a PhD.' He raised his eyebrows and she smiled weakly. 'I know it looks like a step back. But it's not. It's a step sideways. It's a lateral move. Ever heard of "think outside the box"?'

'The puzzle?'

'Yeah. Ever thought of moving to California?'

'No,' she said, with feeling.

'There you are. I'm offering you the chance to step outside the box. It may be a very nice box—Mo says you have a boyfriend.'

'Well,' said Hannah, 'sort of.' Robin gave a slow smile and nodded his head several times, amused. 'Beaches,' he said. 'Warm winters. Legal working status. No leg work except finding a place to live. Know anybody in the Bay Area?'

'The what?'

'San Francisco, sweetheart. Home of the electric kool-aid acid tests. The Golden Gate bridge. The gay Mecca of the Western World. And should you wish to pursue your academic interests, you've got three or four of the finest universities in America practically on your doorstep.'

'Stop, stop, stop!' said Hannah, laughing. 'Overload! Gimme a minute, will you?' She sank her head in her hands and ran them through her hair, coming up as though for oxygen. 'Phew! You're some sell!'

'I've got something good to offer,' he said simply. 'Let me say one last thing. I haven't mentioned what I get out of this, and it's only fair to be honest. The work visa you'd have, because sponsored by me, would mean you could only work for me. To get a full resident status, a green card, you'd have to apply through a lawyer. The deal is, you work for me for at least two years, if we both like each other. If we do, there's no reason you couldn't stay longer. While in my employment, you'd have a decent benefits package, but the usual fairly sub-optimal waitress pay, with supplements from tips of course. Americans generally tip 15%. If they like you, 20%. If you have an English accent and a pretty smile, you can run laughing to the bank. After two years you'll have the option to leave. I have a lawyer friend who works with immigrants. It's expensive, but if you wanted to stay you'd have to do it. Unless, of course, you walked the aisle with a Yank.' He checked his watch. 'Time to meet Mo. Ready?'

Hannah sat back in her seat and stared at her empty coffee cup. Then she nodded once.

'Absolutely,' she said.

'Robin's offered me a job in California,' she told Mo at lunch.

'Yes I thought he might,' said Mo.

'Did he ask you too?'

'Yes, the sweetheart. I told him I'd never been north of Finchley before I came up here and that I'd have to take things in little steps. A move like that could kill a delicate bloom like me.' She smiled at Hannah and the question hovered unasked between them for a moment, and was gone.

'Back to London tomorrow then?'

'Yes. Busy weekend. Harry's party, Hugh's operation, Dad to keep out of trouble.'

'Gets into trouble does he, your Dad?'

'No. He just trundles along really. Watches the rest of us—though I don't know that he actually sees us most of the time.'

'Must have been hard after your Mum died.'

'Mm. Did you know your heart valves open eighty million times a year?'

'Darling, that's for skinny fit people who do lots of running around and aerobics and things. For fat lazy people like me, it's only forty million. That's why we live longer. Less strain on the old valves.'

'But Hugh's fat and lazy,' said Hannah.

'Yeah, well, trust your uncle to mess up my statistics.'

'He's not going to die, is he? People don't die in open heart surgery any more, do they?'

'Absolutely not. They stopped doing that years ago. It's strictly contrary to current medical practices. Speaking of things medical, I had a call from Julia this morning. Failed two papers. She's coming back to London next week to study for repeats. Wants to know can she live in Leighton Road. Can you stand two Altons in your home?'

'Golly! Which papers did she fail?'

'It's a miracle there were papers she passed. She only studied for about ten minutes. But she's got Alton brains.'

'I'm finally going to see the residence, at the party on Saturday.'

'Oh yes—Julia said you're going to be on show. Harry's told the family you're his girl. First time that's happened, by all accounts. Don't worry,' she added sympathetically as Hannah grimaced, 'you're his girl for the party, aren't you? Doesn't matter what comes after.'

'Yes,' said Hannah. 'Funny, that first day I met him in our sitting-room I'd have killed to be called his girl. I'm still proud, you know. I still think, golly, I'm Harry's girlfriend.'

'What's funny to me is that Julia and I laid down money he'd break your heart. Now it looks like you might wring a tear or two out of his.'

'Oh I hope not,' said Hannah solemnly. 'I hope not.'

Fifteen

Hannah went straight up to Hugh's from the Sheffield train. She found him sitting in his armchair, some cello music turned up uncharacteristically loud on his record player.

'Bach,' he called to her as she stood in the doorway. He didn't turn it down until she came in a few minutes later with tea.

'How are you feeling about tomorrow?' she said, sitting on one of the high-backed dining chairs. It felt unusual, to sit there instead of in the armchair. She felt grown-up, able to say what she wanted to say to Hugh, not afraid of somehow putting her foot in it, as she had always seemed to be until now. *I must have grown up*, she thought.

'Very frightened,' he said, without looking at her. *Maybe I'm not so grown-up*, she thought, as a hot flush prickled unpleasantly at her scalp. 'But I am not, as I might have been in former times, feeling unavoidably lonely. Pablo Casals,' he continued, almost in the same breath, 'at the age of twelve played a three-quarter size cello for three hours a night seven days a week at a café in Barcelona. He was paid the princely sum of four pesetas a night.'

'When was that?'

'Oh, the late 1880s, early 1890s perhaps. One day, while searching through second-hand sheet music at a Barcelona music store, he found a copy of Bach's Six Suites for Cello. As far as he knew, nobody had ever played any of the suites in its entirety. They would play parts of them, a sarabande, or a gavotte. He practised them, in their complete form, in private until he was twenty-four years old. Only then had he the courage to play them in public, and it was another thirty-five years before he would agree to record them.'

'What a great story!' said Hannah.

'What great fortune,' said Hugh as the music stopped, 'that it was he who found them. Oh, a young man called—I believe it was Harry. He said to tell you he has gone home to prepare for the festivities and he'll see you tomorrow.'

'Bummer,' said Hannah. 'Now I have to get the train down and arrive at the party alone.'

'Never mind,' said Hugh. 'That is the young man's misfortune, for you will be snapped up instantly by the best of them and his carelessness will cost him his queen. He will be left to weep disconsolately into his beer while you dance with princes.'

'Are you lending me your glass slippers then?'

'Not at all. I'm going myself as an ugly sister.' He stood, lifted the needle from the record and turned the player off. 'Goodnight dear girl. I shall see you—' he stopped.

'After,' she said, and taking his arm, she kissed him lightly on the cheek. 'No catastrophes allowed,' she warned, and he nodded. 'I'm placing you in the excellent care of Saint Ventricle of the Auricles.'

'I feel safer already,' he announced. She watched him leave the room. A moment later he returned. 'And there was this,' he handed her a postcard and watched her turn it over. It was a picture of Notre Dame, blank on the other side except for the address in neat capitals, postmarked Paris, June 26th. She looked up at him. 'He's in Paris,' she said flatly. 'That's nice.'

'I expect,' said Hugh gently, 'he just wants to let us know he's alive and well.'

'Alive,' said Hannah, and she tossed the postcard onto the table and left the room.

Hugh listened to her go upstairs and heard her room door close. He picked up the postcard and studied the picture of Notre Dame. Still with the card in his hand, he crossed to the dresser and rummaged in one drawer, then another. He drew out an old photo album and took it closer to the light. Standing in the middle of the room, he thumbed through the pages. He flipped quickly through the early photos of his parents, of him and his sister as children. When he got to photos of his sister and her husband and first child, he stopped. A sallow baby, serious in a white knitted cap, taking tentative steps down the path at Westbourne Grove. René with his parents on the beach, for three years an only child. Then another baby, a girl, lying in a froth of baby lace. René with his little sister by the hand, outside Charing Cross Station. Then a schoolboy, serious again in cap and school tie, staring straight out at the camera. René and Hannah on the pier at Brighton, René with Hannah by the hand, grinning at the camera, Hannah in tears with the wind blowing her baby hair across her face.

'Oh dear.' He ran a hand over the photo as though to smooth it down. He examined it closely and shook his head. 'The things nobody sees,' he muttered to himself. Then with a deep sigh he closed the album and returned it to the drawer.

Hannah didn't arrive at Harry's party alone, nor did she get the train. Julia returned from Paris three days earlier than planned and was hauling her many bags up to her old bedroom in Leighton Road when Hannah arrived.

'You didn't think I'd miss my little brother's birthday party did you?' she said.

'What on earth have you got in here?' said Hannah, dumping a giant suitcase with difficulty on the bed.

'Goodies,' said Julia mysteriously. 'From Paris.' She unzipped it and drew out a dark silk dress. 'If you've nothing special bought, you can take a look at these. I know just the thing.'

'Julia!' said Hannah. 'You're my fairy godmother, aren't you.'

'Remember dressing me for that party where you were going to run off with some chap called Payton?' she called out later, when Julia was in the bathroom waxing her legs, and she was trying on Parisian creations in front of the mirror. 'That was the night I kissed Jeremy.' She held up a long narrow black dress that swayed sensuously under her hand. She held it against her body to see how it would look. She moved a little from side to side, tilted her head, ran her eyes down her own reflection. She looked OK. She felt strong, suddenly. She'd dress up for Harry. If he was showing her off to his family, she'd make herself something to be proud of. She put the dress aside and picked a short black-and-red tartan skirt from the suitcase.

'Where did you get all this stuff?' she called out, looking at the label. 'This is designer wear. How could you afford it?'

'Consignment,' Julia called back. 'Woman in the place I worked got it all on consignment. Cost next to nothing. Compared to the price it would be new, of course,' she came sailing in in a long Chinese dressing gown with a dragon embroidered down the side. 'No, no, no, darling, put that down. You haven't even seen what I've got for you. It's downstairs in a dress bag. There are two perfect dresses in this world,' she sat at the dressing table and began plucking her eyebrows, 'and they are both downstairs in this very house. I couldn't decide which to wear till I saw you today and then I realized that one of them is just made for you, and the other—ouch!—is made for me. We shall wow the entire county of West Sussex tonight, you and I.'

Hannah's dress looked like a tutu.

'Think outrageous,' warned Julia, seeing her eye it doubtfully. 'Tulle is absolutely the rage in Paris. The gorgeous bimbos at American Embassy cocktail parties would kill for this dress. And luckily,' she began easing it over Hannah's head, 'I bought an extra pair of silk stockings. You look tremendous,' she said seriously when Hannah stood fully dressed before her. 'You look stunning.'

'Thanks,' said Hannah.

Julia was wearing sequins. When she was dressed, they linked arms and stood in front of her mirror, carrying on a nonsense cocktail-party conversation until laughter overcame them.

'I've something to tell you,' said Julia when they sobered up. 'Something's come up and I want you to know about it.'

'What?' said Hannah. 'What's happened?'

'Well, my idiot young brother invited this *girl* to the party—an ex called Ariadne. I told him not to. I told him it wouldn't be a good idea, but he did, and she's coming, all the way from Aberdeen.' She sighed. Hannah studied her fingernails.

'So he'll end up with her tonight?' she said. 'Is that how things will be?'

'I don't know. But it's possible. Especially if he's drunk. And we know how likely that is.'

'Yeah, well,' said Hannah, 'you have to let stuff like that take its course.'

'Oh sweetie,' said Julia, putting her arms around her, 'I knew the boy would break your heart.'

'He's not breaking my heart,' said Hannah quickly, extricating herself from the embrace. 'He doesn't have it,' she finished quietly.

Ten minutes later, Julia found her at the kitchen table, crying into a glass of wine.

'Oh Hannah,' she sat down opposite, 'please don't be upset. Maybe it won't happen. Maybe Harry really means what he says about you. He does say nice things, you know.'

'Yeah,' said Hannah, drying her tears. 'We have fun together. That's all I want, really.'

'Finish your wine, I'll pack the car, then we're off.'

When she was gone, Hannah turned over a postcard on the table and read the postmark again. London W2. June 26th, 4PM. No message. Just her name and street address in neat capitals. The picture was of the Tower of London. 'Ancient fortress on the bank of the Thames,' she read, 'built 1078-1300, it has been palace, prison, arsenal, and mint. Execution place of Thomas More and Anne Boleyn. Its last prisoner was Rudolf Hess.' She sobbed once, bit her knuckles, wiped the tears fiercely from her eyes, then tore up the postcard and threw it in the bin.

Hugh was in a very slightly larger room than the one after his heart attack, and he was by the window. The curtains were drawn round his bed, and Hannah stood a moment at the door, trying to make out if she could hear voices. Then she tiptoed out and went to find a nurse. The girl at the nurse's station couldn't have been older than Hannah herself. She was a red-head and introduced herself in a strong Scot's accent as Judy. Mr. Johnson had come through surgery very well, she said.

'Yes I know. I rang the hospital earlier. Is he awake? Can I see him?'

'I'm sure he'll want to see you,' said Judy cheerfully. 'Let's see if he's awake.' She came round from behind the station. 'I want to check if he needs anything, anyway. So sad about your aunt,' she said sympathetically as they walked down the corridor towards Hugh's ward.

'My aunt?' said Hannah.

'Dying so young like that,' said Judy.

'Did he…have her photo by his bed?' said Hannah. 'In a silver frame?'

'Aye,' said Judy. 'And you know a funny thing,' she stopped near the ward door and lowered her voice. 'He only took it out when we were prepping him for surgery. Said she'd watch over the empty bed while he was in the theatre. He asked me to take it down when he got back to his bed, while he was still under, and put it back in the drawer.' She cocked her head, puzzled. 'Isn't that the strangest thing?' she said.

'Yes,' said Hannah. 'He loved her very much, though.'

'I know it,' said Judy. 'I could see that, the way he looked at the photo. When I asked how long she'd been gone, his eyes filled with tears. Poor love, he said no one would ever replace her.' She sighed and went ahead of Hannah into the ward.

Hugh took a while to wake up properly. His breathing was very wheezy and Judy plumped up his pillows until he seemed comfortable. When she'd gone, Hannah took his hand.

'I suppose this means I don't get the house,' she said. He smiled, and squeezed her hand.

'Is it Sunday?' he said.

'Yes. About 8 p.m.'

'How was the party?'

'I danced with several princes.'

'Did Harry behave himself?'

'Not so's you'd notice. He introduced a ravishing ex-girlfriend into the mix and got stupendously drunk.'

'Oh dear. What a foolish boy.'

'Yes. He was. How are you feeling?'

Hugh peered down at his chest. 'Like somebody prized my sternum apart and taped it shut,' he said. 'Surprisingly. Pass me some water, dear girl, would you?'

They chatted a little more, but he soon seemed to flag and once, when he moved his arm too quickly, he gasped and the colour drained from his face.

'Take it gently, Hugh,' said Hannah. 'The worst bit's over now.'

'Yes,' he said, but he passed a shaky hand across his forehead and seemed exhausted.

'I'll go now. Dad'll be here on Wednesday. I expect I'll meet him here.'

'Yes,' said Hugh, 'Lovely.'

'Hugh,' she said uncertainly, 'I got another postcard. He's back in London.'

'Dear me,' said Hugh. He thought for a moment. 'Perhaps we'll hear from him. Perhaps he'll call you.'

Hannah said nothing. She looked down at the bedspread.

'There really is nothing you can do about it, dear girl. Don't be troubled.'

She nodded. 'I think he's in some awful pain,' she said.

Hugh closed his eyes. He seemed to be asleep for a while. His face was very grey. Then he opened his eyes again. 'His pain, dear girl. Not yours. Not yours.'

Every time the phone rang in the studio on Tuesday, she tensed up. Shortly before leaving work, she searched for *Article1* and deleted it without reading it again. 'Are you sure you want to delete *Article1*?' a message asked. She hit 'Yes' and switched the computer off. When she got home, Harry and Julia were in the sitting room, smoking and listening to The Doors. Harry got up when she came in, and Julia picked up a magazine and began flipping boredly through it.

'Hi babe,' said Harry, and kissed her on the cheek. He followed her out to the kitchen and watched her open a can of soup.

'Want some?'

'Nah.'

'When did you get back up?'

'I was in work yesterday but I went home last night to help clean up after the party.'

'You didn't clean up on Sunday?'

'There was stuff left to do.'

'Harry, if you're lying to me about the fling you're having with Ariadne, don't. I'm not an idiot.'

'I know, I know.' He opened the fridge and took out a beer. 'Ariadne's gone back to Scotland.'

'That makes everything OK? We can just take up where we left off?'

'No. Hannah—I'm sorry. I got drunk. I was a shit.'

'Harry,' she put her bowl of soup on the table and sat down opposite him, 'even if I hadn't decided it was over before this, I still would've been hurt. I heard you were introducing me to your family at your party,' she felt tremendously cool, level-headed, 'and instead you fucked off with an ex-girlfriend. Wait a minute—' she stopped him from interrupting, 'I have something to say. It's not that I've stopped loving you, cos I haven't. And it's not that I think we should break up in a big loud fight over some old girlfriend, cos I don't. As a matter of fact, what I think we should do, if at all possible, is stay together for the rest of the summer and have as much fun as we always have, given good weather, quantities of beer, and anyone who wants some fun too.'

'And then what?' said Harry, obviously taken aback by this approach.

'Then,' she took a mouthful of soup and swallowed it quickly, although it was too hot, 'I'm emigrating to California.'

Sixteen

It seemed the decision had been made a long time before. It seemed as though everything had been leading up to it, and now everything unwound from it, and yet she couldn't recall the exact moment she had made it. Yet everything looked different now. It was like the first day of autumn, when the first cold breeze blows and suddenly there are dead leaves everywhere and even the warmth in the sun at lunchtime casts an elegiac light on the summer. It is over; something has turned and it can't turn back and when the sun sets, although the colours are the same, the air is full of sadness.

What am I doing, thought Hannah, *walking up Harley Street at quarter-to-ten on a Thursday morning? I should be at work, but I'm not at work. I'm not at work because someone I've never met, a doctor, telephoned me and asked me to meet him in his office.*

She stopped by some railings and put her hand out as though afraid she might fall.

It is Thursday July the eleventh, she told herself. *I am twenty years old. Soon I will be emigrating to America.*

A receptionist took her name and asked her to wait. She sat in a velvet-upholstered chair. The waiting room had tall ceilings and casement windows. The traffic noise of North London seemed muted and faraway, swallowed up by the velvet and the heavy dark-red curtains. She looked around the room, wondering if he had sat there and if so, in what chair; and what had he been thinking? Had he felt anything like she did—a jumbled rush of anxiety and guilt and fear? And curiosity; she realised she felt that too. Her name was called and she stood to meet a kind-looking man who ushered her through to his office. It was a room similar in appearance and decoration to the waiting room, but larger, and filled with books.

'Hannah, it was good of you to come. I'm Dr Henley. Alan Henley. Please sit down.'

He sat her in a deep comfortable chair and took another like it close by, rather than returning, as she'd expected, behind his desk.

'Now,' he said in a kindly but businesslike way, 'I want you to understand first of all that nothing said in this room goes beyond this room.' He paused.

'OK,' she said.

'And secondly, I want you to feel as comfortable and relaxed as possible. I understand you are not here of your own volition—at least not at your own instigation, and you need to know that you're not under any obligation to say or do anything. But anything you *want* to do or say is alright too,' he finished cheerfully, and smiled. She smiled back. She liked this doctor. He had something about him she trusted instinctively. She felt herself relax a fraction.

'My dear,' he leaned forward concernedly, 'you look terribly frightened. Please don't be frightened.'

'No,' she said, but she didn't trust her voice with any more.

'Perhaps I should begin, since I initiated this meeting. Actually, to be precise, my patient initiated this meeting. My patient,' he steepled his fingers in a way that made Hannah think of headmasters and clergymen, 'and your brother. He has been my patient now, very intermittently it's true, for some years. Do you know how many?'

'No,' said Hannah.

'Let me see. Your mother died in 1979. I knew your mother well too,' he added as an aside. 'She first brought your brother to see me when he was seven years old. I saw him a few times that year. He was wetting the bed. She was worried because, although he was very bright, he seemed unduly upset by school and she was afraid he was being bullied. Well, he outgrew that, and I didn't see him for a long time. He first came to see me himself in the late summer of 1982. He continued his visits throughout the autumn and winter. After you moved to Ireland in the spring of 1983, we continued to correspond by telephone and in letters through the summer and into the following year. Our correspondence ended some time in the spring of 1984.'

'Why,' began Hannah hesitantly, 'was he seeing you?'

'I'll get to that in a while. First, I want to establish why you're here today. I didn't hear from René for several years, apart from the odd short letter, until a couple of months ago. He wrote me a rather troubled letter. I think you know,' he paused, 'what he was so troubled about.'

Hannah sat frozen in her chair. She could feel the blood pumping out of her heart. *This man knows* was all she could think. *This man knows.* It didn't feel so bad. She nodded.

'Then he called me. A few weeks ago. Said he'd be passing through London and he'd like to see me. He said it was somewhat urgent. I made the time.' He smiled wryly. 'I would always make time for a member of your family. So I saw him, here in this room, about a month ago.' He paused. 'Would you like something to drink? Tea? Coffee?'

'A glass of water,' said Hannah, 'would be lovely.' She cleared her throat. He filled her a glass from a water dispenser in the corner. She took it from him and held it in her lap. A month ago: that would be when he sent her the postcard from the British Museum, with the pyramids.

'He told me some things then that were on his mind. It was quite a garbled story and I knew I wasn't getting the whole truth, but I realised I would have to let him tell me that in his own time, if that time ever came. I tried to persuade him to stay in London, told him he could stay with Marjorie and me, but it seemed to upset him that you were in London, and he said he needed to leave the city and get out into the countryside where he could get some peace. All he would tell me at that point was that he had stolen something very valuable from you and he was afraid of meeting you because he would be ashamed.'

'Stolen something,' repeated Hannah slowly.

'Yes.' The doctor crossed his legs and leaned forward, one arm on the arm of his chair, one on his crossed legs. She looked at his socks. They were black with a tiny pale design up the sides. His shoes looked expensive. 'René's had a problem before with stealing things.'

'No,' she said. She gritted her teeth, held on tightly to the glass of water.

'That's what I saw him about, primarily, when he was at school. I can tell you this without violating his privacy because he said it was alright for you to know. But I came to realise that that was not exactly the problem here. Let me continue with recent events before we backtrack. Okay?'

'Okay,' said Hannah. She felt very alone. The man sitting opposite her was kind and he knew. She must listen carefully to what he had to say. He was a psychiatrist. He could help.

'He went north, to Yorkshire, for a week or so. He called me once, asked if he could take me up on my offer of a bed for a couple of nights. He was very distressed. I said of course. He returned to London, let's see, it was a Saturday—the second last in June. Marjorie and I were entertaining, a small dinner party. René turned up, and he was rather drunk.'

'He never drinks,' said Hannah, 'hardly ever.'

'These are exceptional times,' he replied. 'He was very troubled, very upset, and there was a scene.' He pursed his lips. 'Marjorie and I got him to bed. He kept asking me to make sure you were alright. He was most afraid for you. The next day when we got up he was gone. To Paris. He left us a note and some money.'

'What...sort of scene?'

'Nothing extraordinary. Just the usual unhappy dredging of emotions and events that often happens when troubled people drink too much. I understood a little better what had gone on from what he said that night. But I couldn't help him. Not when he wouldn't stay and ask for my help. However, when he returned from Paris he once again came to me and this time he was a lot more settled in himself, a lot calmer. We talked for a long time. He explained what he believed he had stolen from you.'

There was silence in the room for a little while. *I should be in work*, thought Hannah.

'Do you know what he meant?' asked the doctor.

'I think so,' she said, 'but I'd like to hear what he said. Where is he now?' She had the sudden panicky thought that he might come into the room, might be waiting in an adjacent room, listening to their conversation. She glanced around. There were two doors leading out of the room.

'He's at my house. Marjorie's feeding him up, trying to put a little weight on him.'

René in shirtsleeves. His small, strong forearms with the soft baby hair. Thinner now. Too thin perhaps. She tried to picture him drunk, falling down drunk, making a 'scene'. What kind of scene? In front of Alan and Marjorie's dinner guests, obviously. Perhaps he knocked things over, or tripped and fell. Perhaps he wept, in front of Alan and Marjorie, and their friends.

'What he told me,' the doctor continued, 'was that he had done you great harm. More harm than he could ever have imagined himself capable of. He blamed himself for robbing you of a normal childhood, a normal adolescence. He said over and over that he was certain he had damaged you and that he must try to put it right. He asked me to help you, to find out if you are alright.' He sat back in the chair and looked at her. 'Would you say,' he said carefully, 'that you are alright?'

Hannah looked him straight in the eye. He had a long, intelligent face; dark curly hair. His eyes were too close together and his nose was a little big. On the whole, it was a frank and honest face. 'Yes,' she said.

'I know there are many levels below the surface, and there may be damage to any or all. On the other hand, there may not. Damage may take time to manifest itself. You mustn't think that because René believes he has damaged you, this is necessarily so.'

'Tell me about the stealing,' she said.

'Not an uncommon reaction to great stress. At the time, he was overworking at school, trying to cope with your mother's sudden death, his new responsibilities towards you and your brother. His exams. The prospect of leaving England.' He spread his hands. 'Adolescence.'

'What did he steal?'

'Small things. From shops. He returned some. He was never caught.'

The terror, the shame. She tried to picture him doing it. Maybe some of the things he'd bought her...she tried to shake the thought off.

'People who react in this way often throw away whatever they have taken as soon as they are out of eyesight,' said the doctor gently. 'They don't know why they are doing it. It's a compulsion. René overcame this compulsion when he was about eighteen and he says it hasn't recurred since.'

'Does he want to see me?'

'Do you want to see him?'

It was hard to swallow over the lump in her throat. She must not, she really did not want to cry.

'Could I smoke in here?' she asked.

'Of course.' He fetched her an ashtray from a drawer in his desk, and while he did so, she fought back her tears. She fought also to keep her hand from shaking when she lit her cigarette, but it shook and she knew he saw.

'This is about both of you, Hannah,' he said. 'It's about healing. René has asked me to tell you, you must do what's best for you. If you don't want to see him, he'll understand. If you do, he's at my house, waiting.'

She blew out smoke, crossed her legs, still holding the water glass. It was warm in her hand.

'What do you think?' she said, and before he could answer, she added, 'I'm going to California. For good. In September.'

'Are you?'

'I have a job offer, visa, everything planned.' She knew suddenly that his approval of the plan was essential. She wanted him very badly to say the right thing.

'That's wonderful.'

'Do you think it's the right thing?'

'Yes. I think it's a very smart thing to do.'

'I didn't come far enough, coming here.' Now the tears began, but she fought them, choked them back.

'You can cry, you know,' he said gently. He lifted a box of tissues from a table behind him and held them up. 'See?'

'Lots of people cry then, do they?' She smiled a little.

'Some people cry.'

'Did he cry?'

'Yes. He cried.'

She looked around the room, fighting the tears, willing herself to be calm.

'How did you know my Mum, Doctor Henley?'

He smiled, reached back and replaced the tissues. 'Please call me Alan. I knew her when I was a medical student and she was training to be a nurse. We went out together for a little while. Before she met your father.'

'And you met Marjorie.'

'Yes. She was a lovely woman, your mother. Full of a natural joy. When she died, I was in Africa, at a conference. I had a paper to deliver, an important one, or so I thought at the time. It felt as though a star had just gone out. Before I gave the paper, I told the assembly—there must have been a thousand people there—that a wonderful person had just died in London. We observed ten seconds of silence in her memory. Not a sound, in that giant conference hall, in the centre of Harare.'

'That's very touching,' said Hannah.

'Ah, yes,' he spread his hands out, as though remembering that night and the restless silence in the giant conference hall.

'I sometimes think,' said Hannah, 'if Mum hadn't died...' She didn't finish.

'Who knows why things are the way they are, my dear,' he said. 'You really can't put the blame or the responsibility on any one factor, as a general rule. Hannah—'

He leaned forward again and she felt, almost against her will, beguiled by his candid manner. Frank, she thought, honest. 'Can I speak plainly?'

'Please do,' she said.

Yes, she thought, *plain speech. Here it comes, then. And I'm ready. At last, I'm ready for the truth, out, out in the open.*

'Incest,' he said, 'is derived from the Latin "castum", meaning "chaste". You see, in our culture the term carries with it much baggage: emotional, historical, and indeed, hysterical, including the idea of impurity. In other cultures, the landscape of the word can be quite different. In Chinese, for instance, the notion is of disorder, rather than anything impure. In German, *Blutschande*—blood shame.'

'I know,' said Hannah.

'In some societies, the liaison would provoke no strong emotions whatsoever; no disastrous consequences to the union. It would simply be thought a little strange. In other corners of the world, it is an act punishable by death to both parties.'

'I know,' said Hannah again. 'He told me lots of stuff like this in a letter. He knew all about it. Did he mention some book he's writing?'

'A book? No. We did discuss these things a little, though, he and I. I merely mention them to sound out, as it were, your feelings. I want to find out how you are coping.'

'I'm coping very well thank you,' said Hannah, in a tone she thought sounded pretty believable; relatively calm and unemotional. Perhaps this interview could be over sooner than she'd thought. 'Do you think I should see my brother?'

He considered, but she felt he already knew the answer in his own mind, that he had known all along.

'No. I don't think that would be a good thing for him just now. I'm going to try and persuade him to spend some time at a place I know in Kent.'

'A hospital?'

'Treatment. He needs some help, but mostly what he needs is peace and quiet and time.'

'I'm leaving in September. Perhaps before I go.'

'Perhaps then—that would be ideal. And Hannah, I do hope you will consider that you can come and see me, or give me a call, any time you like. Do you feel convinced of that?'

'Oh yes. Thank you.'

He nodded a few times, and though she didn't meet his eyes, she knew he was looking for something, some final sign or gesture; but she didn't know what it was she was meant to give him.

'Can I ask you something, Doctor?'

'Of course.'

'You could arrest us, couldn't you? We've committed a crime.'

'Ah, Hannah. Not in my book. I took an oath, generally considered the most valuable statement of medical ethics and good practise. I swore to heal my fellow humans. I consider it neither my business nor my right to bring the laws of this country into my surgery when I am dealing with damaged or unhappy human beings. I have no interest in the law in this instance. My interest is in extending whatever help I can to those in pain.'

Hannah stood, put her glass on the desk, and smoothed down her skirt. She looked at him boldly.

'Thanks. I'm not in pain, but I know my brother is, and I know you can help him.' She held out her hand, and he took it and shook it warmly, letting go before she could begin to feel uncomfortable.

'Then you and I are interested in the same thing. I hope you're right, I really hope so. May I call you with news, or would you rather call me?'

'I'll call you, unless something happens. Please ask him…only to send mail to the post office box. My uncle's moving and I may be too. That's the only place he can definitely reach me. He was sending mail everywhere,' she added quietly.

'And you haven't told anybody.'

'No. Never. You can call me at work, OK?'

'I'll let you know if I persuade him to go to Margate. Goodbye Hannah.' He looked at her searchingly. He was asking for more, she knew it, and it bore in on her. She felt the old urgency to be out, gone from this room, for everything to be over and finished and something new to begin. She felt a little panicky and breathless. She almost ran out of the building.

It was a relief to be on her way to work. The studio would be quiet and dull and she could work solidly till six or seven to make up the hours. She sat on the top of the bus to White City planning her day and how she would get through the work. It was all quite easy. Nothing too demanding. She could relax, concentrate on work alone, shut the rest out. She didn't need to think about any of the rest, it could all wait for another day. Just work, and then go home, maybe out for curry with Harry, and early to bed. She closed her eyes in the warm sunshine coming through the window and tried to picture California. Palm trees. The beach. Everyone blonde and tanned and beautiful. She could see pictures, flat like shiny postcards, but she couldn't put herself in them. She tried to choke down the rising ache in her throat. The new life would be fabulous. Everything would work out. It would all, always, be alright.

'Theberton Street,' said Hugh with great deliberation. 'Sixteen Theberton Street, London N7. Very historic part of London, old Islington. Best fish and chips in town too.'

'The Upper Street Fish Bar,' said Hannah. She was putting books in boxes, pausing as she did so to read the spines and sometimes to flip through the pages. It was taking her a long time.

'Fish Shop,' corrected Hugh. 'And across the road, the King's Head, with a theatre, where they still charge for a pint of bitter in pounds, shillings, and pence.'

'Cool,' said Hannah. 'So a pint's fourpence?'

'Alas, no. But in truth, my local will be the Old Pied Bull on Theberton Street itself. The pub where, it is said, Sir Walter Raleigh smoked his first pipe.'

'Rotten idea,' said Hannah. 'Don't smoke myself. Haven't for some days now. Did Dad really only manage to pack that paltry number of boxes the whole week he was here?'

'He did the garden,' said Hugh mildly. 'And the front room. Painted. He really turned out to be rather useful.'

They were clearing the Harrow house. A buyer was in escrow, Hugh was moving to his flat on August 1st. Under strict instructions from his doctor, he sat in his armchair directing Hannah's packing efforts and stirring himself only to make tea and walk to the corner shop for the newspaper. He was beginning to get his colour back and was generally in good spirits. He hoped to be back at work by the end of September. *You'll be going back, I'll be finishing up*, thought Hannah, but so far she had said nothing about her plans. As time went on, it somehow became harder to broach the subject. There had been opportunities during the week her father was there but without really thinking about it she had let them all go by.

'So what's it like then, Theberton Street.'

'Oh, big old rooms. High ceilings. Mock-pillar front. Named after the country seat of Thomas Milner Gibson who built the surrounding streets and Gibson Square in the 1930s.'

'Who was he? How do you remember this junk, Hugh?'

'Lord knows. I think the question ought to be why, when I can't recall my own phone number. Plainly, all this important information leaves no room for such trivia. And birthdays. Thomas Gibson and Walter Raleigh and the history of Islington leave me no alternative but to consign to oblivion the birthdates of immediate family members.'

'You remembered mine. *The Art of Loving*, you gave me.'

'Ah yes. And Christian?'

'December 16th.'

'Your father's in the spring. René?'

'September 10th. He'll be twenty-four.' *Old enough to know better*, she thought, and she packed in silence after that until she had cleared the room of books. They filled twenty five boxes and she gazed at them in admiration. 'I'm going to have that many books when I grow up,' she said.

'You're going to have that many books when I pass on to greener pastures,' said Hugh from behind the paper, 'to do with as you will.'

'Don't do it anytime soon,' she said, 'because I shan't be around to collect my library. I'm going to California in September. To live.'

Hugh brought his paper down. She told him about Robin, the bar, the conditions of the deal. She spoke quickly as though trying to persuade him of the wisdom of her intentions.

'My goodness,' he said when she had finished. 'My goodness.'

She waited nervously. If Alan Henley's approval had meant something, Hugh's, she felt at this moment, could make or break her resolve.

'I believe this calls for a drink.' He struggled to his feet.

'I'll get it.'

'No, no. It's only ten feet away.' He crossed the room and opened the old dresser, whose contents she had suspected but never seen. Glasses. Old glass, almost yellowed, crystal tumblers, thick shot glasses, long-stemmed red and white wine glasses. And liquor. Bottles of Jameson, Baileys, Harvey's Bristol Cream. 'I believe I shall crack this,' he lifted out a dusty bottle of Glenfiddich. 'I've been waiting for an adequate excuse.'

She watched the light catch the whiskey as he poured a finger into each of two heavy tumblers. She took hers and held it reverently. 'Is there a special way to drink this?' she asked.

'Neat,' he said, 'without water or, God forbid, ice. Without excess discussion. Without show.' He held up his glass to her and they stood, ceremoniously, among the boxes and the dust. 'To my niece, Hannah Jane Newell, wishing her success in her every endeavour.'

The whiskey caught in her throat and made her eyes water. 'I talked with a friend of René's last week,' she said. 'He might be going down to Margate for a while. He might be sort of…convalescing there.'

Hugh sat down and rested his tumbler on the arm of his chair.

'Ah good,' he said. 'I'm glad to hear he's in touch.'

She swilled the rest of her whiskey in the glass. It tasted sour. 'Shall I start packing upstairs? The front room?'

'I don't think so,' said Hugh. He sounded tired. 'That's a job for another day.'

'Well,' she said, and raised a smile, 'here's to Sixteen Theberton Street and all who sail in her.'

Seventeen

Thursday, 1st August, 1991. Westgate-on-Sea.

Dear Hannah,

It is definitely coastal here. Cool out there. Sun in the distance against the small cliffs, but the sea creeping up the beach in flat waves to high tide is steel grey. I am definitely not in London. This is definitely good. I am trying to be careful about admitting how comparatively good I feel. As you see, this is not being very effective. The bus from Victoria at 1:30 yesterday stopped at Westgate itself. Drove down through Kent, all the hay high like Oklahoma. That was beautiful. I got here, to the quiet, just after 4. Asked the way in a teashop. Westgate-on-Sea is a teashop sort of town. I got the attic room you would have wanted; overlooks the sea. The window-frame is rotten so you hold the little-paned window closed with some white string. That's okay by me. Last night I didn't go to the filmshow and I didn't play Scrabble. I just stayed here and the sunset came and went and all the colours went by and that was fine. As it got darker I felt memories fill the space—all the space there was, but that was alright too. I am reading Wallace Stevens. 'The light he gives $-$ /It is how he gives his light. How he shines.' I am full of ideas and hope, though tired. I do need to sleep a lot and to start to put some weight back on. On the whole, however, things are pretty good. With you too, I hope. If you want to write to me here the address is at the top.

René.

Saturday, 3 August, 1991. London.

Hi. Got your letter Thursday. Westgate-on-Sea sounds like it may have fallen asleep a hundred years ago. Better not to wake it, it might die of shock. I am lying on a bare mattress in my new bedroom. I have moved in with Hugh who, coincidentally, moved in with me today. Yes, the house on Bethecar Road is finally sold and Hugh has rented a flat in Islington until he has enough energy to buy another place. Though he says with the market the way it is in London now he might be better off renting a decent flat like this fairly close to the centre of town than buying what he could afford because, as he says himself, it would be no small discomfort for a man of his build to inhabit a shoebox in East Ham. Moving Hugh was no mean feat. Still under house arrest after the surgery, he directed operations from an armchair in his living room. Yours truly got to pack. Dad did some when he was over. Tip of the iceberg. I tell you, René, I found stuff in those wardrobes upstairs that our grandmother wore when she was my age. It was quite astonishing, the day we packed that upstairs room. Three big old wardrobes and a dresser stuffed full of clothes, photos, shoes, even the bag mother used when she got married—when she and Dad went away to Florence. Yes, lots of Mum. I know you would have felt as I did, uncovering all those pictures of her. Hugh gave lots of them to me, told me essentially to take what I wanted apart from some special ones he wanted for himself. I now have two boxes of stuff. He's going to store them for me in 'my' bedroom on Theberton Street. I'm here for a month. Islington is fun. More on that later.

Yesterday, with almost everything in boxes in the front rooms and the hall and landing, I found Hugh in the back room downstairs—empty but for the record player on a kitchen chair, playing Verdi's 'Requiem'. Loud. He looked so very sad. I left him there. I was afraid to say anything. What could I say?

The flat is large and draughty. Casement windows. Deep windowsills. The streets here are very leafy and when the light's going, as it is now, the white houses glimmer in the orange streetlights and the green of the trees deepens. From our windows we see balconies and balustrades, tall graceful windows, bow windows, narrow attic windows (none held with white string that I can see), and out the kitchen window at the back a confusion of brown brick and iron fire escapes. Who wants to escape? I love London. I love it here.

Last night I watched *Brief Encounter*. Their tearing apart, I know exactly: that is how I will always feel unless one of us goes further and further away.

I would like to see you, if you'd like to see me—perhaps in about a month. If you'll still be there, perhaps I could go down and visit on your birthday, bearing twenty-four lit candles. It might be considered a fire hazard on the bus, but maybe I could bribe the driver. I can stay in touch with Alan Henley—I'm sure you know I met with him and we had a talk. It's hard to talk about this, especially in a letter. I do not think I am especially, as you fear, damaged. I am not terribly unhappy, just the same as I always was since I came to London. It's not so bad.

I wish you wouldn't worry, but concentrate on getting well instead, on getting better. Alan will always know where you are, I assume. Don't go off into the deep blue again, will you? You were almost lost. Lots of people love you. People need you. But in the end, you must do what's right for you. Isn't that the truth?

I've been gaining and losing friends all summer. Mo went to live in Sheffield. I visited her there. Julia went to Paris and failed two exams and came home to repeat them and then packed it all in and told her father she's not going to be a doctor after all, she wants to go into dress design. There was a huge row. Her father says she'll have to pay him back for two years of med school, but Harry says he'll never hold her to it; he's too soft at heart when it comes to his kids. The Alton household is in uproar, however. In the midst of all this, Harry and I sort of called it a day, though I'm not entirely sure how or when this happened, it just seemed to be a *fait accomplit* all of a sudden.

Julia's trotting back to Paris for a few months. Harry has moved back in with his old friends down in Acton, and I am slave-in-residence (a.k.a. loving and dutiful niece) to our funny, wonderful old uncle, who is beating me roundly at backgammon every single night.

I hope you are being sent to sleep every night by the sound of the sea through your window. Throw away the white string! Let in the sea air!

Love always,

    Hannah.

Westgate-on-Sea. August 8th

Dear Hannah,

What do we know of fear? Not very much, I am forced to conclude. I realise that I have spent most of my life teaching myself to minimize it, at best to avoid it and—not to appear too selfish and narrow-minded in this pursuit—trying to protect you from it too. Perhaps that was not the right approach. To have taught you to cope with it and understand it would have been better, but as I had little experience of it myself, I couldn't very well consciously expose you to it so as to teach you how to survive.

I am learning about fear here. It is the single most prevalent emotion in the place. A close second is boredom, and that too is hard to take; although some days it is a relief. The alternatives are wearing.

It seems to me as though the last ten years were a long hot summer. The leaves are falling. I'd like to see you—don't worry about coming on my birthday or later than that. Let me know a week or so in advance if possible. I think I will still be here in September. The general philosophy here is not to look too far in the future until you're ready. Alan is, as you suspected, taking care of things for me. He has been a good friend to me. If ever you need help Hannah, you couldn't do better than to turn to him. Apart from his having loved Mum, and being very fond of her memory, he is a good human being: honest, stalwart. Marjorie is also very kind and patient, understanding, gentle, one of those strong women. Behind every good man, eh? And before, or beside. You are one too, Hannah, only I don't think you're allowing yourself to believe it yet. Perhaps you're too young to have seen it in yourself. What can any of us know of another human being? So little. I thought I knew you, in my arrogance, I thought I knew you through and through: I thought I'd made you the way you were. Forgive my presumption. Now that I see you may have escaped without great damage, the best thing I can do for you is to let you go. You understood this before I did, apparently.

Some of the people in here are funny, behind it all; some interesting; some just sad. One man fell off the edge when he found his wife had loved another man for twenty years. She had had an affair on and off with this other man for all that time. I'm not supposed to divulge anything that goes on in the group sessions, but I can tell you about casual off-the-record conversations. 'I saw I had two choices,' Ted told me. 'I could exhibit rage—physically hurt the two of them and myself, take it out on the blasted furniture; or I could do what I had always done before and pretend I was two years old. I went for the second option. It was easier and I didn't have to wake the neighbours.'

Another chap tried to commit suicide by sleeping out in the garden all night. He thought he would get hypothermia and sort of slip off into oblivion like Scott of the Antarctic. But it was May, the temperature never dipped below 15 degrees and all he contracted was a head cold. You have to laugh or it all becomes very tedious. Some days easier than others. I have not recovered my attention span very well. It has taken me three days and much revision to write all of this.

Take care

    René.

Islington, August 15th.

Dear R,

Life may go down, but it comes up again. Nothing looks lovelier these days than London, sitting calmly under the giant dome of the sky, clear, and, as the light goes, turning more colours than simple man thinks have been invented. I'm reading enormously. John Cheever stories—the man has a touch as light as gossamer, but he weaves the stories closely. Those characters, they never say a word, they just present themselves. I'm also dipping into *Chaos*, by James Gleick. Finding poetry there. He talks about a certain point, the 'point of accumulation', beyond which periodicity gives way to fluctuations, chaos, that never settles down at all. He talks about Mandelbrot and how, in his scheme, the errors approach 'infinite sparseness'. Wouldn't that be a way to live.

Hugh has a big photo of Mum framed in the hallway here. I'd never seen it before. She's wearing a broad-brimmed hat, with her hair up loosely. More than half my life she's been dead. Swimming far out, into the deep waters, further and further. I don't think she knows what we did. I don't believe there's any possibility for shock or unhappiness after death.

Sometimes I look a little into the future now, when I can bear it. You'll be 24 soon. I can sort of imagine being 24, and 34, and 50. I'm very scared of the no-way-backness of old age, though; also of the disease of nostalgia and the disease, as you know, of fear.

Hugh just said 'Is it augmented by or augmented with?' I said, 'augmented with.' 'Ah,' he said, 'I was right.' 'Who was wrong?' I asked. 'Me,' he said, and gave me a big cheesy grin.

He is much better. Able to walk halfway down Upper Street now; just as far, he says, as St. Mary's church;

or, he adds with a twinkle, The King's Head. He's mostly drinking mineral water, or a half of Guinness (for the iron of course). We sometimes go for a drink at the Old Pied Bull on the corner of our road. Hugh is proud of the fact that Sir Walter Raleigh is said to have lived there. And he knows all about the famous people buried at St. Mary's. Hannah Lightfoot (what a gorgeous name!), who had a daughter by George III and might even have married him, is said to be buried there in a grave marked 'Rebecca Powell.' And a godson of James I, plus Sir George Wharton (I just got his name again from Hugh) who killed each other in a duel right here in Islington are buried there too. In one grave. That's what the king wanted.

Why should I be afraid? Life will take its course like a river. It will take us away from each other, it will bring us back together.

x Hannah.

Theberton Street, August 16th.

Dear boy—I'm not much at writing letters. I have heard you are getting sea air and the peace of the southeast coast: or is it merely placid? I have set up camp in what the Domesday Book referred to in 1086 as 'Isendone'. I feel as though I was indeed around at that time, if not available for comment. Of late, I have become a little more familiar with my coronary circulation, my systoles, diastoles, and atrial pressure than I am really comfortable with. The medical community has seen fit to deprive me of all food that actually tastes of anything. Luckily I have a duplicitous ally in my niece, who sees to it that I get ice-cream (low fat) at least once a month. She knows how to play eccentric little melodies on the *chordae tendinae* of her old uncle.

I hope the end of summer sees you improving in health and spirits. I expect Hannah has mentioned she is off to the New World in a month or so. She will be greatly missed, but there is no brighter light than a free spirit.

    Yours, Hugh.

Westgate-on-Sea, August 25th.

Hannah,

I hope Alan has rung you to tell you I'll be returning to London late next week; I shall be staying in St. John's Wood. A short stay, I think. No more than a couple of weeks. I think I arrive on the 2nd. Alan can give you the particulars. Perhaps we could meet there.

I feel as though I am trying to fit a new skin, a new box, and find the spaces in it. There will be plenty of space, once I've worn it in. Some days, nothing. Muffled voices. I know they could be louder. They're meant to be. Life is rather shabby at the moment. What do I mean to say here? Bursts of good intention, of enthusiasm (undirected, useless). A lot of numbness. What happened to all those beautiful mornings? Autumn coming in now like a slow ship. I dreamed of Armageddon. An upheaval, a terrible natural catastrophe of the earth, fire, breaking up, a rushing, lava, and water, and burning. You and I: the wave almost reached, then we plunged into cool water and were saved. I am not going under. It's true that I feel autumnal, the leaves down, the odd, brilliant, moody skies affect me; I often feel sad. I wonder what's going to happen in the winter—I heard from Hugh that you are planning a trip, that's good news—but I may be reaching an even place where things are calmer. Most of all, I don't want to see anybody just at the moment. This will change, no doubt. When Lenin was in exile in Southern Siberia (I am slowly reading his biography), he befriended a Polish hatmaker called Prominsky, also in exile with his wife and children for a single act. His allowance was mysteriously reduced while Lenin knew him, and no one was buying his hats. More than 20 years later, in 1923, he applied to Lenin to go back to his native Poland. Lenin allowed it. But Prominsky died of typhus on the train.

It's not cold yet. Life is here, all around. I am not plumb in the centre of it, but slightly off to one side. Hope to see you in London.

    René.

Islington, August 30th.

Dear You,

I'm holed up in my peachy room, listening to the Beeb. A gang of women are talking about working in't'mill. One woman's been there 38 years. Lots of laughter at that. A 'tattler' has a bad reputation in the textile industry, they are saying.

Well, you, everyone has their stories and here is mine. I bought a ticket today. More money than I have ever spent on any one thing. London Heathrow to JFK, New York. JFK New York to San Francisco. Tuesday October 1st. I'm leaving on a jet plane, don't know when I'll be back again…remember that song? I'm scared, René, you know I'm scared.

I was meant to go out tonight with Harry and the gang, but I made an excuse. I suppose it was really because I know there'll be another girl there whom Harry is crazy about. Linda is her name and I'm not really ready for all that. The effort of pretending to all the others that I don't care would be even greater than the effort of pretending to myself. The thing is, I really don't care very much, I just don't want to have to see the look in his eyes as he watches her. I'd like to remember it when it was for me. I'm on my own now though. Single. One. Do I give a flea's underpants? I do not. Because it's Friday night—no work till Monday—and because fleas need their underpants to keep them warm.

I've read your letter lots and it doesn't get any happier. I know you are going through a dark time and tonight I'd like to keep you company. Well, let me say this anyway: I do not agree with Erich Fromm. Love is not a decision.

When I told Hugh I'd bought my ticket, I said I felt as if I were being blown about by the winds of chance. He said 'chance is a link that joins us with eternity. It is older than religion.' I said that sounded very deep. He said he thought so too—he surprised himself, he just opened his mouth and that's what came out. Now we think some ancient dead philosopher has taken over Hugh's body and we should charge people to come to Theberton Street and tell him something that's troubling them and he can open his mouth and the philosopher will say something profound. We tried it again, but all that came out was 'How about some crumpets and strawberry jam?'

I'm going to miss Hugh extremely.

What's happening is this: I fly out on the 1st, stop in New York for a few hours, then on. Mo's friend and landlord Robin, who is giving me the job out there, will be there already with his girlfriend Sandy and I can stay in their place till I find a place to live. I start work on the 10th. Robin owns pubs. He's opening an English pub out there. I'm going to waitress and do bar work first. If he likes my work he'll train me in managing the restaurant side. He's planning to open a B&B upstairs, so there's a chance I could train into hotel management in a small way somewhere down the line. For the moment I'm happy I'll have a work visa and a job and a roof over my head in San Francisco. I'm learning to drive. Robin says it's really easy to pass the test out there and then I can pick up an old jalopy. That's what they call old bangers out there. Mo has an old banger of a Fiat. She and I painted it last weekend. I visited her in Sheffield again to sort some paperwork out with Robin. The car was meant to be sort of happy Day-Glo green but when it was finished, it looked more sort of snotty. Mo drove me to the station in it. It's very noisy and doesn't always go again when she stops at lights. Coupled with its colour, these characteristics attract some looks. I wore dark glasses and a wig. Mo went as Mo. She is falling in love with a barmaid at Robin's pub. Mo lives upstairs in a flat above the pub. I asked her to come to America with me. She said perhaps in fifteen to twenty years, once she'd acclimatised to having moved outside the Greater London area.

I do love London. There she is out there, spreading out her skirts. The last light hasn't quite left the sky. Tomorrow will probably be another day just like this one. Take care of you.

Love Hannah.

P.S. Tomorrow I'll ring Alan. Hope I'll see you soon then.

16 Theberton Street, 1 September.

Margaret my dear,

I scarcely know where to begin so I think I shall begin somewhere around the middle. Then I can go forwards or back with equanimity. For her 20th birthday in June, I gave my niece *The Art of Loving*. Dipped into it again tonight. 'To love somebody is not just a strong feeling—it is a decision, it is a judgement, it is a promise. If love were only a feeling, there would be no basis for the promise to love each other forever.'

I have thought about love, on and off, for all these years.

I had some heart trouble and then they tinkered with it and now it's working again. Who knows for how long, but I think I have some life in me yet, like a tough old boot. The house got too much, though; perched on the rim of London like that, full of memories and old rubbish. I sold it to the highest bidder for ten shillings and fourpence and moved down here to Islington to hang out and be cool with the young people of today. Sadly, none of the young people of today would be seen dead with me except aforementioned young niece, whom I don't think you ever had the good fortune to meet, and who is, happily for her, about to fly to sunnier climes and try her luck in the New World. I shall miss her company. She has proved a challenging backgammon adversary and makes a handsome cup of cocoa. I am still a member of the rat race in the City. Nowadays I run slower. If the intention ever actually *was* to win, I forgot that long ago. Was it Lily Tomlin who said that the trouble with being in a rat race is that even if you win, you're still a rat?

Margaret. Do you remember the angels in Berlin who fell to earth? Cassiel and Demiel. I saw the second film last week, playing in the Islington picture house. My niece asked me to go with her. I was interested, remembering *Himmel Uber Berlin*. In this second film, both angels are on earth. Demiel has a family—he married the trapeze artiste. Cassiel's in trouble with drink. 'You think we're so far away,' he told us, 'and we're so close.' I hope they are. The silence is no good to me when it is prolonged. The stillness drives my spirit into hibernation; underground. I suppose it is my spirit; or you might call it my soul. But even burrowed underground, you can stretch out a finger and write in the dirt. Make something concrete of the abstract. That's what I'm trying to do with this letter, you see? Put memory here, put time, put the past to rest on this page. Here, Margaret: here is our past. What does it mean now? How does it seem? How have you presented it to yourself? What words would you, do you choose? I know my angel is close, though she is far away. I don't see or hear her; but I know she is there.

Of course I will never send this letter, but recently I have been in a letter-writing frame of mind and it has helped to pen this. Given that your dear sweet eyes will never read it, may I nevertheless allow myself the liberty of saying that I have missed you every single day since you left: I have lain awake long nights and thought about our time together. Love was a decision. It is a decision. To paraphrase the old verse: with Margaret gone, whose eyes to compare with the morning sun? I always did compare, and I do compare, now that she's gone.

Hugh.

The National Gallery, London, September 7th, 1991.

Dear You,

I have just made the call at a payphone here and asked whoever answered the phone [a nurse? A bored voice, whoever it was☐ to let you know I won't be coming to see you this afternoon after all. This letter is not just to explain why—that can be done in three words: failure of courage—but to say some things I have been thinking about, and that I wanted to say to you in person today. But I can't do that; so here is this letter.

I used to think I wasn't angry. You told me I might be, in your early letters, when you so reasonably tried to smooth the way for me. I think you tried to tell me that one day I might be angry and confused, and that was okay. I didn't listen then: six months ago I wasn't feeling confused *or* angry. I think I was riding a big wave away from you, eager, experimenting, not looking back. I missed you terribly but I was determined not to look back. Then I think I started to get confused. Maybe around March. I sorted things out, maybe in the last month. I decided to take my own life into my own hands and go very far away from you. Now I'm angry.

There. An inventory of Hannah's emotions in the first eight months of 1991. I'm up to September, and it's anger.

I just spent a couple of hours going round the gallery here with Hugh. It was his idea. He wants to sate me with cultural London so that by the time I get to the States I shall be ready for, as he puts it, Hollywood and the Coke bottle. He has the English scorn for America, but he's being very supportive of my decisions. And before I leave, he wants me to have seen every John Singer Sargent, every Christopher

Wren, every Nicholas Grimshaw in the entire city. He hasn't returned to work yet (possibly the end of September) and I've cut down my hours at the studio to three days a week, so on Wednesdays and Thursdays we are About Town, the two of us. This really is a special time. We've been to the Transport Museum (I bought a model red London bus—a number 12—and a London Underground pencil to remind myself of those institutions of public transport that we know and love). We went on a trip to Canary Wharf—took the Docklands Light Rail and Hugh showed me Nicholas Grimshaw's Financial Times print works, built in the docklands three years ago. [Remember how I used to run all the way home from school to tell you what I'd learned? Here it is again, that feeling that something isn't real till I've told you about it. I've tried so hard to learn new ways of making things real, but here it is again and René, I can't help giving into it just in this one letter. I do love you.□ He told me how Grimshaw is part of the engineering tradition in architecture and he's part of the tradition of the industrial architects of the 19th century; I can't remember their names, Paxton I think was one: I think he designed Crystal Palace. Blimey, Hugh just knows so much and once he gets warmed up it all comes spilling out and I just can't keep up. Now I know he really has read all his books, and remembers what's in 'em! He's my hero, Hugh Lloyd Johnson. He said he once read of Grimshaw saying 'Rigour is vital, whatever you are using.' I like that, in an art form. Or is architecture a science? Probably both. Or neither. They're just boxes, aren't they, those terms? So anyway, after we'd seen the FT building (lots of glass with metal rivets and bolts, looking as though they were suctioned onto the glass) we got the DLR back to the city and Hugh brought me on a

Magical Nicholas Tour. All he would tell me was that we were going to see a threshold, also designed by Grimshaw. It was very exciting. We got off the DLR at Bank [Hugh's work station: he calls it The Beast☐ and walked through all those labyrinthine tunnels to Monument, where he says he is going to take me to see the site of the start of The Great Fire, and took the Circle Line to Embankment and then walked along by the river, past Cleopatra's needle, and across Waterloo Bridge, where he said we were getting very warm. We went all the way into Waterloo Station, and then he said we'd arrived. And there it was: the channel tunnel railway terminal, threshold between Britain and continental Europe, herald of a new age of rail travel, and Grimshaw Piece Extraordinaire. René, you have got to see it. It made me want to be an architect. [Bar work is a great start along this road, don't be fooled by the cynics...☐ Waterloo is the world's busiest railway station. Did you know that? I didn't. This new terminal thingie (plane metaphors spring to mind naturally—it's only going to take 3 *hours* to get from Waterloo to Paris!!) is going to take care of 15 million passengers a year. Hugh says he read that the idea is to exhilarate people with the experience of travel. Arriving passengers will be able to sweep into the station, gaping at Westminster and the Thames through a wall made entirely of glass. He said the panels of the glass in the wall will probably be held together by the sort of stainless steel castings that we saw on the FT building. They allow for the glass to move with the rumble of the trains going by. I think it's something like 5 or 6 millimetres they have to be able to move!

So here's the plan: I go to America, work in a bar for two years, study architecture in my spare time, get qualified, and come back to work for Nicholas

Grimshaw, who will be so bowled over by my student portfolio he'll offer me an undisclosed sum to join his inner circle. Alright, I'll say, but only if you let me work on stuff for my family and mates. First I want to build my uncle a house, okay? Okay, Nick will say, do what you do Sweetheart.

Sometimes during the day or when I'm trying to go asleep at night I feel an unnamed dread steal over me. It begins to squeeze in on my heart until I look into its face and name it. Yes, it has a name. Leaving. I say to myself 'in a month you will be leaving England; leaving London and Hugh and Mo and Harry and Julia; leaving the familiar places, going into the dark unknown. Soon you'll be saying goodbye on this side. There is no one on the other side, no one you know.'

I can't bear it! I'm scared! What am I doing?

Hugh and I wandered at just the right pace around the gallery. I hate walking too slowly or too fast in an art gallery. There is a pace that is just right. Most of all I liked Cezanne and Matisse. An old woman with a rosary. Take a look at that one if you come down here one day. She looks so terribly worried. She looks like the past has been all heartbreak and the future terrifies. She looks a little like I feel. Hugh likes John Singer Sargent. He stood for a long time before a portrait of Lord Someone-or-Other, looking like a camel, holding a riding whip. Hugh said Sargent died twenty years to the day before he, Hugh, was born. I have come to the conclusion that Hugh knows everything in the world. Before I leave, I intend to ask him to tell me the meaning of life. Well, I need to leave now and post this on the way home and I see it is raining and I've no umbrella. Oh bother, said Pooh. I'll loiter in the gallery shop looking at postcards till it stops raining. Then I'll walk up Charing Cross Road looking in bookshops. Can't buy any books though: I need to travel light. I'll be going with just what I can carry. Here's that dread again. Must move on.

Love,

Hannah.

Harry wanted her to have a party. It would be the perfect time, he said; the very end of summer, the weekend before classes began; an emigration party, he said.

'I'm not emigrating,' said Hannah, 'I'm just...going to America.'

'I knew you'd say that,' said Harry sadly.

'Well I'm not!' she said. 'I'm just going to see how this two-year thing works out.'

'Everyone says that,' he said.

She agreed to the party. Mo said she'd come down. All the old gang would be there. She even thought of calling Jeremy, but then she remembered she thought he was a pillock, so she let Harry take care of the invitations. Invite everyone, she told him. She surprised herself by asking several people at the studio and was even more surprised when they all said they'd love to come. Harry insisted they have it in his new place in Hackney and that he'd organize the food and booze.

'Food?' said Hannah, surprised.

'Yeah, we have to have something substantial for the stoned food-cravers,' he explained, 'and something insubstantial to help the mere drinkers soak up the booze. Otherwise we'll never survive the night and see the dawn. So,' he started scribbling with a pencil on a scrap of paper, 'we'll need crisps and peanuts, sliced pans, peanut butter, Mars bars, Jaffa cakes...'

'Mars bars?' said Hannah. 'Couldn't we have Twixes? I feel sick when I eat a whole Mars Bar.'

'Yeah, Twixes, and those big Fun Packs of mini-stuff. Milky Ways, Marathons. Yum!' He surveyed the list. 'Something's missing though.'

'Marshmallows?'

'Pickled onions. Cheese. Branston pickle. Mayo. Mustard. Ham. This is going to be a *feast*!'

'What time does it start?' said Hannah. 'Because I'm going to see my brother first.'

'Whenever people show. Being the guest of honour and the reason for the entire party and all, you get to show up whenever you like.' He leaned over and kissed her gently on the cheek, then took her in his arms and rocked her.

'Scared about going?' he said.

'Yeah,' she said.

Hugh said he'd drive her if she liked. He'd looked it up on the *A to Z* and it wasn't very near the tube. It might be raining. She said no, it was fine, she'd go, and she'd come back to Islington after to change for the party; it was on the way anyhow. On the Thursday, she called Alan from work. She told him she was planning a visit Saturday. He said he hoped she expected to find René somewhat changed from when she last saw him. Yes, she said, she did. When she put the phone down she was shaking. She had to leave the office and get some air.

London, Thursday.

Dear You,

From today it all changes. All the change I could want. Sometimes there are only weak links to life. I finished work today. There was a small party at the studio, they got sparkling wine and drank to Good Health, Good Luck, and Happiness for Hannah in America. I felt dizzy but terribly calm. Yes, I am going to America. Things are beginning to blur. Part of it is the time of year: the sudden dark, the constant rain, and the beginning of cold. Everything feels less safe anyway, and here I am pulling up the only roots there are. I wish it was April, with the promise of summer.

I have always told you everything. Today I don't know what everything is.

The sky is lovely over London: light behind grubby clouds, but there are storms forecast. I'm going to see you in two days and I'm scared as hell. I've had lots of dreams about you where I was scared, and many where we hurt each other. You were often a figure of authority, sometimes even of violence, in these dreams. Sometimes I was the violent one. Let's be gentle with each other on Saturday. Good and gentle and not angry—let's forgive each other.

Hannah.

Eighteen

She noticed everything with painful clarity. The cracks in the stone steps. The different shades of faded red and salmon pink in the tiny tiles of the front porch. The silver surround of the doorbell. It looked like there was a row of silver balls, tiny and moulded, surrounding the white ceramic bellpush. It seemed difficult to press. She had to push her finger hard into it. There was a distant ponderous chime, reminding her of the chimes at the dentist's years ago in a giant old house on Westbourne Grove. She thought of the drill, of the pink mouthwash she'd had to spit in a tiny sink. Still, the dentist's would be better than this. This was worse than the worst exam. She tried to think of something more awful than this so she could be glad she was only doing this. Nothing came to mind.

A young girl opened the door. She said nothing when Hannah asked for René Newell. She just opened the door wider, closed it behind Hannah, and began to climb the dark wooden stairs. Hannah followed. To the gallows, she thought. I know what it feels like now. He's in this building, he's somewhere in this building. Mum. Don't look down on us with bitterness. We were good kids.

Alan greeted her first. Stood up from the low armchair he'd been sitting in and crossed the floor, holding out his hand, filling the space between them with comfortable energy.

'Hannah,' he said, 'I hope you don't mind my being here. René asked me and I thought it a good idea.'

'No,' she said, letting him shake her hand, take her by the elbow as though to steady her momentarily against other forces that were in the room.

He came forward then, and took her hand too and held it a moment and smiled. He wore a dark shirt and trousers. He looked thin and immensely pale under his naturally sallow skin. There was a bad mushroom colour around his eyes. She looked for him and didn't see him there.

'Hi you,' she said. They didn't know what to do then, where to look. A hug was possible for a split second, then quickly out of the question.

'Why don't we sit down, and then you can let me know if you'd like me to stick around or leave,' said Alan.

'We can have tea. You want tea?' René said.

She said yes, she'd like tea, and sat in one of the deep, dark green armchairs facing the other two. Alan sat down. René left the room. She took some deep breaths.

'Are you nervous?' said Alan. 'You look nervous.'

'Is he alright?' she said.

Alan moved his head a little from side to side, as though weighing up an answer. 'Alright,' he said, 'is a relative term. He is emerging from a breakdown. See what you think.'

Nervous breakdown, she thought, and the words shocked her with their glib familiarity, sounding trite and yet terribly wrong. Is that what he had? Then it suddenly seemed obvious. Of course. That's what happened. Emerging from—it made him sound like a slow train coming out of a long tunnel.

'Shall I stay a while?' Alan said.

'No,' she said. 'Thanks. It's fine. Thanks though.'

He stood up. 'René actually wanted me here for you. In case,' he said.

I wonder, she thought. *In case what?*

'You'll give me a ring before you leave?' he said.

'Of course. I'm going on Tuesday. Thank you,' she extended her hand and they shook again. 'Thanks for everything.'

'Ah you have your mother's cheekbones,' he said. 'High and fine. You take care, now, and I'll watch out on this side of the ocean. Make sure nobody loses their way.'

As he left, René was coming back and they exchanged a few words just outside the door. Then he came in, and shut the door behind him with a muffled click.

'Tea for two,' he said. As he sat in an armchair, she noticed how thin his legs were in the dark pants. Like two sticks.

'Have you been alright?' he said.

'I've been—around and around. Met myself coming back a few times.'

'Dizzy?'

'Very dizzy,' she said, and she picked at a piece of fluff on the arm of the chair. 'I'd like to stop going round.'

'Most people would.' There was no irony in his voice. There was nothing. She strained against the silence, and the blank tone of his voice. Where had he been? Where was he now?

'So I'm going on Tuesday morning.'

'Early?'

'Eleven. Heathrow. I'm getting the bus out,' she hurried on, afraid he'd think she was asking him to see her off. She didn't want to be talking about this. She didn't know why she'd brought it up. It had come up by itself, jostled ahead of all the other things she could have said.

'Do you want to go?'

'Yeah. I do.' She looked around the room, caught in a lie she didn't even want to tell. 'It's okay here. Not like a...well, a bit like a hotel.'

'Not quite,' he said. 'It's good care.'

'The girl who let me in didn't look like she cared much.'

He said nothing. His stillness was unnerving. He wasn't doing the things normal people do when they talk, moving their heads, nodding, gesturing. He seemed to be held in by something.

'Are you alright?' This was the question. She was glad she had asked it without thinking, but she was scared. She could feel her blood pump. *I'll follow you. I'll stay here and follow you in a heartbeat, you know that.*

'Hannah,' he said, and he moved at last, shifting in the chair as though he were uncomfortable. 'It's warm here. It's—' he searched for a word, 'simple. I don't have to give much.'

'Give much to whom?'

'The sessions,' he said. 'Group therapy. If I say one or two things they're satisfied.'

'You're like a prisoner,' she said.

'It's not like that. I can leave if I want to.'

'That's not what I meant. You're trying to persuade them you're getting better, recovering—trying to play it their way? Is that what you're doing?'

'My recovery,' he said slowly, deliberately, 'is really not as important as you think.'

Was this him? This was more like one of her worse nightmares. Would he suddenly snap out of this, come back? She swallowed.

'What does that mean?'

There was a knock on the door and the sullen girl who had answered the doorbell came in balancing a tray with tea and a plate of biscuits. Hannah wanted tea. Something hot and sweet. It was a relief to concentrate on something physical, like where to put the cup. She kept it between her hands and left the saucer on the floor by her chair. The girl went out again without a word. How did people like that get jobs in a place like this, wondered Hannah. Perhaps she was a patient. She wanted to make some comment, some joke about the girl, but since she couldn't think what would come out right, it died on her lips.

'Remember Nutmeg?' said René.

Nutmeg. She took a gulp of hot tea, felt it scald her all the way down to her stomach. But it was nice. Nice and hot. 'Yeah.' She smiled.

'How you asked me if she washed herself every day?'

'Well, cos she spent so much time washing. I mean, it was basically eat, sleep, and wash for Nutmeg, wasn't it.'

'And playing.'

'Yeah, she played a lot.'

'Perhaps you can get a Nutmeg in America.'

'Maybe. I wouldn't call another cat Nutmeg, though. She was the only one.'

'I may be making a journey myself.'

'Oh yeah?'

'To Morocco.'

She nodded. The tea moved a little in the cup, sloshing very faintly with the movement.

'Why Morocco?'

'To see the dunes at Merzouga,' he said, as though it were something he had to, rather than wanted to, do. He crossed his legs and began talking, but he didn't look at her and she had the eerie sensation that he wasn't really talking to her at all.

'Morocco's true desert, where the first sand dunes of the Sahara start. Life adapting to the least hospitable of all living conditions. In the early spring, a lake forms just west of Merzouga from the only rains. Hundreds of pink flamingos flock to the lake. Imagine, all their colour against all that colour. See, the dunes aren't just yellow. They are red and pink—many shades, when the light changes throughout the day and evening. I've read that you can sleep on the rooves of the local auberges, even on the dunes themselves. In the evenings, the local kids sand-surf down them on plastic bags.' He stopped abruptly.

'But the lake won't be there any more, will it?' she said. 'In September.'

He re-crossed his legs, looked at her briefly for the first time. 'I may be there for a while.'

She nodded once. They both looked elsewhere. *This is torture*, she thought, *this is more awful than the worst dream.*

'This is torture,' she said aloud, keeping her voice low and steady. He took a deep breath, brushed something imaginary from his shirt. She *would* call him back. Before she left, she would see him behind his own eyes. 'Why don't you look at me?'

'The big date-palm oases of the Ziz valley are mostly infected with a fungus that kills a tree in less than a year. When a tree dies, there's a gap that allows the wind to blow through—'

'René—'

'—which leads to erosion. Most farmers only have about thirty palms each—'

'René! Stop!' She sat forward in her chair, resting her cup back on its saucer. 'I don't want to hear about date palm fungus,' she said. 'I want to hear about you.'

She looked at him. He stared back, then smiled a little, as though apologising.

'Me?' he said. 'There's not much to tell.'

Go, she thought. *Go before the worst happens and you start to cry. Don't let him see you cry.* She picked up her jacket.

'I have to go,' she said. 'I'm meeting the others. What time is it?' She looked around the room.

'Time to go,' he said. There was only mildness, no real hint of anything.

'You're not angry,' she said.

He shook his head, smiled. 'Oh no. Neither of us should be angry. Like you said, we must be gentle.'

'And forgive each other.'

'I have nothing to forgive.'

'Then neither have I.'

'Yes,' he said, and he stood up and moved close to the door, but not close enough that she would have to touch him as she passed. 'You have.'

She stood four feet from him, her jacket slung over her clenched hands, hiding them.

'Did you want to show me something? Something you were writing?' she said.

'No.'

'A book or something?'

'No,' he said. 'I destroyed it.'

'Why?' she said, hesitantly.

'It was no good.'

'Oh. Well, I'll go then.' Her voice failed. Light was sucked from the room. He stood with his hands by his side. 'You'll write to me,' she sobbed, 'from Morocco.'

'Yes. I'll tell you about the flamingos.'

'René.' The sobs were racking, she couldn't say any of it, it would all be lost. She put one hand to her mouth, drew her jacket with the other up to her chest, pushing it hard against herself so she could feel the metal buttons hurting her chest. 'We weren't wrong.'

He put a hand out, palm up; it seemed he meant to ask her to move forward so she could touch his hand. When she didn't, he let it fall and closed his eyes. She thought he might be trying to find his way back so that when he opened them she'd see him there, as she longed to. He put his head back, resting it against the wall as though he were very tired.

'Please don't cry,' he said, in such a low voice she could barely hear. She stopped crying. He looked at her. 'In order,' he went on in the same low tone, 'to recover, as everyone says that I'm supposed to do, I have found I need to sever certain...ties. Bonds, I suppose. Or perhaps nerves. In severing them, I may have unavoidably severed other...nerves too. Other chords. Do you follow?'

'It's not over,' she said. 'It'll keep getting better, won't it?'

He didn't answer immediately. He looked puzzled, as though the concept of an improvement in his circumstances was one he couldn't grasp.

'Yes,' he said eventually. 'It'll get better.'

She wanted to run at him; not to him, but at him, as she had when she was a child, down the hallway of the Bayswater house.

'So, I'll go then.' She reached for the door-handle. Like the doorbell, it seemed to require tremendous exertion to operate. The door swung towards her, she stepped to the side, they almost touched—the fabric of their clothing may have brushed together, particles of dust and other matter being exchanged in the disturbance. He moved to touch her but she didn't see.

'Bye René.'

'Bye Hannah.'

Nor did she see how, when she had begun to descend the stairs, her vision once again scalded by violent tears, he shut the door and leaned his forehead against the painted wood and stayed that way without moving, long after she had left the building, walked through the darkening streets of St John's Wood, and descended to the muggy warmth and sudden stale breezes of the Jubilee line.

Nineteen

Tuesday, 1st October, 1991.

Dear Hugh,

I'm about to do what you said, and just get on the plane. That was good advice: thanks. In fact, there's still nearly an hour till we board, but I'm glad I sent you away just now, and I'm glad you went because I hate long goodbyes.

However, I can't just sit here in the departure lounge for a whole hour without doing something because I'm afraid I might leave my check-on luggage in the lurch and get on a tube to Islington. So I thought I'd write you a letter. Of course, nothing has happened in the half-hour since you left, but maybe I could write a short dissertation on how wonderful life is in America to stop this page from going blurry with my tears.

In fact I have no idea how wonderful life is in America. I suppose it is not a great deal more or less wonderful than life anywhere else. But while I am in a philosophical frame of mind, I shall take the opportunity to disagree with M. Rimbaud that life is elsewhere. In my situation, I think this would be a foolish belief to entertain. Life is right here, in Heathrow Airport, ready to board Flight 608 to New York. I hope life will travel a little faster than my planes and be there in San Francisco to greet me. I'll arrive there at 4:40 this afternoon. Not very long after I took off, when you consider I'll have travelled about 6,000 miles on two flights, for eighteen hours, and crossed over into a brand new lifetime.

Thank you for your words before you left. Of course I was too upset to show you I'd heard, but I assume you knew. Thank you also for the Philip Larkin collection. I opened it briefly and read the line 'What remains when disbelief has gone?' So I know it will provoke thought.

Disbelief has not gone, but I'm beginning to find comfort in little things—the copy of John Berryman's *Dream Songs* I brought for my in-flight entertainment. Oskar in *The Tin Drum*, which I'm also reading, who could sing glass to pieces and stayed three all his life. (A very fine age, though what about the delicacy of six? Or the fine upstanding age of twenty?) Sting is singing in my Walkman, 'I change my clothes ten times before I take you on a date...' I'm sitting beside a man who keeps surreptitiously looking over to read what I'm writing. If he reads this I hope he turns red and gets all embarrassed. I think that would be fitting, don't you?

I wonder how Theberton Street is doing: missing me already? I don't think so.

I didn't tell you much about my last few days and with your impeccable diplomacy, you didn't ask. I think my throat was aching constantly from about last Thursday with the ache of leaving. My friends were fab. Mo came down from Sheffield to go to the farewell party in Harry's house. Harry was completely good to me—he didn't kiss a single other girl!—in fact, at the last minute, in his kitchen at 5 in the morning, he told me he'd really loved me and if I hated America and decided to come home, I'd always get a hug and a six-pack and a pillow in his bed. It was sweet of him to say that. The thing is, even though I know he's probably given that pillow to some other girl already, I know he meant it. And the hug and the six-pack would mean a lot more than the pillow anyway. Julia and Mo clubbed together and bought me a complete set of the most amazing silk lingerie ever made. Harry gave me a copy of *Ulysses*, in honour of my Irishness, and our common awe of genius and Guinness and all things literary. I shall attempt to read it. I immediately cracked it open when he gave it to me. Leopold Bloom was cooking liver for breakfast. A bit much for us at 5AM in view of all the beers we had consumed, so I put it away quick, but it's in a suitcase waiting.

Hugh, I don't really know what I'm doing, but other people seem to have a firm grasp of it so I've decided to jog along and wait for it all to dawn on me. Probably ten years down the line. Isn't that how it goes?

They're starting boarding in a few minutes. I'm off to see if I can post this somewhere nearby. Surely they must have postboxes in the departure lounge for people who are emigrating and need to write long letters to their uncles just before they get on the plane? I can't deny I'm terribly excited and scared and thrilled and feeling a little reckless and mad. Before signing off I'd like to tell you how it was when I saw René on Saturday, but I'm not sure there are words for it. I don't know where he has gone but I hope he returns. As I told you, he's talking about travelling to Morocco. He hasn't mentioned this before. I don't know if it's true. He was worse than I could have imagined. Empty and blank and trying to fool people he's getting better. That's what I saw. But as I saw it through the predictable tears, I can't be sure.

I love you, Hugh. There—I've never had the courage to say that before. I wanted to at the airport. Be kind to that good heart of yours.

 Hannah.

Hannah stood and picked up her bag. She wandered down the length of two gates, past a pizza stand, to the bank of TV screens. There it was: Flight 608 to New York. On time. Some other flights said Boarding, and the word Boarding flashed, as though it was urgent and passengers should be running to the gate. She walked back to the same row of seats, sat in one at the end, and took out the letter she'd written to Hugh. She had used her last English stamp on it but now she couldn't find a postbox and she didn't want to leave the departure lounge. Maybe Flight 608 would start to say Boarding in flashing capitals while she was gone. Maybe she'd get lost. She looked at the stamp. It was a mushroom. 'Endangered species' it said. 'Devil's bolete'. Now she'd have to post the letter in America, cover the English stamp with an American one. She had a sudden image of a giant stamp, the shape of the United States, coming down over England and its teddy-bear-shaped neighbour, blotting them out. *I'm going to live in America*, she thought. She stood up. There wasn't enough air in airports any more. Better to walk around. Better to get on a plane, watch the world from thirty thousand feet.

 He was standing near the ticket desk, searching the crowd. He hadn't seen her. She moved quickly behind a pillar. People were beginning to form a line at the gate. She felt rigid, paralysed with fear and excitement and dread. Should she move out where he could see her? What would she say to him? Could she somehow get on the plane without him seeing her? She had a terrible urge to run, leave the airport, be far away; at the same time, a fierce urge to go to him. But she couldn't erase the image of him in the room in St John's Wood, with his hand out and his eyes a blank. Please don't cry, he'd said. And he'd said he had nothing to forgive.

She tightened her hold on her bag and walked out into the space in front of him. Someone bumped her from the side with a luggage cart.

'Oh, sorry.' She turned, tried to get out of the way, and then he was in front of her, not smiling, holding a raincoat over his hands at the front.

'Hannah.'

'Hi,' she said. It sounded like someone else's voice, higher, too bright.

'I came to see you off,' he said.

She nodded. People were beginning to crowd around them and the First Class passengers were boarding.

'Come here,' he took her hand, led her by the hand through the people and out to where there was more space. He took her to a corner by the windows, and let her hand go. She quieted, everything calmed in her, they might for a moment have been alone in the busy space.

'I wanted to see you,' he said, 'before you left for the New World.'

'America.'

'Scared?'

'Not really.' She looked over to where a small boy was trying to climb up on a low window ledge. 'Yes, scared. Excited.' She looked back at him. 'I don't know what. How did you get through the ticket barrier? All the security?'

'I begged,' he said. He took her hand again, between his two. 'I didn't want the other day to be our goodbye.'

'Me neither.' She looked at the ground. His shoes, she didn't recognise them. Were they new? They weren't like his other shoes. 'I missed you a lot,' she said.

'Don't—' His hands jerked as though she had hit him.

'I'm not, I just…I'm glad you came here.' She put her other hand around his and he squeezed the hand he held. They stood like that, their hands a tight knot, and when she looked in his eyes she could see him there, the way he had always been, looking at her the way she remembered. She couldn't meet his sorrow with her own; that would be too much sorrow for either of them to bear, so she closed her eyes.

'I'll never regret what we did,' she said.

She tried to imagine what he was thinking, but it was dark and she couldn't tell.

'Alright?' she said into the dark.

Over the public address, a stewardess announced that Flight 608 to New York was boarding rows 36 to 50. She thought she heard him sigh.

'Good,' he said. He dropped her hands. There was a row of empty seats facing the window. He walked over and sat in one. She picked up her bag and sat in the seat next to him. Outside, the planes crouched on the tarmac. The sun was brilliant on the concrete and on their metal backs. Small airport vehicles manoeuvred around the planes, delivering luggage and food. He was staring at the floor, his elbows on his knees, his hands gripping each other so the knuckles showed white.

'I'm going to be alright Hannah.' He turned his head a little as he spoke but he didn't look at her.

'I know.'

'And you'll be alright. You'll be more than alright in your new life, you'll be fine.'

'I hope so.' She didn't think she would ever feel alright again. Not in a thousand years. She couldn't remember what alright was meant to feel like. 'I have to get on my plane. They're calling my row number.'

He looked out at the planes and the little vehicles making their small journeys from here to there.

'Do you still love me, Hannah?'

'Yes. I do.' She watched him, searching his face, washing it into her memory. She didn't think she'd see him again. This was all they had, this moment. She might think of this moment for the rest of her life.

'Finch,' she said, 'Why were you a finch?'

'Sparrows and finches,' he said, 'they're related somehow. I think they're from the same family along the line somewhere.'

'Weaver birds,' she remembered. 'They weave elaborate nests.'

'Some affinity,' he said. 'It doesn't matter. Of all birds, you seemed most like a sparrow to me.'

'I'm not that fragile.'

'No. I don't think that way now.'

'What do you think now?'

'I don't know,' he said. 'I don't have any metaphors now. Come on, I'll walk you to the gate.' He stood up, took her bag and they began walking towards the gate.

'I sometimes think in shapes,' he said, 'patterns.'

'What's a good pattern?' she said. 'A safe one.'

He thought. 'Tumbling,' he said.

'Tumbling? That doesn't sound particularly safe to me.'

'Controlled tumbling,' he said. 'The tumbler is a type of pigeon who turns over and over backwards during flight. A tumble-over is a toy that rights itself no matter which way you push it.'

'Tumbleweed,' she said, 'blown across the countryside.'

'That's for survival,' he said. 'They're rooted part of the year, then they break off and travel to survive. Nature's grand design.'

The queue of people was moving quickly now, filing past the flight attendant taking tickets. She put her hand out for her bag and he gave it to her. She felt weak, momentarily desperate, like a child going in the school gate alone. A hot flush prickled down her body, and after it had passed she felt a deep calm, a resoluteness. They were at the head of the queue now, and she handed the flight attendant her ticket and hesitated.

'Sir?' said the flight attendant.

'I'm not boarding,' he said, and he moved to the side, to the barrier that separated the seating area from the gate. Hannah walked on and stopped when she was across the barrier from him. They stood facing each other across the flimsy rail.

'Is that how you see yourself?' she said quietly. 'A tumbleweed?'

'No.'

'How do you see yourself?'

'A darker part of the picture,' he said. 'In the shadows somewhere.' He leaned across the barrier and kissed her lightly on the cheek. She smiled a little, and turned, but she hesitated, as though she knew he wasn't finished. When he said nothing more, she nodded.

'OK,' she said. 'OK,' and she started to walk. He watched her until his view was blocked by the passengers who followed her.

'Something of a necessary companion,' he continued, more to himself than anyone, 'to the light.'